PRAISE FOR *THE MERMAID'S MIRROR*

THE
MERMAID'S
MIRROR

All rights reserved. Published in the United States by Graphia, an imprint of
Houghton Mifflin Harcourt Publishing Company. Originally published in
hardcover in the United States by Houghton Mifflin Books for Children,
an imprint of Houghton Mifflin Harcourt Publishing Company, 2010.

Graphia and the Graphia logo are trademarks of
Houghton Mifflin Harcourt Publishing Company.

For information about permission to reproduce selections from this book, write to
Permissions, Houghton Mifflin Harcourt Publishing Company,
215 Park Avenue South, New York, New York 10003.

www.hmhbooks.com

The text of this book is set in Bembo.

The Library of Congress has cataloged the hardcover edition as follows:

Madigan, L. K.
The mermaid's mirror / by L. K. Madigan.
p. cm.
Summary: Lena, almost sixteen, has always felt drawn to the waters of
San Francisco Bay despite the fears of her father, a former surfer, but after
she glimpses a beautiful woman with a tail, nothing can keep Lena from
seeking the mermaid in the dangerous waves at Magic Crescent Cove.
[1. Mermaids—Fiction. 2. Identity—Fiction. 3. Surfing—Fiction.
4. Magic—Fiction. 5. Fathers and daughters—Fiction.
6. Family life—California—Fiction. 7. California—Fiction.] I. Title.
PZ7.M2583Mer 2010
[Fic]—dc22
2010006771

ISBN: 978-0-547-19491-2 hardcover
ISBN: 978-0-547-57735-7 paperback

Manufactured in the United States of America
DOC 10 9 8 7 6 5 4 3 2 1

4500318788

For Michelle . . .
forever a California girl,
no matter where
she lives

PROLOGUE

Lena woke up on the beach.

She knew she should feel afraid—sleepwalking to the beach in the middle of the night could not be a sane thing to do—but the salt scent and roar of the ocean calmed her. The moon shone down on the waves, making them glitter like thousands of tiny lights flickering just beneath the surface, rolling over and over.

Lena stood on the wet sand, searching for landmarks. About a hundred yards away, the craggy finger of Shipwreck Rocks jutted into the sea.

Somewhere out in the darkness, the foghorn crooned its faithful call. The familiar sound reassured Lena. A few miles away, the lighthouse flashed its beacon.

Wrapping her arms around herself to keep from shivering, Lena looked down at her clothes. She was wearing her pajamas, but she must have put on her hoodie in her sleep. She was barefoot, which made sense. She never wore shoes on the beach.

She turned and followed her footprints back along the moonlit stretch of sand. The crash of the surf sounded much louder in the dark. *How did I walk all this way without waking up? And what time is it?* She quickened her pace. If her parents woke up and found her missing, they would freak out.

Her footprints disappeared in the dry sand, but by then Lena was close to her usual path. She found her sandals near the base of the cliff, apparently kicked off and waiting for her return, just like always. She slid them on and made her way up the path to the parking lot, long sea grasses whispering against her legs.

At the edge of the parking lot, Lena turned back for one last look at the ocean. It rolled and glittered, vast and inscrutable. Lena turned away and headed home.

◻ ◻ ◻

The mermaid woke from a dream of humans. She was surprised to find herself adrift in a restless sea, with no memory of leaving home. Before turning to go, she raised her head above the surface and gazed at the empty shore.

CHAPTER 1

A patchwork of paper waves surrounded Lena. The walls of her room were covered with every shade of blue, green, and gray water imaginable—some images were photos she had taken herself, and others were pages torn from magazines: surfers riding through translucent green barrels . . . surfers surrounded by miles of limpid blue tropical sea . . . surfers about to be flattened by dark gray walls of water.

As Lena lay sleeping, the oceans of the world sparkling all around her, her cell phone rang. It was the Kai ringtone. Eyes closed, Lena rolled over and reached out from under the covers, fumbling on her nightstand for her phone.

"Hi," she croaked.

"Her name's Selena, and she dances on the saaaand," sang Kai, mangling the words to some old '80s song. His voice sounded overly loud to her half-asleep ears. "Leen? Did I wake you?"

"Mmm-hmm."

"But it's seven o'clock. You *never* sleep this late. Are you okay?"

Lena squinted at her clock—7:04—and blinked in surprise. She was usually up by six, or six thirty at the latest. "I'm fine." She yawned, then added, "And I don't dance on the sand."

"You know what's weird? I don't think I've ever woken you up before. That means . . . oh, wow. That means you're just *lying there in bed.*"

"That's what it means," she agreed, closing her eyes. She felt like she could go right back to sleep.

"Leen! I just realized that I don't know what your pajamas look like. I'm a terrible boyfriend. I'll be right over to check."

She snickered. "Great. Just knock and my dad will let you in."

"Oh, yeah. Your *parents,*" he joked. "They're always messing me up." He lowered his voice. "But what *are* you wearing?"

Lena stifled a laugh. When he used that sexy voice, it always made her feel like cracking up, instead of flirting back. "My wetsuit, of course. Doesn't everyone wear rubber pajamas?"

Kai groaned. "Oh, nooo. My eyes . . . my mental eyes! You've scarred them. But since you've already got your wetsuit on—"

She giggled.

"I'm heading out to Back Yard. No school today, remember? Want to come?"

At the mention of the local surfing spot, an image of moonlight on water floated into Lena's mind. Her eyes snapped open.

She sat up, looking around her room. Her hoodie hung in the closet, and her sandals sat in the shoe rack, same as always. *Was it all a dream?* She slid her feet out from under the covers and examined them.

There were grains of sand between her toes.

"Leen? You there?"

Lena lay back down slowly. She didn't remember getting out of bed, or going downstairs, or unlocking the back door. All she remembered was the shock of finding herself on the beach. "Yeah," she said. "You're going to Back Yard. Right now?"

"The early bird catches the wave, Leen—you know that."

I should tell Mom and Dad, she thought.

Almost before the idea could take shape, she backed away from it. No, they would just worry . . . maybe even make her go to the doctor. Lena frowned. It was a completely random episode, probably a one-time thing.

"Lena, helloooo? Are you falling back asleep?"

"No, sorry," she said. "I'll meet you there. Is Pem coming?"

"She is."

"Okay. I'll be there in twenty minutes." After she hung up, Lena realized she hadn't told Kai about her sleepwalking. *I'll tell him later,* she thought.

But she knew she would not.

◻ ◻ ◻

Lena stood in the wet sand, foamy wavelets lapping at her feet. The surf at Back Yard was breaking long today. Lena could see that the surfers in the water were spending a lot of time waiting around for decent waves.

"Hey," said Pem, joining her at the water's edge. "Where's your wetsuit? You're not going to swim?" Even wearing a full-body neoprene suit, lips coated with sunblock, and long black hair secured in a braid, Pem looked like a model.

"Not today," said Lena. "But you know cold water has never stopped me from a good game of GOTCHA!" Before she had even finished speaking, Pem had anticipated Lena's move, and they bent down simultaneously, flinging water up at each other. Lena took off down the beach, splashing through the ankle-high surf, Pem right behind her. Lena stopped and faked to the right, throwing Pem off long enough to spatter more seawater up at her.

"Don't you think"—Pem laughed—"we're getting a little old for this?"

Lena paused to catch her breath, clothes and hair drenched. "Way too old!" Then she spun and scooped.

Pem yelled, dodging the spray.

"Okay, okay," said Lena, laughing, hands on her knees.

"I'm only showing you mercy because you're already wet," said Pem, "while *I'm* nice and dry in my wetsuit."

They headed back to the blanket spread out on the sand. Pem's surfboard, an eight-foot board with blue hibiscus flowers painted on top, was lying next to it.

"See you in a few," she said, grabbing her board. "Want to go for coffee after?"

"I can't," said Lena. "I'm going to the city with my dad."

"Oh. So you just came to watch Kai?"

"Well, yeah." Lena hesitated. "Both of you." She knew that Pem was sensitive about the fact that Lena and Kai were *together* now.

The three of them had been best friends since sixth grade, but a couple of months ago, on a warm July evening, Kai had called and invited Lena to the movies. When she got there, Pem was nowhere around. Even when they were walking out of the theater and Kai took her hand, she just thought, *Huh? Kai doesn't usually hold hands.* As they made their way down Main Street, he pulled her into the skinny alley between the art gallery and the bookstore, where creeping vines of honeysuckle covered the fence. Then he turned to her with smoldering eyes, and Lena had finally understood. When he leaned close and kissed her, she was ready.

Pem snapped her leash around her ankle. "Here comes Kai. I'll talk to you later, okay?"

Lena nodded and watched her friend paddle out.

Kai dropped to the blanket next to her. "Hi," he murmured, pulling her close. "Oh, Leen, you're soaked!" He opened his duffel and pulled out a huge towel, wrapping it around her shoulders. "You must be freezing."

She let him fuss over her, though she didn't feel cold.

"Hi, Lena," said someone behind her.

Lena turned to see Kai's sister, Ani. "Hi," she said. "I didn't know you were home from school."

"Yeah, I don't have classes on Friday, so I can drive home for the weekend." She knelt down and rubbed wax onto her board, using circular motions.

Kai studied the waves. "Long lulls," he said.

"Yeah, not perfect," said Ani. "But better than a day *not* surfing." She grinned and headed out.

Kai waxed his board, gave Lena a kiss, then followed.

Lena watched her friends in the water, smiling at the way Kai tried to conquer every wave, while Pem was more cautious. Ani had a breathtaking grace in the water that made the other surfers look like beginners. *I should've brought my camera,* thought Lena.

Ani was the first one out of the water. She set her board down on the sand and stood watching Kai and Pem, who were sitting astride their boards, waiting for good waves. She looked down at Lena. "Don't you get tired of just watching?"

The words slapped Lena like icy spray.

Ani sat down on the blanket next to her. "Sorry. That came out wrong." She combed her fingers through her short blond hair. "But it looks like you want to be out there."

Lena bowed her head. She always felt a little nervous around Ani, who was tall and athletic and a crazy-smart physics genius. She'd had her pick of colleges, but had chosen Stanford so she could stay near the ocean. "I do want to be out there. It's just that my dad—"

"Oh, right," said Ani. "He had some surfing accident, right?"

"He almost drowned," said Lena.

"But . . . wasn't it a really long time ago?"

Lena nodded. "Before I was born."

"And that was it? He never surfed again?"

"No. I've never even seen him go in the water."

"Wow." Ani stared out at the sea. "That's some serious fear."

They sat in silence for a moment, watching the surfers.

"I do want to surf!" Lena burst out.

"Yeah?" Ani looked at her.

"Of course. But I was hoping to do it with his blessing, you know?"

Ani nodded. "That's cool. Respect, and all. But what if he's never going to say yes?"

Lena shivered.

Kai and Pem emerged from the waves, dripping and laughing.

"When you're ready to learn," said Ani, standing up, "with or without his blessing . . . let me know. I taught Kai and Jamie. They can tell you I'm a pretty good teacher."

Lena didn't answer. She stood up to receive Kai's kiss, his lips cold from the water.

CHAPTER 2

Lena began to feel uneasy the moment she saw the building. Impossibly tall, it stretched up into the sky like a giant steel beanstalk. As she tilted her head back to try to see the top, her stomach gave a little lurch.

"Here it is," said her father, looking as proud as if he'd built it. "Come on." He pushed through a revolving glass door.

Lena followed more slowly.

"Wait till you see the office—you won't believe it," he said, stepping onto an escalator. When they reached the top, he greeted the security guard and headed for a bank of elevators marked 16–30.

Lena could see that he was trying to be cool, but he was bouncing up and down on his toes slightly as they waited for the elevator.

The doors of the elevator slid open, and a rush of power suits, briefcases, and expensive haircuts streamed past them.

Lena's dad pulled at the cuffs of his white oxford shirt, as if to make sure they covered his tattoos. His blond hair curled over the collar of his shirt.

He's probably going to get one of those stockbroker haircuts now, thought Lena. *Sad.*

They stepped onto the elevator, and a woman in a crisp business suit stepped on behind them, fingers flying on her cell phone. She punched the elevator button for 27.

As the doors whooshed shut, her father said to Lena, "Push the button for twenty-nine."

"Really?" said Lena. "Twenty-*nine?*"

He nodded, beaming. "Practically in the clouds."

The woman glanced at Lena's dad, her gaze lingering. She closed her cell phone.

Lena was used to women ogling her dad. Her mom called him a computer nerd trapped in the body of a hot guy.

Reaching for the 29 button, Lena said, "Wow, Dad. Practically the penthouse. Or do they just want to keep you far away from the general public?" She pressed the button. A moment later, her stomach dropped as the elevator shot up. She reached out to grasp the handrail at the back of the elevator. "Why is it . . . so fast?" she asked, feeling as if she couldn't catch her breath.

"This express elevator only goes between the sixteenth and the thirtieth floors," said her father. He grinned, his blue eyes shining. "Fast, huh? Did you leave your stomach on the first floor? Lena?"

She closed her eyes and held tighter to the handrail. *Almost there,* she told herself. *Just hold on.*

"Lena? What's wrong?"

She couldn't answer. There was a growing pressure in her ears.

"Selena." She felt her father's hand on her arm.

"Are you okay?" shrilled the woman.

The elevator halted with a ding, and the doors opened at 27.

Lena clung to the handrail, trying to catch her breath.

The woman moved toward the exit, looking concerned. "Do you want to get off?" She held the doors open.

Lena shook her head.

The woman took her hand away, and the doors slid shut.

"Honey, what's going on?" asked her dad.

The elevator rose, and the pressure in Lena's ears ballooned. *Ding.* 29.

Lena stumbled out. The floor seemed to tilt under her feet. She opened her mouth in a yawning motion to clear the pressure in her ears. "Nothing," she said finally. "I just felt weird for a second."

"You did? Are you okay?"

"Yeah. I'm fine." She shrugged away from his hand. "Let's just go see your new office, okay?"

He studied her for another moment, then nodded. "Okay. Then we'll get an early lunch. Did you eat this morning?"

"Dad, I eat every morning." Hadn't he *seen* her sitting at the breakfast table, eating the same English muffin and yogurt she always ate? No, he'd been too buzzed about visiting the office. And of course Cole was yammering on about football, and Mom was muttering about caterers (she was an events planner), so Dad had been distracted, to say the least.

They reached a pair of heavy glass doors, with two ws etched on them, and stepped into the reception area. A gray-haired man was speaking to the receptionist and turned to glance at them.

"Brian." The man approached, hand outstretched. "You made it. Good."

Lena's father shook the man's hand. "Don. Good morning," he said, his voice deepening into what Lena thought of as Dad's I'm-Being-Serious-Now voice. "This is my daughter, Lena. Lena, this is Mr. Wolinsky."

Wolinsky and Wellman Consultants. *Must be one of the bosses,* she thought. "Nice to meet you, Mr. Wolinsky."

"Call me Don, please." He smiled. "We're all looking forward to working with your father."

She smiled, too. "Great."

"This is Karen," continued Don, indicating the receptionist.

"Nice to meet you, Lena," she said. "What lovely hair! You have your father's blond hair."

"Thanks."

"In ten years I probably won't have any of it left," her father said, chuckling. "I'll have to look at Lena to remind myself what it looked like."

Lena cringed.

Karen laughed. She held up a bowl of M&M's. "I always offer candy to the kids when they visit, but I guess you're not a kid anymore, are you? Let me see—are you fourteen? Or fifteen?"

"I turn sixteen next week," said Lena. She took a couple of M&M's. "Thank you."

"Oh!" said Karen. "You're so petite, I guessed too young." She winked. "When you're my age, you'll appreciate that."

The three adults shared a slightly-too-hearty laugh, and Lena smiled, putting the M&M's in her mouth so she wouldn't have to respond.

"Well," said the Boss Guy. "Shall we give Lena the grand tour?" He turned to lead them down the hall.

The guy—*Don,* Lena reminded herself—introduced Lena to the other people in the office, most of whom had already met her father. Lena thought it was the politest group of people she had ever met, everyone smiling and saying nice things about her dad.

"Let's take a look at the view from my office," said Don.

Lena followed them into a spacious corner office, dominated by a floor-to-ceiling window that curved around the edge of the building.

"Come look, Lena," said her dad. "Isn't this something?"

She stood next to him, the glass of the window so crystal clear that it seemed as if they were standing at the edge of the twenty-ninth floor with *no* window in front of them . . . nothing to keep them from falling. She took a breath and looked down. Cars and taxis, buses, and bicycles flowed up and down the streets, advancing and stopping in a traffic dance. People moved along the sidewalks, colorful and distant. There was a grassy park across the street, ringed with trees and flowers. A bubbling fountain was the centerpiece of the park, with a bunch of little kids running around it in circles. San Francisco Bay glinted in the distance.

Lena's face grew warm, and a light sweat broke out on her forehead. It felt like the building was swaying, as if in a heavy wind. But the flag on the flagpole across the street hung slack.

She lifted a hand, as if to hold on to something. But there was nothing there. She focused on the park across the street to regain her perspective. The water in the fountain sparkled and splashed, sparkled and splashed. As she watched, suddenly she felt like she might plummet out the window, not falling straight down, but sailing through empty air like a bird, against all laws of gravity, until she crashed into that bubbling fountain.

The pressure in her ears returned, along with a roaring sound.

Lena opened her mouth, trying to take in more air. The back of her neck felt hot, and she thought, *Oh, no—I'm going to throw up in front of my dad's new boss!*

She fell forward against the glass, which was suddenly hard and reassuring under her palms.

Darkness swam into her eyes, and the last thing she heard was her father calling her name from far away.

CHAPTER 3

"Absolutely. Yes. You're right." Lena's dad, his voice brittle, talked on the phone while Lena stared out the window of the car. Her mind kept replaying the moment when she woke up in that guy's office with a bunch of scared faces looking down at her. She would never forget it, no matter how long she lived. That Karen woman had wanted to call 911! *Errgh*. She leaned her head against the side window.

"We'll be home in less than an hour," said her dad. "Okay. Here she is." He handed the phone to Lena.

"Hi, Mom."

"Hi, sweetie."

The sound of her mom's voice caused a lump to form in Lena's throat. "I don't want to go to the hospital."

"I know, sweetie. Dad and I talked about it, and we decided it's probably not necessary, but I'm going to call Dr. Feldman."

"Mom, I'm fine!"

"Of course you are. You probably just had a little attack of vertigo, but I still want to talk to Dr. Feldman."

Lena sighed, even though she knew her mom was right.

"See you in a little while."

"Okay, bye." Lena closed the cell phone and handed it back to her dad.

He plugged it into the charger and started the car. "Sorry about the shopping, Leen, but—"

"I don't care," said Lena. Her dad was supposed to take her shopping after the visit to his new office, but now they were going straight home. Which was fine with Lena. She didn't exactly want to start passing out all over San Francisco.

Her dad drove out of the city and headed south on Highway 1.

They passed a big green highway sign:

MOSS BEACH 17 MILES
DIAMOND BAY   28 MILES
SANTA CRUZ 73 MILES

Santa Cruz, thought Lena. *There's a bunch of surf schools there. It's only forty-five minutes away. Dad's been asking what I want for my birthday . . .*

She looked at him hunched over the steering wheel, his expression taut, and decided that now was not the time to bring up surfing.

◻ ◻ ◻

Her mom did her best to act calm and unworried when Lena got home, but her being home in the middle of the day was proof enough that things were not normal.

"What did Dr. Feldman say?" asked Lena.

Mom kissed her forehead, and Lena knew she was checking for fever. "Her nurse said to make sure you ate something, and to call back if it happened again. Apparently fainting can happen sometimes during puberty. We might want to take you in for a blood test to make sure you're not anemic."

17

"I'm fine," said Lena, for what felt like the twentieth time. "I just got dizzy. It was so embarrassing!" She cringed all over again at the memory of waking up surrounded by strangers. "At least I didn't puke in front of Dad's new boss."

"Oh, honey!" said her mom. "No one cared about that. They were just worried about you fainting."

Lena's father said, "Yeah, well, you should have seen the Oriental rug in that corner office. I was glad she didn't puke, too!"

"Brian!"

Her dad put his arm around Mom's shoulder. "Kidding, honey."

Cole came crashing down the stairs into the living room. When he saw their parents hugging, he threw his arms around both of them. "Group hug!" he yelled.

Mom held out an arm to Lena. "Come on, you know the drill."

Lena moved into the family circle, putting one arm around her mom, and reaching out with the other to rumple Cole's hair.

He ducked out from under her hand. At six years old, he was starting to resist rumpling. He turned his bright blue eyes—so much like Dad's—up to Lena and asked, "Want to play catch with me?"

"Maybe later, Coley," she said. She heard that question from her brother at least once a day—she and her parents rotated shifts of playing catch with him.

"Okay," he said. "Tell me when you're ready?"

"Sure."

He bounded out of the room and headed back upstairs.

"Have you had lunch?" asked her mom.

"Yes," said Lena. "Dad and I stopped at Pink Cottage on our way home."

"You stopped at the Pink Cottage and didn't get me scones?" said her mom, mock-aghast.

Lena left her parents to discuss the lack of scones, calling over her shoulder, "I'll be in my room."

She climbed the stairs and went into her room, closing her door. She logged in to her IM. Pem was online.

Sea_girl: Hey.

PemberLoca: Lena! Ur home early.

Sea_girl: Yeah.

PemberLoca: How come back so soon?

Sea_girl: Umm . . .

PemberLoca: ??

Sea_girl: This weird fainting thing happened.

PemberLoca: Wha??!!

Sea_girl: Yeah. Felt rly weird, then I fell over.

PemberLoca: OMG scary! Were u with ur dad?

Sea_girl: Yeah, his new work. ☹ We were by this huge window way up high n I guess I got dizzy.

PemberLoca: Going to doctor?

Sea_girl: Prolly.

PemberLoca: Too freaky! U ok, bff? ☹

Sea_girl: Yes! Just a one-time thing.

Lena lifted her hands from the keyboard, suddenly chilled. *Just a one-time thing.* That's what she'd told herself about the sleepwalking.

Sea_girl: Lets not even talk about it, k?

PemberLoca: K. See u tomorrow?

Sea_girl: Yes!

PemberLoca: Bye.

Lena logged off and went back downstairs to get something to drink. As she walked into the kitchen, her mom was saying, "... if the vertigo was caused by something else?"

"She's never had any blood work done," said her dad. "It would be—"

Her parents stood close together, their heads bent. They fell silent as Lena entered the room, and Lena caught the worried expression on her dad's face before he saw her.

Glancing up, he made an effort to smile, then said with fake casualness, "What's up, Lena?"

She hesitated, then said, "Nothing. Just getting a drink."

She grabbed an energy drink and hurried from the room, because she did not want to talk about fainting anymore.

◻ ◻ ◻

Kai was singing into the phone. *"Lena said knock you out ... I'm gonna knock you out ..."*

Lena laughed. Even though Kai looked like the quintessential California surfer boy—whose life would revolve around "brews and bros," and who would only listen to speed metal—he was actually a drama geek who loved all music, from power ballads to punk. Lena had heard Ani accuse him once of having "ludicrously undiscriminating taste in music," to which he had replied, "Love Ludacris!" Lately he'd taken to inserting Lena's name into whatever song was on his brain radio. "I did *not* say to knock anyone out," she said. "And I think you've reached your limit on oldies for the day, haven't you?"

"Oh, Leen," he said. "There *is* no limit. Hey . . . that sounds like it should be a slogan, doesn't it? And you might as well prepare yourself. Drama Club is voting on which musical to put on. It's down to three: *Brigadoon, Grease,* and *Guys and Dolls.*"

"Whoa," said Lena. "Those are all really old!"

"Don't be ageist," said Kai. "They prefer the term 'classic.'"

"Why not something like *Wicked*?"

"I dunno. Hey, how was your trip to the city?"

Lena reluctantly told him about the fainting, and he begged to come over immediately to confirm in person that she was all right.

"Nooo," she said. "I'm fine, I'm fine! No one seems to believe me. I probably just have swimmer's ear, or something." *Although I haven't been swimming in over a week,* she thought.

"Okay, I believe you," he said. "Let me come over anyway. Just to . . . you know."

Lena giggled. "You know?"

"Right. *You* know."

"Um, I *don't* know. And I'm almost afraid to find out."

"I want to be alone with you. There. How's that for blunt?"

"That might be kind of tough," she said. "Seeing as both my parents are here, and they're all worried about me now, so they probably won't let me out of their sight."

Exhaling heavily, Kai said, "Man. They're such, like, *good parents.* Why can't they be all wrapped up in their own problems?"

"I know, right?" Lena laughed. "I'm practically grown. They should just leave me to my own devices."

"I got your devices right here, baby," said Kai in his sexy voice, which made her crack up some more.

"I'll just see you tomorrow," she said.

"Really?" Now he sounded hurt. "I was serious. I want to see you."

Lena paused. She was still adjusting to the concept of Kai being her boyfriend. *Friend* Kai would have said, "Yeah, catch you later." *Boyfriend* Kai wanted to see her all the time, it seemed like. "Oh," she said. "Okay. Um, why don't you come over after dinner?"

"Perfect."

"But don't blame me if you're bored once you get here."

"Unpossible," he said. "I'll see you later."

CHAPTER 4

Lena dreamed she was falling, the helpless dizzy sensation jolting her out of sleep.

She lay frozen, her heart thudding in her chest, as her eyes adjusted to the darkness. *Practically in the clouds.*

She rolled over and sat up. No more sleeping today. She wasn't going to risk going back to *that* dream. Without turning on the light, Lena got out of bed and went to the window, moving aside the curtain so she could peer outside. A light fog blanketed the empty street, casting a misty halo around each streetlight. Sliding open the window, Lena felt the rush of cold air on her face. Perfect autumn beach weather.

She pulled on sweats over her pajamas, shivering a little. Stepping into the hallway, she listened for early-morning family sounds, but the house was quiet. They must still be asleep. She padded down the stairs and into the kitchen, where she turned on the light, dimming it immediately so the glare wouldn't hurt her eyes. She grabbed a marker and scrawled on the dry-erase board:

6:15 a.m. – went for walk on the beach – L.

Pulling on her jacket, she stepped outside, where the cold air smelled of the sea. Lena took a deep breath, as if inhaling perfume. Why couldn't it smell this good everywhere?

She walked two blocks to the end of the road without seeing anyone else. When the streets were silent and dark, it was easy to imagine she was the only person awake for miles. Behind the dark windows of all these houses, she pictured everyone still curled up in bed, fast asleep, while she roamed the neighborhood alone.

Lena walked across the graveled public parking area and moved down the narrow beach path, a worn stretch of earth in the middle of tall grasses. The dew-covered blades clung to her pants like wet fingers. Stashing her sandals near a fallen log, she gave a sigh of relief as her feet touched the cool sand.

The only light on the shore came from Pelican Point Lighthouse, two miles to the north, where a bright beam flashed in the darkness and winked out, just like clockwork. But the darkness didn't bother Lena; she could walk this stretch of sand with her eyes closed. *In fact,* she thought wryly, *I could walk this stretch of sand in my sleep.*

Lena made her way down to the edge of the water, where the sand was rippled from having been under water a few hours ago. The tide was out, but she could feel the urgency of the sea . . . soon the tide would sweep back in and cover the sand where she stood. The waves pounded as if hungry for shore.

She walked almost a mile, until she came to Shipwreck Rocks, the massive stone jetty that extended into the sea, separating Diamond Bay from Magic Crescent Cove. A weathered sign proclaimed WARNING! DO NOT CLIMB ON ROCKS. RISK OF INJURY OR DEATH. Ignoring the sign, Lena began to scale the rocks. The sign had been there her whole life, and she'd never heard of anyone getting hurt on the rocks, other than the occasional twisted ankle or scraped knee.

Once she reached the top, she settled down on a relatively flat boulder, resting her eyes on the horizon, where gray met darker gray. It was so early even the surfers weren't out yet.

She's never had any blood work done . . .

Lena shivered. She wished she hadn't overheard her parents. She couldn't get that word out of her mind. *Blood.*

I'm fine, she told herself. *My blood is fine.* Restless, she got up and made her way carefully down the other side of the rocks. When she neared the bottom, she jumped onto the sand.

She walked farther down the beach, farther from home, as if she could leave her fears behind. Finally she stopped to catch her breath, staring out at the empty water.

As she gazed at the sea, a sleek head popped out of the water.

She smiled and waved at the sea lion. They loved this stretch of shoreline. She knew it was silly to wave at them— she wouldn't do it if other people were around—but sea lions always seemed so interested in human activity that she couldn't help greeting them. She wished she could swim out to play with them.

The sea lion disappeared beneath the surface again, popping up a few more times in different spots, finally drifting so far north that Lena couldn't see him.

"Bye," she whispered.

. . . never had any blood work . . .

Lena wished she could pluck the thought out of her head and throw it into the sea, where it would be borne away by the waves.

She splashed ankle-deep in the surf, letting the cold water tickle her feet. She grabbed a sandy stick, dragging it through the wet sand, making circles and hearts and stars. Then she wrote in big letters, *I AM FINE*.

Lena tossed the stick onto the sand and made her way back to Shipwreck Rocks. She should probably head home. No point in worrying her parents even more by being MIA when they woke up. Lena climbed to the top of the rocks, glancing back the way she had come, and almost stumbled. A solitary figure had appeared on the beach.

Where did he come from? Was he there when I was there? Was he watching me?

She looked harder and recognized the long, loose coat, the shambling walk. It was just Denny.

Denny was a weird loner who was always wandering up and down the beach. He never bothered anyone, just muttered to himself. Sometimes he shouted at the sea. It was best to give him some space. He didn't seem to be homeless or hungry, but no one knew where he lived, or how he survived.

Lena decided to make her way home *quickly*. She didn't think he would bother her, but the idea that he had been lurking nearby without her knowledge was unsettling. Just before she descended the steep rocks, she glanced back again. Denny was standing on the spot where Lena had written *I AM FINE,* staring down at the words in the sand.

◻ ◻ ◻

The mermaid felt the lure of humans.

She swam closer to shore, knowing that the sun had nearly risen and she must not be seen. It wasn't fair to the humans. Most of them went mad with the knowledge of mer-folk.

They lingered by the sea, wasting away in the desire of seeing them again.

The mermaid surfaced. This stretch of beach seemed familiar, although it was far from her village. Ah, there was a human!

She watched him for a moment as he trudged through the wet sand, shoulders bent, long coat flapping around his knees. He had the look of one who had Seen.

Not wishing to cause him further unrest, the mermaid slipped beneath the surface and swam away.

CHAPTER 5

After breakfast, Lena dragged her backpack over to the kitchen table and started pulling books and folders from it. She frowned down at the pile of homework. Something was missing. Spanish, Algebra II, History, English . . . *Where was the—?* Lena opened her backpack and peered inside at the empty space. She looked at her books again. Everything seemed to be on the table already. She'd left her Biology book at school, but that was because she didn't have any Bio homework. *Hmm.* She shrugged and tossed her backpack to the floor.

Lena's cell phone chimed with a text from Pem:

Want to go to the mall?

Lena hit Reply and texted: Yeah call u later.

She plodded through a half hour's worth of homework before Cole came into the family room—which adjoined the kitchen—and turned on the TV, locating a football game. The sound of cheering crowds and sports announcers filled the room.

I need a break, anyway, thought Lena, and she gathered up her books and papers to put in her backpack. *Where's the—?* She shuffled through her papers a few times, then shook her head. Where was *what?!* It was driving her crazy, the feeling that something was missing.

"Is it okay if I go to the mall with Pem?" she asked her mom.

"Did you finish your homework?"

"Mostly. I have some reading to do."

"Okay. Is Kai going to be there?"

Lena tried not to roll her eyes. "Mom, Kai isn't with me twenty-four/seven."

"I'm just asking."

"He's not going to be there. Can you take us, or should I ask Dad?"

"Ask your father. He's upstairs in his office."

Her dad was tapping away on his laptop at the big oak desk. Lena went to stand behind him. She admired the Chinese dragon tattoo on his left forearm, with its intricate green scales, and the yin-yang symbol on his right shoulder. Although she couldn't see them, she knew her name and Cole's name were inked above his heart.

"Hi, hon," he said.

"Hi. Could you take Pem and me to the mall?"

"Sure. I have to go out pretty soon to run some errands, anyway."

"Thanks." Lena went to stand by the window. She stared in the direction of the ocean, even though only a tiny slice of it was visible from here.

"You've been remarkably quiet about your birthday this year. I thought the Sweet Sixteen was supposed to be a big deal."

She didn't answer for a moment. *Sweet sixteen and never been kissed,* she thought. *That was almost me.* "We don't have to do a big deal," she said.

"I take it you'll be wanting sushi from Miso on Main for your birthday dinner, as usual."

"Yes, please." Lena loved sushi anytime, but especially on her birthday.

"How many people should we order for?"

"I don't know. Eight? Ten?"

"How about *sixteen?*"

She smiled at him. "No, I don't want a big crowd."

Her dad made an expansive gesture. "You only turn sixteen once. Now, what about presents? I know you said gift cards are fine, but I want to get you something special."

She gazed at the distant glimmer of the ocean. *I couldn't ask for a better opening.* "Actually, Dad—"

"Yes?"

"There is *one* thing."

"Great! Tell me."

She hesitated, looking into his beaming face. "I was hoping—"

He waited.

"That this year—" She swallowed and said, "That you would let me take surfing lessons."

Her dad's smile disappeared.

Lena's heart bumped. *Oh, no.* She moved closer to the desk, gripping its hard wooden edge. "Or if, you know, lessons are too expensive . . . maybe *you* could teach me." She heard the tremor in her voice and winced.

Her dad stood up and crossed the room. He paced back and forth, finally coming to a stop in front of the same window where Lena had stood. She imagined him staring out at the sliver of ocean, just like she had.

"No," he said. "I'm sorry."

Her shoulders sagged. "But Dad—"

"You know I can't, Lena."

She took a deep breath and held it for a moment, to keep her response inside: *No, I don't really know that.* "Okay," she said. "What about lessons? Kai's sister said she—"

"No."

"What? *Dad.* Come on. It's not fair! Do you know how it feels to splash around in the water like a little kid while your friends are out surfing? Or worse . . . to sit on the sand watching them? No, you don't, because *you* learned to surf when you were, like, Cole's age! Which, by the way, don't you think he's going to want to surf someday, too?"

Her father didn't answer.

"Dad. I know you had a bad experience—" She stopped and tried again. "I know you're worried that something might happen to me, but I'll be super-careful."

Still no answer.

Lena was breathing heavily. The longer her father stood at the window, the angrier she felt. "Aren't you even going to answer me?"

Her father turned to face her, and his eyes were chilly now. "Yes, Lena, I'll answer you. The truth is that I've been thinking."

She lifted her hands. "About?"

"I've been thinking that my new job in the city is going to mean I spend a lot of time commuting from now on. Forty-five minutes each way. Longer if the traffic is bad."

Lena blinked. What did this have to do with surfing?

"And I've been thinking. That's an awful lot of time away from my family."

Lena frowned. "Yeah, but you knew that."

"Too much time, I think." He sat down heavily behind his desk.

Lena looked at his slumped shoulders, and had a terrible understanding of what he was saying. She began to shake her head.

"Maybe it's time we moved closer to the city," said her father.

Lena couldn't answer, just kept shaking her head. An aching lump filled her throat. Finally she said, "Leave Diamond Bay?"

He nodded.

"Just because I want to learn to surf?!"

"Not because of that."

"Then why?" Tears slid down Lena's cheeks.

Her dad put his hand over his eyes. After a long moment, he said quietly, "I don't think I . . . we . . . can go on living here anymore."

"But this is our *home*. Why would you say that?"

"We could get a lot of money for this house. We could start over somewhere."

Lena stared at him. "I don't want to start over," she said, and headed for the door.

She stumbled down the stairs, hardly seeing where she was going.

I'll live with Pem, she thought. *I don't care what he says, I am not leaving Diamond Bay.*

"Is Dad going to take you to the mall, honey?" asked her mom.

Or I could live with Martha. Or maybe Leslie, thought Lena, walking past her mom and out the back door.

"Lena? What's wrong? Are you crying?"

As she headed toward the beach, Lena's mind raced. *Even Kai,* she thought. *It might be weird, but his parents would probably let me stay there.*

By the time she reached the narrow beach path, Lena's tears had slowed. At the sight of the sea, relief flooded her body. Lena walked across the sand and into the knee-deep surf, letting the waves wash away her fears.

After a time, she became aware that someone was saying her name.

Her mind felt curiously empty, except for a wordless little song that was playing over and over . . . It was very soothing, combined with the sound of the ocean in her ears. The counterpoint of the foghorn added a note of longing to the melody.

The sound of her name grew more insistent. Someone touched her shoulder. Lena blinked and looked around.

She was seated on the dry sand, which was warm and gritty beneath her, although she didn't remember sitting down.

Her mom was squatting next to her, a look of fear on her face. As Lena's gaze focused, her mom said, "Oh, thank God." She put a hand to her chest. "Lena, what happened? Are you okay?"

"Sure. Why?"

Her mom continued to stare at her for a long moment before she answered. "I've been calling your name from all the way back there." She pointed back to the beach path. "Then I came right up to you, and you didn't seem to hear me. You—" The expression on her face was strained. ". . . were humming. Your eyes were open, but you acted like you were in a daze, or something."

I wish I could remember that song, thought Lena. It was gone from her mind.

"Lena." Her mom's grip on her shoulder tightened. "Honey!"

"What?"

"You're scaring me. You're not acting like yourself."

"I'm fine." There was that phrase again. Lena spread her hands out in the sand, running her fingers through the soft grains. *It's weird that I don't remember coming over here and sitting down,* she thought.

"Okay," said her mom. "Let's get you home. I'm going to call Mum." Grandma Kath was her mom's mother, and a nurse-midwife. Whenever there was a minor illness in the house-hold, Mom always called her first. "What happened? You were crying when you left the house. Dad said the two of you had words."

Lena's gaze came back to rest on the sea. "I'm not leaving," she said. "Dad said he wants to sell the house. I don't really believe him, but if he does . . ." She looked steadily at her mom. "I'll move in with one of my friends. I'm not leaving Diamond Bay."

A series of emotions swept across her mom's face before she finally said, "Of course not, honey."

"Why would he say that?" cried Lena, tears threatening again.

Mom pulled her close and patted her back. "Shh, it's okay. I don't know. Your dad . . . he gets overwhelmed, sometimes. He worries about . . . us."

Lena relaxed under her mother's touch, but she heard the slight hesitation in her words. It sounded like she'd been about to say, "He worries about you."

CHAPTER 6

When they got home, Lena's mom made her a cup of tea, which was the first solution to most problems in their house. Strangely enough, Lena felt better after she drank the hot, milky tea.

Cole asked her to play Ninja-Cat with him on his Mindbender, so she picked up a controller and joined him on the floor.

". . . eyes were open . . . conscious . . . seemed almost like a fugue . . ." Her mom was speaking quietly into the phone, but Lena could still hear fragments of her sentences. There was a pause, then her mom said, "Yes. All right. I'll see you soon, then."

Fugue? thought Lena. *Isn't that a music thing?*

Her dad was pacing between the kitchen and family room. He had apologized to Lena already, saying, "I'm sorry I upset you, sweetheart. We're not leaving Diamond Bay. I was just . . ." His voice had trailed off, and he resumed pacing.

When Grandma Kath arrived, she bustled in with her usual English good cheer. "All right, love?" she asked, kissing Lena's forehead.

Cole hugged her. "Grandma!"

"Yes, yes, darling, hullo!" Grandma Kath gave him a cuddle, then went to the kitchen sink and washed her hands with soap before examining Lena. She removed an electronic thermometer from her bag, pressed a button on it, and said, "Open up, love, there's a good girl."

"Is Lena sick?" asked Cole.

"No, darling," said Grandma Kath. "It's just a quick checkup."

Lena held the thermometer under her tongue.

"Can I listen to her heart?" asked Cole. He was fascinated with Grandma Kath's stethoscope.

"In a few minutes," she said. "Go back to your game."

But Cole stood watching for another moment, then raced upstairs.

The thermometer beeped, and Grandma Kath took it out of Lena's mouth. "Perfect," she said. "Now let me take a look in those lovely eyes . . . the color of a stormy sea, your dad always says." She shone a light in Lena's eyes, and down her throat. Then she took her blood pressure, and listened to her heart, all the while keeping up a soothing patter. "Breathe in. Your mum says you were upset. And that you seemed a bit dazed when she found you on the beach. Breathe out. Do you remember what happened just before that?"

"Nothing happened. I just went to the beach." Lena adored Grandma Kath, but she felt fine now, and resented this minor medical drama. "Can I call Pem now? We were supposed to get together. She's probably wondering what happened to me."

Cole reappeared, dragging Lena's quilt with him. "Here," he said. "In case she feels cold."

Lena looked at her sun-and-moon quilt—made by Grandma Kath—and smiled. "Aw, thank you, Coley." Normally he wasn't allowed in her room, but she couldn't get mad at him when he was trying to take care of her.

"Which side do you want?" he asked.

"The sunny side," she said. One side of the quilt was sky-blue flannel with a yellow velvet sun stitched in the middle; the other side was midnight-blue velour spangled with white stars, and a satiny moon in the center.

Cole struggled to drape the heavy quilt over Lena's shoulders. When he was satisfied she was warm enough, he went back to his game.

Grandma Kath resumed her ministrations. "Breathe in," she said, placing the stethoscope on Lena's chest. "Did you fall down at any point? I know you sometimes climb on the rocks."

"No." Lena inhaled.

"And breathe out. Did you go in the water?"

Lena exhaled, rolling her eyes. "Yeah, I went in all the way up to my *knees*."

"Do you remember if the sun on the water was especially bright or shimmering?"

"It just looked normal."

"Did you hear anything unusual?"

Lena hesitated. "No," she lied.

Grandma Kath gave her a sharp look. "Right. One more big breath in. Good. And let it out. Did you see anyone else? Speak to anyone?"

"Grandma, it's the weekend. Of course there were other people on the beach. But no, I didn't talk to anyone."

"And how are you feeling now?"

"Fine."

"Not feeling sleepy or nauseated?"

"No. Can we be done with this?"

"Certainly." Grandma Kath smiled and packed up her things. "You're fit as a fiddle. Would you be a love and let your brother have a listen to your heart?"

Lena sighed, but agreed. Cole sat next to Lena, and Grandma Kath put the ends of the stethoscope in his ears. Then she showed him where to put the chestpiece so he could hear Lena's heartbeat.

A rapt look came over Cole's face. "Lena, I hear your heart," he said, his blue eyes shining.

She smiled. "How does it sound?"

"Like this." He imitated the sound of a heartbeat. "Want to listen to mine?"

"Of course." She reached for the stethoscope.

Grandma Kath carried her bag of nurse-y tricks over to the kitchen table, where Mom and Dad were hovering.

Placing the stethoscope against Cole's little boy chest, Lena pretended to listen to his heart, but she slipped one of the ear tips out of her ear so she could hear what Grandma Kath said.

". . . blood count would be a good idea, but she seems fine. Keep her home today, so you can observe her. Watch for lethargy or irritability."

Lena kept her expression neutral, but she thought, *I'll be irritable if you make me stay home, duh!*

"I want to be a nurse when I grow up," said Cole.

"Do you? Turn around and I'll listen through your back," said Lena.

As Cole scooted around, Lena heard her mom say, ". . . straight to the ER next time."

Lena's eyes bugged out slightly before she could compose her face. *The ER?!*

"Or a quarterback," added Cole.

Lena regarded his small shoulder blades, so fragile-looking. She was tempted to place a kiss right between them, but he probably wouldn't appreciate that, so she just placed the stethoscope on his back, murmuring, "Hmm."

Then she heard her dad's voice, low and urgent. She couldn't make out what he was saying, but she caught one word: ". . . Lucy."

Lena kept her gaze fixed on Cole's back, but her heart thumped harder. No one ever talked about Lucy, her real mother. She had died when Lena was barely four. Her dad had married Allie—Mom—when Lena was nine.

"What do you want to be when you grow up?" asked Cole.

Lena strained to hear the adults' conversation, but they were whispering.

"Lena," persisted Cole. "What do you want to be when you grow up?"

Her parents and Grandma Kath had stopped talking and were looking at her now. Lena raised her eyebrows at them and said to Cole, "Happy."

◻ ◻ ◻

Lena's parents did, indeed, make her stay home for the rest of the day.

Lena texted Pem that she'd had a fight with her dad, leaving out the part about the beach and the *fugue* and the drama.

She just said she didn't feel good, and would talk to her tomorrow.

By four o'clock, Lena was going stir-crazy. "Mom, please," she said. "I feel totally fine! Kai called and asked if I could go to the Creamery with him. Please?"

Her mom shook her head.

"I'll bring you home some ice cream," Lena wheedled.

"No."

"Caramel Mocha Madness? Come on, you know it's your favorite . . . those little chunks of dark chocolate . . ."

Her mom laughed and put her arm around Lena. "*No,* honey. Not even for Caramel Mocha Madness. Grandma told me to keep an eye on you, and I take her orders very seriously."

Lena heaved a sigh. "Mom, I know you think I . . . zoned out or fugue'd out or whatever . . ."

Her mom frowned at this evidence that Lena had listened in on her conversation.

"But I've been thinking about it, and I'm *sure* I was fully conscious the whole time I was on the beach. I just didn't hear you calling."

"I'm glad you feel better, honey. You're staying home, though." She let go of Lena and said, "But if Kai wants to come over here, he's more than welcome." She moved into the kitchen. "We're planning a wild night of football watching. Cole and Dad are fired up about the Raiders game. I'm fired up about lying flat on the couch."

"Fine."

Lena went to call Kai. "My mom won't let me out of her sight. Do you want to come over here?"

"So your parents are home?"

"Kai! Of course they're home. They're going to watch the Raiders game on TV."

"They are?"

"Um, yeah, why?"

"Well, even I—who knows nothing about football—know the Raiders suck."

"They do?"

"Pretty reliably."

"Aw, that's too bad. Cole likes them because they're pirates. Which is also why he likes the Buccaneers. So do you want to come over?"

"I'll be there in ten minutes."

When the knock on the door came, Lena opened it and Kai burst into the house, his hand on his heart, singing, *"Summer lovin' . . . had me a blast!"*

She laughed. "I take it the Drama Club decided on *Grease.*"

"Yes, and *you* are going to help me practice for the audition."

"I am?"

"Of course you are. And Lena, seriously, with your voice, you should try out for the show, too."

"Not even maybe," she said. "But thank you. That's sweet." She headed for the stairs.

Kai followed. "Well, yeah, I *am* totally sweet. But for real, Lena, you should audition. It's just not right to keep that amazing voice hidden. And wouldn't it be great if we both ended up with the lead roles? You and me . . . Sandy and Danny!" At the top of the stairs, he caught her in both arms and kissed her.

Just then Lena's mom came out of her bedroom, and her eyes widened.

Kai and Lena sprang apart.

"Hi," he said.

"Hello, Kai."

Then no one spoke for a long moment. Finally Lena's mom said, "Why don't you two join us downstairs for the game?"

"Uh, Mom?" said Lena. "We're not into football."

"Neither am I," said her mom. "But it's nice to be with the family, right?"

"Sure."

"Lena's going to help me practice some songs for an audition," offered Kai. "We're doing *Grease* this year."

"Oh. How nice."

Nervous, he added, "I told her she should try out, too."

"Lena does have a beautiful voice," said her mom, smiling. "But the only person she ever sings for is Cole."

"Come on," said Lena, pushing him down the hall toward her room. "We'll join you later," she called back to her mom.

"Don't forget to—"

"Yes, Mom, I'll leave my door open." She rolled her eyes.

Flopping down on her bed, Kai crossed his arms behind his head. "I guess I'm pretty special."

"Why is that?" asked Lena, sitting down next to him.

"Your mom thinks you only sing for Cole. But you sing for me, too."

"That's only because you *heard* me singing to Cole and wouldn't shut up until I sang to you, too."

He grabbed her hand and pulled her down next to him. "I

remember. It was his bedtime. You sang, 'I Can See Clearly Now.'" His expression softened. "It was so beautiful."

"Oh, yeah, that's one of his favorites." She rolled on her side and looked at Kai.

"So will you help me practice for *Grease*?"

"I guess. But I'm not trying out, so you might as well give up on that idea."

"Oh, Sandy," he sang. *"I sit and wonder why-yi-yi-yi . . ."*

She giggled. Kai trailed off, gazing at her, and she knew what was next.

They kissed for a few minutes, until Lena heard her dad making a lot of noise coming up the stairs. She and Kai sat up hastily, and Kai moved to the chair beside her desk.

Her dad appeared in the doorway, wearing a Raiders bandanna and carrying Cole's plastic sword. "Arrgh!" he cried. "Come downstairs, me hearties."

"Oh," said Kai. "Yo ho."

Lena stood up and walked out of her room. Kai followed, and her dad brandished the sword at him as he passed, saying, "Ye scurvy knave! I'll teach ye to eye me daughter with yer filthy peepers!"

"Right," said Kai. "Um, argh."

After the Raiders lost, Lena walked Kai out to his car.

"Sweet dreams," he said.

She kissed him, then backed away, singing, *"My head is saying, 'Fool, forget him' . . . My heart is saying, 'Don't let gooooo' . . ."*

Grinning, Kai put his hands to his heart in a display of theatrical devotion.

◻ ◻ ◻

When Lena woke up on the beach that night, she sank to her knees.

Oh, God, she thought, her heart leaping with fright. *There is something wrong with me.*

Shipwreck Rocks were closer this time. She watched the sweep of light from the lighthouse and listened to the call of the foghorn. After a few minutes, the terrified pounding of her heart was calmed by the regular pounding of the waves.

One thing she knew for sure: it was time to tell Kai and Pem.

CHAPTER 7

"Would you stop looking at me like that?" said Lena.

Kai jumped. "Like what?"

"Like I'm dying!"

They were eating lunch in the middle of a noisy bunch of drama people—Kai's friends, mostly—who kept bursting into songs from *Grease* and doing the hand jive.

"I'm sorry! I can't help it. Are you sure you're okay?" Kai put his arm around Lena, even though they had resolved not to force Pem to witness public displays of affection.

"Of course. Don't I look okay?"

"You *look* fine," said Pem. "But what if—" There was a tightness to her voice that Lena had never heard before.

She's scared for me, thought Lena. *She's scared I'm really sick.*

And what if there *was* something seriously wrong with her? Would Pem be able to handle it? Pem hated sad movies and sad songs and sad news in general. She still talked about the time her parents had let her watch *E.T.* when she was eight years old. "He was dead," she always said. "The bag was zipped up. It was horrible. I had nightmares for weeks."

In the cheerful light of day, Lena's sleepwalking seemed less ominous. But coupled with her fainting episode, she could see why her friends were worried.

"Pem," she said, making her voice as reassuring as she could, "I'm sure it's nothing. But . . . well, I wanted to tell you guys. I thought maybe one of you would say, 'Yeah, I sleepwalk all the time.'"

"No, I'm glad you told us," said Pem. "But you really have to tell your *parents.*"

"What? No." Lena shook her head. "No way."

"Lena, I've never heard of anyone doing that before. It doesn't sound like normal sleepwalking. What if you have—?" But she wouldn't finish the sentence.

Lena finished the sentence inside her own mind: *a brain tumor.*

"Fine," said Pem impatiently. "If you won't tell them, I will."

Outraged, Lena burst out, "NO! Do *not* tell my parents."

"Lena, we're talking about your *life*—"

Kai waved his hands between them. "Wait a minute, wait a minute. It's so obvious what's going on. Don't you see it?"

"See what?" asked Pem. Her arms were crossed, and she was glaring.

"The reason she's sleepwalking."

"The reason?" repeated Lena.

"It's so obvious," said Kai again. "I can't believe you didn't figure it out. It's the surfing."

"The . . . what?"

"Okay, listen: Lena has been obsessed with learning to surf, right?"

"So?"

"So she talked to her dad about surfing lessons again, and he said no, like he *always* does, and she's been upset about it. So her subconscious has been fixated on that, right? And even though she's asleep, her subconscious is trying to figure out how to . . . to make her dad change his mind. And for some reason, her subconscious makes her leave the house and go to the beach. Where the surfing is."

Both girls stared at him.

"That's crazy," said Lena finally.

"No, it actually makes sense," said Pem.

"It does not!"

"Right," said Kai. "*I'm* crazy. Meanwhile, *you're* not the one zombie-ing around at midnight." He stood up and staggered around, arms outstretched, groaning, "Brainz!" Then he pretended to be a zombie doing the hand jive.

Pem cracked up, and even Lena smiled. She got up and tossed her apple core into the trash. She opened a bottle of iridescent white nail polish and began to apply it to her fingernails, signaling the end of the discussion. "Pem, if it happens again, I'll tell my parents. But not right now."

Pem frowned. "You're making a mistake."

"I'm starting to think it was a mistake to tell you," said Lena.

Kai froze, mid-jive.

"That's harsh," said Pem.

"Can I trust you?" Lena looked up from her nail polish, all hint of humor gone from her expression.

After a moment, Pem nodded.

There was an uncomfortable minute while Lena continued to paint her nails, Kai focused on his pizza, and Pem sat in wounded silence.

Finally, with an attempt at lightening the mood, Pem said, "Guess who I saw on my way in this morning?"

Lena and Kai exchanged looks.

"No idea," said Lena, smirking.

"Do tell," said Kai, propping his chin on his hand and making wide eyes, as if hanging on her every word.

"You know who," said Pem. "Max." She beamed.

"Mad Max?" said Kai.

"Quit calling him that!"

"I'll quit calling him that when he quits gunning his motor like a poser."

"Kai, he drives a 1971 Mach One. Of course the motor is loud. That's why they call them muscle cars."

"Pemberley, there's a difference between merely *driving* your muscle car, and revving the engine like it's an extension of your manhood," said Kai.

Lena hid her smile with her hand.

Pem narrowed her eyes. She hated to be called Pemberley. "You don't even have your driver's license yet. I think you're just jealous."

"What does having a license have to do with your boyfriend's overcompensating?" said Kai. "I have *ears*. He revs his engine. Loudly."

"He's not my boyfriend," muttered Pem.

Max had been a senior at their school last year, and he went to San Francisco State now, so he still lived at home. He drove his brother to school sometimes, which allowed Pem to maintain her crush on him.

"He was looking at me, though," added Pem, glancing at Lena.

Of course he was, thought Lena. *Who wouldn't?* Pem was all big chocolate eyes, clear tanned skin, and bright white teeth. Her black hair hung almost to her waist. She was like a tall drink of gorgeous. Lena pondered her own boringly pale face, with its freckled nose and cheeks, and the scattering of zits that showed up like clockwork once a month. Next to beautiful Pem, Lena knew she was a single shot of nondescript. More than once, Lena had wondered what made Kai choose her.

"He's got the poutiest lips," continued Pem, staring off into space. She opened her vintage *I Dream of Jeannie* lunchbox— which she used as a purse—and extracted a tube of lip gloss.

"Hmm." Lena thought Max's pouty lips made him look spoiled.

"Hey, Leen," said Kai.

"Yeah?"

He folded his second slice of pizza in half. "Why don't you ask my sister to teach you to surf?" He took another massive bite.

Lena hesitated. "Did she tell you about that?"

"Abou' wha'?" he asked, mouth full.

"She offered to teach me."

"When?"

"The other day at Back Yard."

He swallowed. "Oh, cool. I didn't know. She's a really good teacher. She taught me and Jamie."

"That's a great idea!" said Pem.

"I don't think so," said Lena. "She's too intimidating."

"Nah," said Kai. "It's true she's a big old Amazon, but don't let that scare you. She just *looks* fierce. She actually cries every time she has to go back to school and leave her cat."

"What about a board?" said Lena.

Kai swallowed, then scratched the dozen scraggly whiskers on his chin. "There's a soft-top board in our garage. It's the one we all learned on."

A thrill of rebelliousness fluttered in Lena's belly. She could almost feel the waves lifting her on the board, could almost taste the salt of the sea on her lips.

"Want me to ask her?" said Kai.

"Yay!" said Pem. "Finally!"

Lena opened her mouth to say yes. "I better not," she answered. She was almost as surprised as Pem and Kai to hear those words.

CHAPTER 8

After school, Lena went home to an empty house. Her mom was still at the banking conference she had organized. Cole stayed at after-school daycare when both parents worked.

Lena cranked her favorite band—the Blue Lunatiks—on the iPod stereo while she searched through the cupboards in the kitchen. *Where's the—?*

She reached for a bag of chips, then stood looking at them. *The chips?*

She opened the bag and munched a few. No, but there was never a wrong time for chips. She looked around the kitchen, even opening the freezer. *Not in here.*

Lena wandered out to the living room. She opened the hall closet and peered inside.

This is crazy, she thought. *WHAT am I looking for?*

She ate a few more chips and put the bag away. She went upstairs and stood in the middle of her room, frowning. It must be in here . . . whatever *it* was. She went to her bureau and looked at her collection of cobalt-blue glass—started for her by Grandma Kath, whose birthplace was Bristol, England, famous for blue glass. Lena had some animals—a cat, a swan, a seal, and an angelfish, plus a few little perfume bottles and a sea-glass marble with veins of cobalt in it. She even had a miniature blue teapot with creamer and sugar bowl, all on a tiny tray. Nothing was missing.

Her gaze fell on the wooden hope chest at the foot of her bed. It was full of old toys, books, schoolwork, and photos. *Hmm . . . maybe it's in here.* She lifted the lid and propped it open.

Her favorite stuffed animals—the ones she had not been able to part with when Cole was born—lay on top in the chest.

Aw, Pinky, she thought, pulling out a stuffed pink hippo. She set Pinky down on the floor next to her, then extracted a plush bunny, a chenille teddy, Puss-in-Boots (complete with shiny black boots and feathered hat), and a green sea turtle.

The next layer down was a bunch of file folders containing elementary-school assignments and artwork. *I really can't draw,* she thought, perusing her crayoned stick figures.

Oh, here was her family tree. That was the big fourth-grade project. Lena remembered worrying that her tree would look strange, with three parents on it. But when she saw her classmates' family trees, she stopped worrying. Pem had two moms—she had been adopted from Guatemala when she was a baby—as did Zoe. Their friend Ryder had two dads. Andre and Kenny, who were twins, lived with their grandmother.

Lena slid her old school papers back in the file folders and set them aside.

Underneath a fuzzy pastel baby blanket, Lena found a photo album, its pages tied shut with yellow ribbon. She lifted it carefully out of the trunk. It was full of photos from her early childhood, before her mother died. She hadn't looked at it in years.

Even as she opened the cover, Lena knew the photo album wasn't what she was looking for. *It's too big,* she thought, then made a frustrated sound. *What* wasn't too big?

Lena flipped the pages in the album. Here she was as a new-born, plump and squished-looking, without any hair. There was a shot of her parents surrounded by flowers and balloons that said, "It's a girl!" and "Congratulations!" She was just a tiny bundle in her mom's arms in that one. Her dad looked so young and happy as he gazed at his wife and baby.

She turned the pages. There were more baby pictures . . . sleeping, posed in various outfits, wide-eyed and solemn, grinning toothlessly through a faceful of mashed peas, clapping, reaching for her dad, laughing . . . so many photos.

Lena turned the last page of the album and stared down at the photo of her mother. Lucy looked radiant in that shot, with her brilliant green eyes and reddish gold hair. The color of honey on fire, Lena remembered her dad saying once, long ago. Despite her beauty, Lucy's heart-shaped face was pale. *She must have already been sick,* thought Lena.

How old would Lucy be, if she were still alive? Lena felt a moment of shame at how little she knew about the woman who had given birth to her. In some ways, she was lucky that Mom—Allie—had filled all her maternal needs so completely that she didn't even miss Lucy.

When she was little—probably Cole's age—Lena had asked her dad a few times what happened to Lucy, but he always said, "I can't talk about it, sweetheart. I'm sorry. Someday when you're older, I'll tell you how we lost her."

What if it's hereditary? thought Lena. *Maybe I have whatever disease she had.*

She thought of the words *I AM FINE* being washed away by the waves.

◻ ◻ ◻

Lena's dad fixed spaghetti—his customary meal when Mom was working late. After dinner, Cole cleared the table and said, "Dad? Want to play catch?"

"Uh—"

Before Lena's dad could answer, Lena said, "I need to talk to Dad for a few minutes, Coley, okay?"

"Okay! I'll play basketball." He headed outside to play with his mini-hoop.

Lena's dad leaned against the kitchen counter. "What's up?"

"Um, I was wondering," said Lena, putting plates in the dishwasher. Then her throat closed as she prepared to utter the next words: *if you could tell me how my mother died.*

"Yes?"

Lena dried her hands with a towel.

Her father waited. Finally he said, "Honey, we're not going to move. I should never have said that. I—"

"No," said Lena. "It's not that. I want to know—" She forced herself to meet his gaze, and he looked at her quizzically. An image of that old photo—with her young, happy parents holding their new baby—came into her mind, and she could not bring herself to say: *how Lucy died.*

". . . if you ordered my cake yet."

Her dad smiled. "Lena. Your mom plans stuff for a living. Of course she ordered your cake! Why? Did you change your mind about having chocolate?"

"No," said Lena. "I was just wondering."

The sound of the garage door clattering open interrupted them.

Lena's dad looked toward the kitchen door. "Speaking of Mom," he said. "She's had a long day. Will you heat up some spaghetti for her?"

"Sure." She heaped pasta on a plate and put it in the microwave.

Cole banged in through the front door as their mom came in from the garage.

"Hellooo!" she called.

"Mom!" Cole raced up to her and threw his arms around her waist.

"Hi, Coley!" She bent over and hugged him. She looked up. "Hi, guys. Mmm, I smell spaghetti. Is there any left over?"

"It will be ready in two minutes," said Lena.

"Group hug!" yelled Cole. "Dad. *Da-ad.* Lena, come here."

Dad and Lena joined the other two, and they all embraced.

"I'm beat," said Mom. "I'm whipped. I'm exhausted. I'm . . . tired." She opened the closet door and tossed her shoes and coat inside. Then she collapsed on the sofa. "Oh, sofa," she groaned, "how do I love thee?"

Cole jumped onto the sofa next to their mom. "Mom, you know what? It's Monday. Can I watch *Monday Night Football?* Dad said I had to ask you." Cole was not allowed to watch TV during the week.

Mom groaned again. "Oh, honey," she said. "Mommy is just catatonic from telling people what to do all day. Please don't ask me right this second."

"What's cantatonic?" asked Cole.

Mom chuckled. "I guess it means I *can't* tell another person what to do today. Dad will have to make the call this time."

"Come on, bud," said Dad. "Let's read some books, then we'll tune in to the game." He and Cole left the room.

Lena took the plate out of the microwave and grated Parmesan cheese on top of the steaming pasta. Handing the plate to her mom, she joked, "I thought you never got tired of telling people what to do."

"Oh, thank you, sweetie," said her mom. "And yes, that's true. Generally, I'm quite comfortable bossing everyone around. As you well know." She took a bite of spaghetti and made appreciative sounds. She swallowed and said, "I guess negotiating TV on school nights is my weak spot. On the one hand, it's a school night, so . . . no TV. On the other hand, he's the biggest six-year-old sports fan on the planet. It seems wrong to deny him his football."

Lena poured a glass of red wine and handed it to her mom.

"Ohhh, Lena, you're the bearer of nectar and ambrosia tonight." She took a sip. "Delicious."

Mom must know, thought Lena. *Dad would have told her how my mother died.*

Scrolling through recorded shows on the DVR, her mom said, "Oh, *Project Runway*! Excellent! You know I love to watch that show while I eat. Those size-zero models make me feel hungry." She pressed Play on the remote. "Want to watch with me, sweetie?"

Lena regarded her mom, exhausted after a long day of work . . . now relaxing with leftovers and reality TV. "Sure," she said, and sat down next to her. The old sorrows could wait.

CHAPTER 9

Lena felt a flash of panic when she woke up. *Am I on the beach again?*

Then she felt her mattress beneath her . . . solid, not sandy. She saw the four walls of her room, covered with glossy waves . . . not the vast expanse of the Pacific. She relaxed, rolling over to see her clock radio. 5:40.

Earlier than usual, she thought, closing her eyes.

She tried to recapture the remnants of her dream. A woman's voice had been singing: *"By the light . . . of the silvery moon . . ."* But wait, it wasn't a *silvery* moon, in her dream. It was some other word—blueberry moon. Lena smiled in the darkness. The mind was a mysterious thing.

Oh! Lena's eyes flew open. *Today's my birthday.*

She climbed out of bed and went to her window. She pushed the curtains aside and gazed out at the darkness. A full moon hung in the sky, looking enormous. *The harvest moon,* thought Lena. Then she smiled. A silvery moon.

She climbed back in bed, snuggling down under the covers, but sleep would not come.

I guess I'm up, she thought. *Might as well go for a walk.*

She pulled on warm clothes and paused by her desk, looking down at the photo of Lucy she had removed from the photo album. She touched a finger to the image, and felt a surge of longing for her mother. "It's my birthday, Mama," she whispered. "I'm sixteen today."

Padding quietly down the stairs, she wrote on the dry-erase board:

OCTOBER 10! — went for birthday walk — back for pancakes — chocolate chip!

She slipped outside and hurried down to the beach. She took a deep breath once she reached the sand, filling her lungs with cold salt air. *My first present of the day,* she mused. *The beach.*

She headed north, in the direction of Magic Crescent Cove. The beam of light from Pelican Point Lighthouse winked at her over and over, as if beckoning her. "I'm coming," she whispered.

Why don't you ask my sister to teach you to surf? she heard Kai's voice in her head. Lena stomped her feet on the packed sand. *I should have said yes.*

She grabbed a long, pointed piece of driftwood and dragged it behind her as she walked. She stopped and wrote the words *I WILL SURF* in the wet sand.

The tide was still out when Lena came to the bend in the cove where Shipwreck Rocks loomed. She walked close to the water's edge, then climbed across the wet rocks and jumped down on the other side.

The sky began to lighten, imperceptibly at first. Just blackness, then a dark gray color, then pearl gray. Lena found a dry log farther down the beach and sat down. She rested her eyes on the sea, listening to the endless roar of the ocean, feeling tiny on the earth.

The sun rose, casting a weak October light through the clouds. Seagulls appeared as scribbles in the sky, wheeling and flapping. *It must be getting close to seven now,* thought Lena. *I should probably head back.*

But she lingered, gazing out to sea, her soul peaceful and open.

After another moment, her eyes focused on a distant rounded shape beyond the breakers. Two shapes. *Dolphins.*

She stood up, trying to see better. It was rare to see dolphins along this stretch of coast, and even more rare to see them this time of year. They circled and dove. Was that a third dolphin? Lena walked closer to the water, looking intently.

A wet head rose between the two dolphins. Was it a sea lion? How cool! It was like they were playing. She lifted her arm to wave at the sea lion.

No, the head was bigger and rounder than a sea lion's, without the characteristic snout. Lena's arm dropped as the head rose farther out of the water.

It was a woman.

The hair on the back of Lena's neck stood up. Her eyes widened. Was she seeing things? How could a woman be swimming out there in the middle of the ocean? *Between two dolphins?* Lena didn't blink.

The woman saw her, too, and seemed to be looking back just as intently. Lena could see the pale face, so definitely *not* a sea lion's face, but the woman was too far away for Lena to make out her features. As they stared at each other, the woman seemed to rise higher on the water in an effort to see Lena. Her bare white shoulders were above the surface now.

It's really a woman, thought Lena. *Not a sea lion. She must be freezing . . . she doesn't have a wetsuit on!*

Just as Lena was beginning to think she should run for help, the woman disappeared below the surface, leaving a ruffled patch of empty water behind.

Oh, my God, is she drowning? thought Lena, her heart racing. *I can't just stand here and let someone drown!*

Agonized, she waited to see if the woman would come up for air again. Just as she was about to turn and run, she thought she saw the head break the surface again, slightly closer now. She peered out to sea, wondering if she should call to her.

It was definitely a woman. Her face was still too far away to be clear to Lena, but it looked as if her mouth was open in astonishment.

They stared at each other, as if no one else on earth existed, a long silent moment of vision. Then, as Lena opened her mouth to call out, the woman disappeared below the surface again. As she dove, a glistening silver tail flashed out of the water and disappeared back into the sea.

¤ ¤ ¤

Heart racing, the mermaid dove. She swam in a panic, her thoughts scattering like frightened fish. *No, oh, no,* her mind wailed. *No.*

CHAPTER 10

Lena stood perfectly still in the same spot, trembling, for the next five minutes.

If she could believe her eyes, she had just seen a mermaid. If she had only *imagined* that flashing tail, then there was a woman out there in the frigid ocean. And if there was a woman out there, she was either drowning or swimming under water to some location where Lena could not see her, because Lena's eyes never left the water.

Finally, unwillingly, she turned to walk back down the beach, her legs shaky. The woman was gone, and so were the dolphins.

Lena felt the first tickle of belief in her belly: That was no human woman. That was a *mermaid*.

A tiny laugh escaped her throat. Mermaids were *real*.

She stopped and stared back at the sea. Was she really gone? Was it over, the moment of magic ended already? *Come back,* she thought. *Please.*

The mermaid had been playing with the two dolphins, Lena was sure of it. Out there in the vast deep lived a fairy-tale creature who was real, who was alive. Who played with dolphins. Who probably ate and slept, because didn't all living things need to eat and sleep? Who lived alone . . . or maybe with other mermaids! Lena's breath caught as she imagined a whole gathering of . . . what did you call a group of mermaids? A mist of mermaids? A marvel of mermaids?

She had to go, thought Lena. *They don't want to be seen.*

Lena broke into a run. She needed to do something physical, something that would help her body catch up to the rapid beat of her heart.

When she got to the rocks, Lena stopped and put her hands on the rough stones, feeling the solid reality of them. Already, doubts were surfacing.

It was a woman.

Of course it was.

She was out for an early-morning swim.

With no wetsuit? argued Lena's practical mind. *And what about that tail?*

There was no tail.

It was a trick of the light on the waves.

Lena nodded. She was always seeing things out in the water—that turned out to be nothing more than a random splash or a diving sea lion.

□ □ □

By the time Lena got home, she had convinced herself that she'd seen a woman swimming, not a mermaid.

She stepped into the dark house. *Everyone must still be asleep,* she thought.

"Surprise!" yelled Cole, running in from the living room.

Lena jumped.

"We were hiding," he explained. His eyes blazed like tiny twin gaslights. He threw his arms around Lena. "Happy birthday."

Her parents followed, embracing the two of them.

"Group hug," sang Cole.

"Thanks, guys," said Lena. "You're up so early!"

"That's the only way to surprise you," said her dad. "Mom set the alarm for six, but you were already gone. So we hunkered down in the living room to wait." He yawned.

"Dad fell back asleep," said Cole. He started to sing: "Haaappy birthday to yooou . . ."

Her parents joined in.

They were all gazing at her with such love that Lena found herself wanting to laugh and cry both. "Thanks, guys," she said when the song was finished.

"I'll start the pancakes," said her mom. She brushed back a strand of Lena's hair. "Did you have a nice birthday walk?"

Lena's smile faltered. *If that was a woman swimming, where did she go?*

"Yes," she said. "Very nice." *She just swam away. It was a woman, and she swam out of view.*

"Good," said her mom, and squeezed her. "Now . . . brekkie!" She turned toward the refrigerator.

"Mom," said Cole. "Can we have bacon, too?" He trailed after her.

"I can't believe you're sixteen," said Lena's dad. He blinked a couple of times and turned away. Lena knew he was blinking back tears when he did that. He went back into the living room, saying, "I've got a present for you in here."

Lena followed. Her dad patted the sofa next to him, and Lena sat down. He handed her a small box. "Happy birthday, sweetheart."

She smiled. "Thanks, Dad." Opening the box, Lena found a thin silver bracelet inside. She picked it up—there was a dolphin charm dangling from the links.

She shivered.

"Dad?" asked Lena.

"Mmm-hmm."

I saw something in the water, she thought.

He was looking at her now, so she had to say something. Without thinking, she asked, "Do the words 'blueberry moon' mean anything to you?"

Her dad paused. "As a matter of fact, they do."

"Really? I was thinking about them when I woke up this morning."

"You were?"

"Yes. This song kept going through my head: *'By the light . . . of the silvery moon,'* but then it seemed like those weren't the right words."

He tried to smile. "It was a song Lucy made up for you when you were little."

"Really?"

He nodded.

"How did the song go?"

He glanced at the kitchen door, then sang softly,

"By the light
of the blueberry moon
we sang this song
in Lena's room.
By the light . . ."

Lena joined in:

". . . of the blueberry moon
we sang this song
in Lena's room."

They smiled at each other.

"Why was it a blueberry moon?" asked Lena.

"I don't know. I think it was just because you loved blueberries."

"Oh." Lena looked at her father. "Did she sing to me a lot?"

He nodded, looking wistful. "All the time." A crooked smile came over his lips. "Sometimes—if I was very good—she even sang to me."

Lena glanced at him quickly. Did he know about her singing to Kai?

But her dad's gaze was unfocused, and it was clear he had wandered off into old memories.

Lena felt a strange jealousy—she couldn't remember her mother—she had only fragmented impressions of being at the beach with her.

Hazy memories of her mother were suddenly replaced by the sharp image of a silver tail.

She's real, thought Lena. *That mermaid was real. I did not imagine her. I need to see her again.* "Dad," she said.

"Yes, sweetie."

"It's my birthday," said Lena. "Please teach me to surf. It might be good for you! If we're in the water together, maybe you'll—"

Her father stood up, leaving a cold spot next to her. "I'm sorry, Lena," he said. "I can't."

Lena stood up, too. "Okay." She headed for the stairs.

"Where are you going? Mom's making breakfast."

"I'll be down in a minute," she said.

In her room, she sat down on her bed, reaching for her phone.

Hundreds of waves beckoned from her walls. Lena reached up and trailed her fingers over the collage of oceans.

If I want to see the mermaid again, she thought, *I have to go to Magic's. And the only way to get in the water at Magic's is on a surfboard.*

She texted a message to Kai: `Plz tell ani I'm ready for lessons.`

¤ ¤ ¤

Lena's birthday party that night was three hours of dedicated fun with friends. As she lay in bed that night, she tried to decide what her favorite part had been.

Was it Martha—who'd had a crush on her dad since fourth grade—belting out U2's "With or Without You" on karaoke, or was it Leslie and her boyfriend competing to see who could eat the most spicy tuna rolls? (Leslie, with fifteen.)

Pem's gift of an entire set of hardbound Jane Austen novels was pretty sweet, too. "What the heck," she had said. "I can't exactly ignore the fact that my name comes from *Pride and Prejudice.*"

No . . . the best part was Kai's present—a plush toy otter holding a tiny pink box. When Lena opened the box, a pair of pearl earrings glimmered against a bed of pink satin.

"Pearls for my pearl," Kai had said, then turned dark red.

Lena lay in bed, thinking of that moment. She had kissed him then, right in front of her parents. Because a guy who would do that for you . . . well, that must be love. She fingered the earrings already on her lobes and vowed never to take them off.

I'm so lucky, she thought, and closed her eyes. But as sleep began to wash over the memories of her Sweet Sixteen party, the last sharp image in her mind was of a white-shouldered woman in the sea, staring right at her.

CHAPTER 11

Lena's birthday present to herself was scheduled for Friday afternoon.

The school week seemed to creep and crawl and sometimes lie down for a nap. Lena knew she was driving Pem and Kai crazy with her thrilled nervous energy, but she couldn't help it.

The sight of the city bus chugging to the curb that Friday after school almost made her weep with joy. Lena's stop was before Pem's; as the bus came to her street, she hugged her. "See you after."

"Can't wait," said Pem, and waggled a "hang loose" hand-sign at her.

Lena was so wound up she ran all the way home, backpack slapping against the middle of her back. When she got in the house, she threw it off with a grunt.

No one was home yet; her mom was working on a charity golf tournament today, but she was due home at four, and Lena wanted to be long gone by then.

She took the stairs two at a time and went to her room. She put on her swimsuit, then shorts and a T-shirt. She grabbed her sandals and bounced back downstairs, heading for the garage.

Her wetsuit was hanging on the drying rack, as always. Wetsuits were a part of life for swimmers on the northern California coast—even if you didn't surf, you still had to wear a wetsuit in the frigid water. Lena could still remember her first one, when she was nine years old—it was the traditional black and gray, but her mom had used fabric paint to draw on bright silver stars.

Good thing Mom's not afraid of the ocean, thought Lena. She'd been the one to teach Lena how to swim, and all about safety in the water.

Lena folded the suit into her duffel bag and zipped it up. She grabbed a banana from the kitchen, thinking, *Fuel. My body is going to be working hard.* Then she filled up a water bottle, stashed it in her duffel, and stood waiting impatiently for her phone to ring.

Finally, it did—the Kai ringtone. "We're almost there," he said.

"Okay, I'll meet you outside."

Lena stepped out on the front porch and locked the door. She headed down the driveway just as Ani's red Jeep rounded the corner.

Kai jumped out and put his arms around her. "You ready?" he murmured.

She hugged him back. "Very."

He kissed her gently once. Twice. When he went for a third time, Lena pulled away. "Surf now, kiss later," she said with a smile.

Two surfboards protruded from the back of the Jeep. Kai climbed into the back seat, and Lena climbed in the front. "Hi."

"Hi," said Ani. "Ready to score some surf?"

"I'm ready."

"Good. It's a perfect day."

"You're welcome," said Kai. "I ordered it special for my girl." He reached forward and put his hand on Lena's arm.

"Sit back, Midget," said Ani. "You're interfering with my concentration."

Kai glared, but sat back.

"Do you think I'll be able to stand up the very first day?" asked Lena.

"Sure. It's called a pop-up. And yes, we'll just keep at it until you get at least one ride. Let's drive south a couple of miles. The waves look a little tall today for a beginner."

Good, thought Lena. *Maybe we won't see anyone we know.*

Ani parked on a gravel strip by the side of the highway, and the three of them clambered out. Standing next to the Jeep, they stripped down to their swimsuits and pulled on their wetsuits.

"Need some help?" asked Kai, standing close to Lena. His hand slid down her back. He gazed at her, looking like he might kiss her again, so Lena shook her head. "I've got it," she said, zipping up the wetsuit.

"Kai, grab your board and go," said Ani. "I need Lena to focus, and since you lack that ability entirely . . . please leave."

"You're wrong," said Kai, moving in for one last kiss. "My ability to focus on Lena is highly developed."

Lena pushed him away, laughing. He unhooked his board from the Jeep and headed down the path to the beach.

Ani unhooked the second board and led Lena to the beach.

Kai was kneeling next to his board when they reached him, applying wax. His board was bright blue with a black skull-and-crossbones on it. Ani tossed the green soft-top board next to him and put her hands on her hips, looking at Lena.

"I've heard you're a good swimmer," she said.

"I am."

"That's good. Because a surfer whose board has gotten away from her is just a swimmer, okay? You wear a leash for the board, but leashes can break. And surfing is hard work— you can get tired real fast out there in the water. In fact, I suggest you start doing pushups to build your upper-body strength, okay?"

"Okay."

"Great. Which foot are you?"

"What?"

"Which foot are you? Regular or goofy?"

"Um . . ."

"Don't you skateboard?"

"No."

"Really? I always thought every surfer was a skater, too."

Lena shrugged. She didn't care about rolling on concrete . . . she wanted to be in the water.

"Okay, here's what we're going to do," said Ani. She walked around Lena and stood behind her. "Just relax. I'm not going to do anything to hurt you. Do you trust me?"

"Sure." Lena stood still, waiting tensely.

A long moment passed, while they stood in silence. Lena tried to relax, listening to the lull of the surf, watching the perfectly formed waves roll onto the shore, one by one. Suddenly, Ani shoved her. Lena instinctively put out her right foot to keep herself from falling.

"Aha! A goofy-foot," said Ani.

"A what?"

"I wanted to see which foot you put forward to catch yourself. You put your right foot out first, so your stance on the board will be right foot forward, otherwise known as goofy-foot. Left foot is regular."

"Left foot is . . . ?"

"Regular. Sorry if I startled you. That's just the best way I know to find your stance."

"That's okay."

"Of course, if it ends up feeling wrong while you're surfing, then by all means try the other foot. It's not a perfect system." She smiled. "Now come sit down with me for a while."

Lena sat down on the board next to Ani.

Kai had finished waxing his board and now leaped on top of it, singing the chorus from "Greased Lightning."

Lena cracked up, watching him wiggle his hips and flap his knees open and closed.

Ani rolled her eyes. After a moment, she said, "I'm sorry to say, Midget, but you're no Danny Zuko."

"I know I'm not," said Kai. "I got the part of Kenickie."

"Then why are you learning 'Greased Lightning'?"

"Because we're doing the stage version of *Grease*. Kenickie gets to sing that song, not Danny."

"Oh. Well, that's great, but now I need you to shut up, okay?"

Kai sat down on his board, winking at Lena.

"We're just going to watch the shorebreak for a while, Lena," said Ani. "Every time you get ready to surf, before you get into the water you need to sit with the waves first, to see how they're breaking. Just sit and watch them for a few minutes. Are they breaking big or small? Are they coming one on top of the other, or are they spread out? And watch for a rip. Have you ever gotten caught in a rip tide?"

Lena nodded.

"So you know to swim parallel to shore until you're out of it. Don't try to fight it."

They sat quietly. Lena glanced over at Ani, who was studying the waves intently.

Doesn't everyone know how to do this? thought Lena. She had been "reading" the waves as plainly as if they were books for as long as she could remember. It had never occurred to her that some people had to be taught how to do it.

"Perfect," murmured Ani. "Nice, mushy waves. Good for beginners."

She looked at Lena, and now her expression was stern. "Next thing, before we even get in the water, I want to remind you that this isn't a swimming pool. This is Mother Nature, and she is powerful. Respect her power. Learn to protect yourself, because this Mother has no loyalty. Once you've learned how to take care of yourself, *then* you'll be able to have fun."

Kai stood up and said, "Yeah, yeah, yeah. Just let her get in the water." He caressed Lena's cheek and said, "See you out there."

As Kai splashed into the water and lay down on his board, Ani said, "Let's watch him for a few minutes. Then we'll get in, I promise."

"Okay."

"See how he's got his back kind of arched, and he's using nice fluid motions? That's the right way to paddle. Just your arms. If you put your whole body into it, you'll wear yourself out." Ani pointed to the surfers already in the water. "That's the lineup. Don't get in their way . . . like Kai is doing. If a good wave broke right now, they'd have to try to avoid him. Or worse, someone might decide to ride right over him, to teach him a lesson."

They watched the surfers for a few more minutes. A promising wave rose up, and three of the surfers began to paddle furiously, including Kai.

"See that girl?" said Ani. "She's on the inside of that wave."

Lena nodded, studying the position of the three surfers.

The girl surfer popped up first on her board, on the "inside," as Ani had said, earning the right of way. One of the other surfers cut his board back up over the wave and kicked out to wait for the next one.

Kai, however, continued riding the wave next to her, knees bent, wiry body balancing with the swell.

"Okay, do *not* do that," said Ani. "Do not drop in on someone else's ride. It's not cool."

"Why would he do that?"

"Surfers can be really competitive. Especially to girl surfers. I guarantee he wouldn't do that to a dude. He might get his skinny butt kicked. Which reminds me. As a girl, you have to be hyperaware of the mood out in the lineup. If you ever find yourself in a situation that feels unsafe, get out of the water and leave. Live to surf another day. Now. Let's practice your stance before we head out."

"Okay."

"I want you to lie down on the board, do a pushup, and land on the deck like this." Ani demonstrated, then had Lena practice a few times. After she was satisfied that Lena had mastered the landing, Ani said, "Awesome! Let's go surfing!"

The water was cold, but Lena barely noticed the temperature. It was such a relief to relax into weightlessness in the sea that she nearly wept. Lena hadn't been swimming for ages. The heartbeat of the ocean pulsed around her, as if to say "Welcome back."

"Lie down on your stomach on the board," instructed Ani. "Feet together. Good. Wow, you're doing great with balance! Just staying on the board is hard enough."

Lena smiled. The rocking motion of the swells felt as soothing to her as being rocked in a cradle.

"Okay, Lena, here comes a little wave. Arch your back and grab the rails to do a pushup."

"The rails?"

"Sorry, the rails are the sides of the board. Here it comes!"

Lena did as Ani instructed, and Ani helped push her board over the wave. "Great! That was a little one. When you get a bigger wave coming toward you, you'll have to turn turtle. That means you're going to roll over, holding on to your board, so that the wave washes over you."

They jumped a few more small waves, then Lena said, "I want to try a pop-up."

"You sure you're ready?"

"Yes!"

"Okay, on the next little broken wave, I want you to do a pushup, but this time get to your feet. Remember to put your goofy-foot forward. Here it comes."

Lena felt the swell of the wave touch the board and pass into her very soul. She pushed with her arms, then jumped to her feet. She wobbled a little, balancing, and kept her knees bent, to lower her center of gravity.

"That's great, Lena!" shouted Ani, as Lena rode the white water to the shore. "Fall away from the board."

As the board stalled out, Lena allowed her body to fall away from the board.

"You're a natural!" cried Ani. "I can't believe you stayed up the whole time! It took Kai, like, two weeks to catch a wave and stay up for the whole ride."

Lena smiled. "That was fun!"

"It's the best. You're going to be really good at it, I can tell. Must be hereditary."

Lena cocked her head at Ani.

"Wasn't your dad a really good surfer? You know, back when he used to surf?"

"Um . . . I really don't know."

"My dad says they all used to surf Magic's together."

"They did?"

"Yeah. And Magic's doesn't treat fools kindly, so you know he must've been good."

The mention of her father cast a shadow over Lena's joy. What would he do if he knew she was out here?

"Ani?"

"Yes?"

"I really shouldn't stay much longer. And . . . I'm getting tired."

"Thanks for telling me. Some people don't know when to come in. They stay out so long they get hypothermic. Let's head for the beach. Can you get to shore on your own? I just want to catch a couple of waves. Then we'll call it a day."

"Sure." Lena climbed out of the rolling surf and dried herself off with a towel. She sat down to watch Ani and Kai surf. They were laughing and yelling insults at each other.

"Way to drain out, Midget!" called Ani.

"Don't call me Midget, Gidget!" yelled Kai.

I want to surf with Dad, thought Lena, with a pang. *I want him to tell me I'm a natural. Maybe someday.*

When Ani and Kai had had enough, they headed for the beach.

The three of them peeled off their wetsuits and poured jugs of fresh water over them, to clean the sand and salt off.

Kai put his arms around Lena before she had a chance to slip back into her shorts and T-shirt. He ran his hands over her back and shoulders, causing her bare skin to tingle. "You looked great out there," he said.

"Thanks. It was awesome. I can't wait to be good at it."

He pressed her closer to him, and kissed her. "Trust, Leen. You were meant to surf."

CHAPTER 12

Lena sent a text to Pem: Surfing rulez!

After a moment, a message came back from Pem: Yayyyyy! Woo-hoo!!!

Lena: Ani is a super great teacher.

Pem: I wish I could have gone w/ u but wait til u hear what happened!

Lena: ??

Pem: U will never believe it.

Lena: Do I rly hafta guess?

Pem: Hee! I will tell u when u get here.

Lena: OMG ur evil!

Pem: See u soon. Xoxo

Lena made an impatient sound.

Ani glanced over at her. "Everything okay?"

"Yeah." Lena closed her cell phone. "Pem has some news, but she won't tell me until I get to her house. Thanks for dropping me off there." Lena had asked Ani to take her to Pem's house so she could change clothes and dry her hair before she went home.

"No problem. Do you want to get together next Friday for another lesson?"

"Yes! I already can't wait!"

Ani smiled. "It won't be long before you're surfing on your own. You've got a really good grasp of the basics already. Although I don't mean you should surf *alone*. You should always take someone with you." She cocked her thumb at Kai in the back seat, who was listening to his iPod. "Like Pig-Dog there. He's ready to get in the water anytime."

"Pig-Dog?"

"Kai keeps trying to get me to call him Kaiborg or Flea or Skeleton or something like that. He's dying for a cool surf name." She flipped on her left blinker, then turned down Pem's street. "So of course I torture him with bad nicknames." She pulled up in front of Pem's house and put the Jeep in park. "Okay, Lena, see you next Friday. Same time?"

"Yes, that would be great. Thank you sooo much, Ani. Please let me pay you?"

Ani shook her head. "No, I already told you. I'm not doing this for the money. I love surfing, so it feels like a rite of passage, you know? Sharing the surf-love. Helping a new surfer learn the ropes. Or the rails, I should say. Someday *you'll* help someone and pass on the good karma."

"I will," said Lena. She climbed out of the Jeep, and Kai leaped out of the back seat.

"Call me later," he said, enfolding Lena in his arms again. He was deep in the middle of a goodbye kiss when Ani honked, making them both jump.

Lena laughed. "Bye."

Ani drove away, Kai waving from the front seat.

Lena knocked, and Pem threw open the door.

"I am a surfer now," said Lena.

Pem squealed and hugged her. "I know! I can't wait to surf with you. Come on in. Mama Mia's fixing dinner. You can stay, right?" One of Pem's moms was named Mia, so Pem had grown up calling her Mama Mia. Her other mom was just "Mom."

"Sure," said Lena. "Can I take a shower first, though? I'm all salty."

"Yeah, yeah."

"But first I want to hear your big news!"

"Come to my room," said Pem. From the glow on her face, Lena knew it had to be about Max. Once they were inside, Pem burst out, "Guess who called me?"

"Hmm, let me see," said Lena. "The president?"

"Stop!" said Pem, pushing her shoulder. "You know it was Max."

"I'm stunned."

"I was so nervous I could hardly breathe! We talked for, like, half an hour."

"Really? What did you talk about?"

"Oh, you know. We were just talking. Nothing special. About school, and music, and surfing. He said we should hang out sometime."

"Hang out? He actually said 'hang out'? He's in college! Shouldn't he be a little smoother with the ladies by now?"

Pem cracked up. "Probably. But I like that he's not smooth. He even said that college is totally intense, and he kind of misses high school."

Lena reached for a comb, trying not to feel annoyed that they were talking about Max, as usual. She had wanted to tell Pem all about her first time surfing, but clearly Pem's conversation with Max was far more thrilling to her than anything else. "So . . . are you going out with him?" She worked the comb through her salt-sticky hair.

"I don't know. It was just a phone call."

"Today it's a phone call, tomorrow you're cruising around in that muscle car of his."

Pem giggled. "Can you just see my moms' faces when he drives up in that thing, all loud and kicking out blue exhaust?" Pem made engine-revving sounds. "'Uh, yeah, see you later, Mrs. Er . . . Pem's mom and Mrs. Pem's other mom. I'll have your daughter home early.'" She imitated the sound of tires peeling out.

"Yes," continued Lena, imitating Max. "I'm here to take out your fifteen-year-old daughter in my luuuuv machine."

"I think having two moms is going to make it even harder to date than having the usual parent-combo," said Pem. She fiddled with the braided anklet on her leg. She and Lena had made yarn anklets a couple of years ago. Pem's was three different colors of pink, in keeping with her penchant for all things Jeannie-esque.

Lena didn't answer for a minute, just combed her hair, then she said, "Maybe. They don't want you to date until you're sixteen, I know, but that's pretty standard."

Pem frowned. "I don't want to wait that long, though! I won't be sixteen for four more months. You're lucky."

"I am?"

"That your parents let you start going out with Kai."

"Well, that was different. Kai was already *there*. They knew him. In fact, they didn't even know we were together until my mom saw us kissing on the beach one day, and the cat was out of the bag. Now they're always trying to make us hang out with them in the family room, instead of in my room."

"Still," said Pem. "How can I make my moms let me go out with Max?" She blushed. "If he asks, of course."

"Pem. He's going to ask. He's just too lame to come right out and do it."

"He's not lame!" Pem gave Lena a playful punch on the shoulder. "He's reticent."

"Reticent?" Lena laughed. "Vocabulary much?"

"Dude, you know I can't even help it. With a mom who teaches English, I'm doomed."

"Or fated."

"Preordained."

"Destined."

They giggled.

"I smell garlic," said Pem. "Let's see what Mama Mia is making for dinner."

"Okay, but first I need to get the salt water off me," said Lena, heading for the bathroom. "Do you have an extra towel?"

"They're in the cupboard," called Pem through the door. "You can wash off the sand, Leen, but you can't wash off that smile. You'd better cheer down before you see your parents."

◻   ◻   ◻

The next day Max was waiting for Pem after school.

Lena saw him leaning against his car in his trademark Hawaiian shirt, glancing around casually, as if to say, "I just happened to end up parked here in front of my old high school. No reason."

But Lena knew instantly he was here for Pem, and turned to tell her.

Pem, of course, had already seen him, since she had super-strength Max Radar. Her face was alight. "Oh, my God," she whispered.

"I know!" Lena whispered back.

Just then Henry, Max's brother, walked up to the car.

"Oh," said Pem. "Maybe he's just here to take Henry home."

"No way," said Lena. "He's here for you."

They kept walking, and sure enough, when Max saw them, he smiled and waved.

Pem waved back.

"Hi," he called.

Pem and Lena approached the car.

"Need a ride?" called Max. "I was just here to pick up Henry"—*Right,* thought Lena—"but I'd be happy to take you and your friend home." He nodded at Lena.

"Sure," said Pem, affecting the same casual air.

Everyone stared as Henry flipped down the front seat, indicating that Pem and Lena should get in back. Max frowned, but Henry didn't seem to notice.

The girls glanced at each other, then climbed into the back seat of the Mustang.

That was the last day Pem rode in the back seat.

The next day Max was there again, to "pick up Henry," and he offered them a ride home again. This time when Pem accepted, Max relegated Henry to the back seat with a cock of his head. There was a split second of awkwardness before Lena joined him, then Pem slid gracefully into the front seat as if she owned it.

Lena actually rolled her eyes the third day Max was waiting outside school. Why didn't he just ask Pem out, instead of going through this whole Oh-hi-I-just-ran-into-you-here scenario?

When he offered them a ride home, Lena declined, much to Pem's consternation.

"Come on, Lena!" she whispered.

"Why?" asked Lena. "Why can't you just go without me? Why do I have to be there?"

"Just . . . it seems like it's more natural if you're there."

"What's the big deal? Henry is there."

"Yeah, but you know my parents would get all horrified if they saw me riding around in a car with a college guy! At least if you're with us, it doesn't seem so . . . like, private."

"It's not private! You're riding around in broad daylight with Henry in the back seat. You don't need me. Your parents probably wouldn't mind at all."

"Lena, come *on*. I'd do it for you."

Lena sighed. It was true. Pem would do anything for her, including letting Lena stop off at her house and shower before going home from her surfing lessons. "Okay," she said.

"Thanks," said Pem, squeezing Lena's elbow. Then she opened the door of the Mustang with an air of possession, and pushed down the front seat so that Lena could get in back.

Making a face at her, Lena climbed in. "Hey, Max," she said.

"Hey, Lena."

"Hi, Henry."

Henry glanced over at her, then quickly looked away, his face reddening. "Hi," he said.

They drove without speaking, the hip-hop music of Friendly Frenzy booming from the car's speakers.

Max took Lena home first.

"Thanks, Max," she said. "Talk to you later, Pem."

"See ya."

"Bye, Henry."

Henry lifted his hand briefly.

Relieved to be out of the car, away from the loud thumping bass and the silent slumping brother, Lena went into her house.

CHAPTER 13

The song in Lena's mind was bittersweet, full of lilts and trills, but with a minor-key melancholy. She hummed along, trying to memorize it. *I hope I remember it when I wake up,* she thought.

"Lena," said a voice in her dream.

Yes, she answered.

"Where are you going?"

Magic's, she said.

"Why?"

It's Magic there.

Then someone touched her arm, and Lena woke up.

She was standing next to the sliding-glass door in the family room, her hand on the lock, her mother next to her.

Mom kept hold of her arm. "Sweetie," she said. "Are you okay?"

Lena blinked a couple of times, orienting herself. It was dark outside the glass door, and the family room was in darkness, too, except for a small circle of light cast by the table lamp in the corner.

"I'm okay," she said, noting the worry on her mom's face. "What time is it?"

"It's five a.m.," said her mom. "I got up early because I had some work to do." She released Lena's arm. "You . . . you were humming again. And your eyes were open." Lena heard the unspoken part of her sentence: *Just like that day on the beach.*

Lena flashed on her mom saying, ". . . straight to the ER next time." She scrambled for a convincing explanation. "I got up early, too."

Her mom studied her for a moment, then said, "You did?"

Lena looked at her reflection in the dark glass. Luckily, she was dressed . . . not still in her pajamas. "Yes."

"But you didn't act like you saw me."

"I . . . didn't," she said. "I was thinking about something else."

"You said you were going to Magic's." Lena's mom was still tense, but Lena could see she *wanted* to believe her daughter was okay.

"I couldn't sleep," said Lena smoothly. "I thought I would take a walk."

Now Mom was shifting from worried to adamant. "Absolutely not, Lena! I don't want you out walking in the dark."

Lena shrugged and moved away from the door. Mom would feel better now that she thought Lena was clueless, rather than delirious. "Okay. This is super-early for you to be up, though, isn't it?"

Her mom went to the couch and picked up her laptop. "Yes, well, you know me: the hardest-working lazy person in the world. There were some loose ends I *had* to tie up today before the trade show." She settled on the couch. "You're welcome to sit with me, but you'll have to read or do something quiet. I need to concentrate."

"That's okay. I'll just go back to my room," said Lena.

"All right, sweetie."

Lena felt her mom's eyes on her as she walked out of the room.

Instead of returning to her bedroom, Lena went into her dad's study. She opened the window and stared out into the darkness, hoping to see a sliver of ocean in the distance. She breathed in the sea air and listened to the foghorn.

Why is it called Magic's? she thought.

That stretch of coast was officially named Crescent Cove. That was the name on all the signs on the highway. Why did the locals call it Magic Crescent Cove?

Maybe someone saw something magical there.

Lena closed the window and went down the hall to her room. She climbed in bed. It wasn't even five thirty yet; she might as well try to go back to sleep.

She closed her eyes. Images of perfectly formed waves rolled through her mind. She rode the waves . . . no surfboard necessary. In her waking dreams, she dove and turned and shifted with the tides, all by herself. Not even a wetsuit.

Like the mermaid, she thought.

◻ ◻ ◻

The mermaid woke from fitful slumber.

She had drifted for days in the magical cove, hoping to see the girl again. She knew it was madness to linger here, risking discovery, but she could not depart. When she was hungry, she found a reef full of mussels. When she was exhausted from hours of scanning the shoreline, she allowed herself to sink into restless sleep.

She draws me as powerfully as any Siren, mused the mermaid. *What gifts does she possess?*

Finally, weak and wasted, the mermaid abandoned her vigil.

CHAPTER 14

Lena's pulse quickened at the sight of the red Jeep pulling into her driveway. Of course, she was happy to see Kai—he had rehearsals every day after school except Friday—but she was even happier to know that she was minutes away from immersing herself in the cleansing sea.

Lena closed the front door behind her and ran to Ani's Jeep.

Kai jumped out and kissed her. "Are you ready to ride?"

Laughing, she brushed past him and climbed in the back of the Jeep.

"No, I'll sit there," he protested.

"I don't mind. It's only fair to take turns."

Kai pretended to climb in the back with her, and Ani said, "I'm growing weary of you, Kai. If you want a ride, sit down and buckle up. Otherwise get out and walk to Back Yard."

With a scowl, Kai sat down in front.

"Hi, Leen," said Ani. She put the Jeep in gear and pulled out of the driveway. "Ready for lesson number two?"

"I can't wait!"

"Good. Today's lesson: how to wipe out."

"Yay!" cried Lena into the wind.

Ani returned to the stretch of coast where she had taught Lena her first lesson.

"This is a sweet spot for beginners," she explained. "And it's off the beaten path, so there aren't as many locals to get bent out of shape at us for breathing their air and touching their waves."

Lena hurried into her wetsuit and snapped on her leash.

"All set?" asked Ani.

"Hang on, I just need—" said Lena, reaching into her duffel bag.

Ani waited.

Lena drew her hand out. *I just need what? Not this craziness again!* "Nothing," she said. "I'm ready."

"Paddle out and practice what I showed you last week," said Ani. "I'll critique."

Lena splashed into the ocean and lay down on the deck of the surfboard, enjoying the sensation of sliding through the water as she propelled herself forward.

As Ani watched Lena on the board, she called out instructions like "Bend your knees," "Keep that foot turned out," and "Turn turtle!"

Once Ani was satisfied that Lena was proficient on the board, she called over to Kai, "Hey, Pig-Dog, can we borrow your board for a few minutes?"

"Why would I let you borrow my board?"

"So I can teach Lena how to duck-dive."

"And I'll use the soft-top?"

"Duh, Dog."

Kai considered. "If you call me Maverick the rest of the day, you can use my short board for twenty minutes."

"I'll call you Goose the rest of the day," muttered Ani under her breath. She called out, "You got it, Maverick!"

They exchanged boards, and Ani explained to Lena, "You need to know how to protect yourself in the water, whether it's from a surfer who's out of control, or your own wipeout. Sometimes you need to turn turtle, and sometimes you need to duck. You can't duck a long board, but you can a short one." Pushing down hard on the board, Ani dove under an oncoming wave.

Lena practiced a few times, then it was back to the long board.

"I'm going to let you head out to the lineup in a minute. Your timing is really good with catching the waves. You don't need to keep surfing the mushy waves. So we need to talk about wiping out. Because wiping out is just part of surfing."

"Okay."

"I know you've grown up swimming in the ocean, so you know what it feels like to get tossed around under water when a wave crashes over you, right? You pretty much feel like an insignificant little pebble."

"Totally."

"You've learned just to relax and go with the flow, yes?"

"Yes."

"You can hold your breath a long time. Longer than any wave can last. So just wait till it stops churning, then push yourself up to the surface."

"Okay."

"Are you ready to try the lineup?"

"I'm ready."

"Go, girl!"

Exhilarated, Lena paddled out to the lineup, a huge grin on her face.

"Hey, noob!" called Kai. "Show me what you can do!"

The other surfers eyed her.

"Great," muttered one. "Just what this spot needs. More beginners."

"I know, right?" said his buddy. "Like there aren't enough surfers in the world already. Dang."

Lena saw Kai's expression go tight, and she said quickly, "It's cool. I can wait."

Kai's body was tensed up, but he forced a big smile and said, "Awesome, dudes, you're so right. It's your world . . . we just surf in it. Go ahead and bag the best waves. Then my girl's gonna take a ride and close this place down."

Everyone laughed, and Lena relaxed. Kai was good at keeping the peace out on the water.

"Aww, yeah," said the first guy. "I wanna see you in action now. And no disrespect. Everyone's gotta start somewhere."

They hung back, allowing Lena to get set up. When a good wave approached, the second guy said gruffly, "Hurry up. You can have this one."

Lena waited to feel just the right movement of the wave's swell, then used her arms in a butterfly motion to paddle the last few feet before she popped up. Landing on the deck of the board, feet perfectly planted, she rode the wave like she had been born to do it.

"Tear it up!" shouted Ani.

This was a bigger wave than any of the ones she had ridden before, and the feeling of rushing through the water as if on the back of a dolphin made Lena breathless with joy.

She let herself slip off the back of the board when the ride was finished, and came up laughing, tangled in kelp. Out in the lineup, people were clapping and hooting.

"Just kind of glide out of the kelp. Don't struggle with it," said Ani.

Lena shrugged her shoulders and wriggled her legs, and the kelp slid off. She turned and waved at the other surfers.

"I can't believe how you rock at this," said Ani. "It takes some people years to get good at surfing. It's almost like you anticipate the way the wave is going to move! You really only need me for maybe one more lesson."

"Wow, are you kidding?"

"Not kidding. Next week we'll try a different spot."

"Magic's?" asked Lena.

Ani stood still in the water. "No, not Magic's," she said, giving Lena an odd look. "Magic's is only for advanced surfers, and even then, it's dangerous. The shorebreak comes up out of the deep water and lands hard on the sand. It's not a nice, gradual shorebreak. Besides . . . why would you want to surf at Magic's?"

So I can see the mermaid, thought Lena. "Why wouldn't I?" she said. "I mean, if I ever got to be a really good surfer."

"Isn't that where your father almost . . . ?"

"What?" said Lena.

"Not to mention—" Ani broke off quickly.

Lena stared. "Not to mention what?"

Ani glanced back at the shore. "I think we should call it a day. Why don't we dry off?"

"Wait. What were you going to say?"

Ani refused to answer. "Nothing. Really. Let's get out."

CHAPTER 15

Lena and Henry developed a nonverbal relationship. When Max was yammering on about cars, they pantomimed snoring. When he whined about how hard his college classes were, they used their thumb and finger to play tiny violins. When Pem giggled over-brightly at some attempt at humor by Max, they rolled their eyes and pretended to vomit.

Sometimes Henry was already plugged into his iPod when Lena climbed in the back seat. Then he just nodded at her and returned his attention to his music. Lena figured there were days when he couldn't even muster up the enthusiasm for mockery.

"Bye," called Lena as she hopped out of the car one afternoon. "Thanks, Max."

"Call me later," said Pem.

"Yep." Lena waved at Henry, who made a "Save me!" face. Giggling, she watched Max drive away, and went into the house.

"You're home early," said her mom.

"Oh," said Lena. She had never told her mom about getting rides home from Max. Lately her mom had arrived home from work later than Lena got home from school, so there was no need to account for her time. But it looked like today was the day. "I got a ride home," she said.

"You did? That's nice," said her mom, frowning at her laptop screen. "Darn it. They've double-booked the lower ballroom that day." She began to tap madly on the keyboard.

"Mom," said Cole. "Let's go to the beach." He was holding his Nerf football.

"Pretty soon, sweetie," said their mom. "I have to fix something for work."

"I'll take him," said Lena.

"Oh, that would be great, honey," said her mom. "I'll try to join you guys when I finish."

"No problem. Come on, bud. Let's beach it."

Cole rocketed out the door, football tucked under his arm like he was running for a goal.

As they strolled down the street, Cole chattered about his most beloved subject. "You know what, Lena? You know who my favorite player is?"

"No."

"Ronde Barber. He's a cornerback. So maybe I'll be a cornerback when I grow up. He holds the record for . . ."

Lena made sounds that indicated she was listening, although her mind was on surfboards. If she had her own, would she want a long board or a short board?

As they neared the beach parking lot, Lena could see Max's car parked in the lot. The windows were rolled down, and two dark heads leaned close together.

Maybe they're just talking, she thought.

But even at this distance, it was obvious the occupants of that car had not come to the beach to admire the view.

With a jolt, Lena realized that Pem's relationship with Max had made the shift from friendly to physical . . . and Pem had not told her.

Thinking back over the past week, Lena felt like smacking her forehead. Pem had become more relaxed in the presence of Max-the-College-Guy, and Lena had figured it was Pem's natural confidence. Now she realized it was because Pem and Max had moved beyond casual rides home, and into *parked cars.*

"Come on, Coley," she called, and ran down the beach path.

Cole raced after her.

Lena breathed easier once she reached the sand. Wading into the surf, she felt the familiar delicious shock of cold, followed by a feeling of warmth as her skin adjusted to the water temperature. She stood still for a minute while little waves washed over her feet, a constant, hypnotic ebb and flow.

Cole dashed toward a flock of seagulls, scattering them. The birds rose lazily into the air and settled down on the sand again a few yards away.

Lena stared out at the sea for a few minutes. *Where are you, mermaid?* Then she walked back up the beach and sat down. She dug her toes into the top layer of soft, warm sand and into the chilly layer underneath. She closed her eyes, wondering if she would spend the rest of her life searching the waves for a creature that would never appear again.

"Want to play catch?" called Cole.

Lena opened her eyes. She didn't really want to play catch, but he looked so small and hopeful that she couldn't say no. She grinned up at him, then rolled over quickly, catching him by the knees. He squealed, his legs buckling, and sat down in the sand.

"That's not catch!" He laughed. "That's a tackle."

"I know," said Lena. "Because I'm an awesome football player, and you never knew it."

"You are?" He looked amazed.

She stood up, holding out her hand, and he grabbed it, pulling himself up. "Well, not really. But I'm an excellent tackler. Or wait . . . no, I meant TICKLER!" She caught him in her arms and gently took him down to the sand again, tickling him.

He laughed and squirmed. Finally she helped him up, his blond hair full of sand and his cheeks rosy. They tossed the Nerf football back and forth for a while, then Lena said, "Time to head home, bud."

Cole didn't complain, just followed her back up the beach and across the gravel parking lot—which was blissfully free of classic Mustangs. When they reached the sidewalk, Cole took her hand, this time chattering about his teacher, Mr. Neil, and the classroom's hamsters.

As Lena held his hand, she thought, *This is what's important. Not elusive sea creatures that are possibly all in my head.* A rush of love swept over her, and she squeezed his hand, murmuring, "Really? You might get to bring Nutmeg and Cinnamon home some weekend? That's so cool."

When they got home, their dad's car was in the driveway.

"Dad's home!" cried Cole, and he turned to Lena with wide eyes. "Let's surprise him."

"Okay," said Lena. "We'll sneak in through the garage door instead of the sliding door."

They entered the garage from the side and went to the door leading to the kitchen. Lena turned the knob quietly and eased open the door. She could hear her parents' voices in the family room, but they couldn't see the kitchen door. She tiptoed inside, and Cole followed.

"... not the right time," she heard her dad say.

"Yes, it is. Brian, you can't keep putting it off. It's not fair to her! How do you think Lena's going to feel when she finds out the truth?"

Lena froze when she heard her mom's voice, usually so calm, raised to a cry.

"Allie, I *told* you I just need a little more time. Don't you think I've had enough going on? Starting a new job, and—"

"You're trying to pretend it's not happening, but it is. We can't go on like this!"

Lena had an overwhelming desire to push Cole back out the door so he wouldn't hear their parents fighting, but he was already standing next to her, his face dismayed. She put her arm around him and said, "It's okay, Coley. They're just having a disagreement. Just like you and Austin do sometimes."

His lower lip trembled. Their parents never fought in front of them.

"Mom," said Lena, stepping into view.

There was a shocked silence.

Mom walked into the kitchen and took note of Cole's expression. "Oh, honey." She put her arms around him. "Sorry you heard that. Dad and I aren't mad. We're just talking."

He clutched her, and she stroked his hair. "Did you and Lena have fun at the beach?"

Cole nodded wordlessly.

Lena looked at her dad. He looked back at her, trying to smile and failing.

What's not fair to me? she thought. *What's going on?*

"We wanted to surprise Dad," said Cole.

"Good job, bud," said their dad, and he opened his arms. Cole ran to him. Then Dad reached out an arm. "Group hug?" he asked.

Lena walked over to them, and after a moment, Mom followed. The four of them stood holding one another, as if they would never let go.

CHAPTER 16

Consoled by cuddling and thirty minutes on his Mindbender game, Cole recovered from his parents' argument right away. During dinner, he described in detail the battle between the robot dogs and the ninja cats on his game, then he stopped talking as he fell upon his dessert—a chocolate-chip brownie.

Mom picked at her food, while Dad tried to overcompensate by talking animatedly to Cole and questioning Lena about school. She responded with short, unsatisfying answers, and he gave up.

If you're keeping things from me, she thought, *I don't feel bad keeping things from you.*

After dinner, Lena loaded the dishwasher while her mom watered the flowers in the backyard. Her dad and Cole lay on the couch, reading a book. Lena hovered at the sliding door for a minute, wondering if she should go talk to her mom, or just leave her alone.

As if reading her mind, her dad said, "Don't you have homework, Lena?"

The words *Don't you have something to tell me, Dad?* were bitter in her mouth, but Lena swallowed them and turned to leave the room. She stopped to open the coat closet. *I need my*— Closing her eyes, she fought down a wave of panic. *Okay, this is not even funny anymore. This must be some bizarre syndrome: looking for something and not knowing what it is.*

She forced herself to do some homework before she went online to chat, but she felt annoyed by everyone's banter as she watched variously colored lines of text scroll by. Kai opened a private window:

Kaiborg: Ur quiet tonite.
Sea_girl: *shrug*
Kaiborg: Everything ok?
Sea_girl: Sure, the rents are just bugging me.
Kaiborg: Want me to come over? ;-)

"No," Lena said out loud, then felt guilty. *I kind of suck as a girlfriend,* she thought. *I should be all lovey and telling him how awesome he is all the time.* She typed an answer that she knew would make him happy.

Sea_girl: I wish! U would make everything right. <3
Kaiborg: I'm calling u now.

Lena sighed. Well, that backfired. Now instead of typing words he wanted to hear, she would have to speak them. Her cell rang. "Be a good girlfriend," she told herself, and answered the phone.

◻ ◻ ◻

At eight o'clock, Lena heard her dad going through the bedtime routine with Cole—tooth-brushing and bath time. Lena heard Cole singing in the tub, his voice echoing in the tiled bathroom, *"I love to go swimmin' with bowlegged women and swim between their knees . . . swim between their knees . . ."*

She grinned. Her dad had taught him that song.

After his bath, Cole came to her room and knocked.

"Come in."

He opened the door and ran to her. "Night, Lena."

She hugged him, inhaling his freshly shampooed hair. "G'night, Cole Dog."

He giggled, as he did every time she called him that. "I'm not a dog!"

"Yes, you are. You're my dawg." She hugged and kissed him. "Sweet dreams."

"Sweet dreams." He left, and Lena got up to close her door. She looked across the hall to his room, where their dad was sitting on Cole's bed, holding a Magic Tree House book. Lena always thought of her dad as a sunny, happy guy—with his California-boy blond hair and easy grin—but right now his whole body was slumped and his eyes were focused on the floor. It was hard to stay mad at him when he looked so miserable. When he glanced up at her, she signed *I love you* to him, and he smiled, blinking a little.

She went downstairs and found her mom crashed on the couch, watching a rerun of *Top Chef* and eating a candy bar.

Her mom looked up at her guiltily. "This show is more fun to watch when you eat junk food," she said, indicating the candy.

"Yep," said Lena. "And you didn't eat much dinner."

Her mom returned her gaze to the TV, not answering. She reached up to twist one of her diamond stud earrings. They were a wedding present from Lena's dad; she never took them off.

Lena waited a few minutes, then said, "Mom?"

"Mmm-hmm."

"What's not fair to me?"

Her mom tensed. She hit Pause on the remote, and stared at Lena for a long time before she finally said, "I'm really sorry, Lena. I wish—" She hesitated, then said, "It's not for me to tell you."

Lena stared back until she felt tears approach, then she left the room.

◻ ◻ ◻

Lena heard a soft knock at her bedroom door.

She opened her eyes, disoriented. Her light was still on— she must have fallen asleep while she was reading. She squinted at her clock radio: 12:32.

Then she heard Cole's voice. "Lena?" he called softly.

She jumped out of bed and opened her door.

He stood there in his pajamas, hair tousled, shielding his eyes against the light in her room. "I woke up," he said.

"I see that. Come in, bud."

Cole shuffled into the room and climbed up on her bed. He slid his feet under her covers and pulled the quilt up to his chin. "Can you turn the light out?" he asked.

Lena obliged, then lay down on the bed next to him. When he was little, Cole used to come into her room in the middle of the night sometimes after he'd had a bad dream. But he hadn't done that for a long time.

"What's the matter?" she asked.

"I woke up. I thought I heard Mom and Dad yelling again. But I got up, and it was dark."

"Aw, it was just a dream, bud. Everything's okay."

Cole sighed, already half-asleep. His fingers stroked the satiny moon on her quilt. "Will you sing me a song?"

Lena put her head on the pillow next to him. "Sure." She thought for a minute, then sang very softly:

*"By the light
of the blueberry moon
we sang this song
in Lena's room . . ."*

She repeated the verse once more, then waited to see if Cole had fallen asleep.

"Sing it again," he mumbled.

She smiled and sang the short verse again—twice—getting softer with each line. When she had finished, Cole's breathing was regular and deep.

"Love you, buddy," she whispered. She lay awake in the dark for a long time, her own fingers worrying the satin moon. Finally she got out of bed, tucking the quilt closely around her brother.

Still wearing yesterday's clothes, Lena went downstairs and took her jacket and stocking cap out of the hall closet. She unlocked the kitchen door and went out through the garage. Opening the side door, she stepped out into the darkness.

She shivered and pulled her coat closer as she reached the sidewalk. There was a fine, misty rain falling, which made the night seem even colder and darker. She headed down the street toward the beach, glancing back at her house once to make sure no lights had come on.

I'll be back before anyone else wakes up, she thought.

She peered warily around as she walked. Anyone out wandering around in the middle of the night could not be up to any good. A wry grin quirked her lips. *Unlike me, who is so sane and sensible.*

She turned onto the paved bike path above the beach that led to Magic Crescent Cove. She kept her eyes on the path as she walked, since it was so dark. She didn't want to trip and fall. That would be just her luck: sneak out, fall, break her ankle, and have to lie here in the path until morning, until some jogger or bicyclist came along.

She picked her way along the path cautiously, occasionally pausing to lift her eyes to the sea. Without admitting it, she was hoping to see a head out there in the waves. And not the head of a dolphin or a sea lion.

This obsession must be another symptom, she thought. *Whatever my particular mental illness is, it makes me hallucinate fairy-tale creatures and look for things without knowing what they are. Oh, and sleepwalk. Can't forget that. At least I didn't sleepwalk my way out here this time.*

Lena's jacket was wet now—she hadn't thought to bring an umbrella. She stood uncertainly for a moment, trying to decide whether or not to return home. She would have to hang her coat somewhere to dry where her parents wouldn't see it. She frowned down the path and kept walking. She would just go as far as the edge of Magic's.

Shivering, Lena came to the park bench viewpoint on the walking path and sank down to rest. She gazed out at the sea. The blackness of the ocean met the blackness of the sky. The regular sweep of light from the Pelican Point Lighthouse whirled in the distance.

Shoulders hunched against the rain, she thought, *So this is what craziness feels like. Wandering around outside in the middle of the night, in the rain, looking for something that doesn't exist, and even if it did . . . I can't see it now, because of the rain and the dark!*

Lena stood up, giving one final look at the sea, then turned her face up to the sky. She closed her eyes as the rain slid down her face like tears, and whispered, "I just wish I knew for sure."

She remained standing, emptying her mind, visualizing the smooth interior of a conch shell. And like a conch shell, her mind filled with the sound of the ocean.

As she stood in stillness, her soul opening like a night-blooming flower, words floated into her mind: "I beheld you, child."

Lena opened her eyes. *Where did that come from?* She looked around, although she knew that the words were only in her head. "Beheld" was not a word she had ever used in her life. But the sentence had formed in her mind as fully as if it had been spoken in her ear. Heart beating faster, she looked out at the black ocean again. It was as if she had asked for a sign and been given one.

I will look for you again, she thought. *I will never give up.*

Tears of relief filling her eyes, she turned to walk home.

Before she had gone very far, however, someone stepped out on the dark path, barring her way.

Lena gave a stifled cry.

The figure did not move, just stood immobile. It was a man—she could tell by the size and shape of him.

With a fear that was utterly primal, Lena backed up. *I'm so stupid,* she thought. *I should never have left the house. I'm so, so stupid.* Her heart slamming against her ribs, she looked behind her, trying to estimate how far she could run before the man caught her.

"You saw her," came a rough, low voice.

Lena's heart gave an even harder jar.

"I saw her, too," said the man. "A long time ago." He took a step toward her, and Lena could finally see him. He was wearing a long coat, and she realized it was Denny.

Lena didn't know whether to feel relieved or even more terrified. Everyone thought he was harmless. But maybe they just didn't know. Maybe he had attacked girls before, and no one knew. If he was harmless, why was he here on this unlit path in the middle of the night, blocking her way?

Lena's muscles tensed as she prepared to turn and run back the way she had come. If she could outrun him, she would scream as soon as she got close to someone's house.

But at that moment, Denny turned and gazed out at the sea. "I want to see her again," he said.

Without stopping to think, Lena rushed forward, closing the distance between them in a few strides. Before he could move, she was pushing past Denny and racing to safety.

CHAPTER 17

It wasn't until Lena stood panting at the door of her house—safe, alive, far away from Denny—that she registered his words: *You saw her. I saw her, too.*

Saw who?

But there was only one possible answer.

Denny had seen the mermaid.

Lena leaned against the back door, nearly faint with relief. *She's real.* Denny saw her. She laughed a little, then sobered. *Either that, or I'm as crazy as he is.*

But she was glad he hadn't been planning to hurt her. He just wanted to talk to someone else who had seen the mermaid.

◻ ◻ ◻

"I need to borrow your surfboard," Lena told Pem.

"You do? Why? I thought you were using the soft-top from Kai's house."

"I have been. But that's only when I go out with Ani and Kai."

They were sitting in Max's car, waiting for Max to finish a conversation outside with another Mustang owner.

"So you're going to go surfing without Ani?"

"Yes."

"Already?"

"Well, not right away. I'll have one more lesson with her, but once I'm finished, I won't have access to their board. I need to borrow someone else's for a little while, so I can—" Lena didn't finish the sentence. She could not tell Pem that she wanted to get in the water at Magic's.

"So you can what?"

"So I can . . . uh, go out and surf when I feel like it."

"Huh. Well, what will I do when I want to go surfing?"

"You haven't surfed in, like, over a month. You've been kind of busy." Lena raised her eyebrows, looking out the window at Max.

Pem didn't answer, just looked back at her without smiling. She twiddled the braid around her ankle and turned away, looking out the front windshield. "How are you going to hide a surfboard from your parents?"

"I'll put it behind some stuff in the garden shed, and cover it with a tarp."

"Won't your mom see it? Isn't she always digging in the garden?"

"No, she's been too busy to garden lately. She hardly ever goes out there anymore. And she already harvested the stuff she grew this summer."

Pem continued to look out the front window. "I'm just afraid they're going to find it. Then I'm in trouble, too."

"No, you're not," said Lena. She made an impatient sound. "You know what? Just forget it. Never mind."

"No, I'm just saying—"

"No, seriously. Forget it."

There was a dense silence.

"You could borrow my brother's board," said Henry.

Lena and Pem both turned to look at him. They were so used to his silence that hearing him speak was like hearing the steering wheel talk.

"What?" said Lena.

"Max has two boards, a long one and a short one."

"He does?"

"Yeah."

"Do you think he'd let me borrow the long one?"

"Sure."

"Henry," said Pem. "I don't think your brother would like you promising his stuff to people."

Henry gave Pem a cool look. "We'll ask him when he gets in."

Lena waited until Pem had turned away, then made an exaggeratedly shocked face at Henry. He smiled.

A moment later, Max got into the driver's seat, grinning and saying, "That guy has a 1972 Mach One."

"Max," said Henry.

"Yeah?"

"Can you do me a favor?"

"What." Max's tone was flat, his famously pouty lips pressed into a thin line.

"Actually, it would be a favor for Lena."

"Yeah?"

"She needs to borrow your long board."

Max whipped his head around to peer at them in the back seat. "What?"

"She needs. To borrow. Your long board."

"Why?!"

"She just does. She doesn't have a board of her own yet, and she needs one. For, uh, a few weeks?" He glanced at Lena, and she shrugged, nodding.

Max cursed quietly and added, "Uh, sorry, Lena, but there's no way. Even if I wanted to loan you my board, you're a total beginner, aren't you?"

"Yes. But Ani says I'm really good."

He shook his head. "Yeah, sure, sorry, but—"

"Let her borrow the long board, Max, or I'll tell Mom and Dad that you've been dumping me at the mall so you can go make out with your fifteen-year-old girlfriend."

Everyone else in the car drew in shocked breaths. No one spoke for a long minute.

Finally Max said, "You little—"

"Who knows? They might even decide to take your car away."

After another stunned pause, Max said, "I'm an adult! They can't take away my car, you f—"

"You're right," said Henry. "You are an adult. Which reminds me of the word *statutory*. Do you know that word?"

"What the—shut up! I'll deal with you later. All right . . . your little girlfriend can borrow my board," he sneered. "For two weeks. That's it. I'm not going to just hand over my board for the rest of the season. The waves are biggest in winter."

Lena waited for Pem to say something in her defense, like "She's not his girlfriend," but Pem remained silent.

"And if you damage my board, Lena . . ."

"I won't! I'll be really careful. I swear."

He drove her home, blasting Pone on his stereo. He stopped in front of Lena's house and parked. "Bye," he said.

"Um, so when can I have it?" she asked.

"Gee, why don't I rush home and bring it back right now? If it's convenient for *you?*"

"That would be awesome," she said, giving him a big smile.

His eyes bugged out, then he threw up his hands. "Fine. Whatever. I'll get it now, and your two weeks starts this minute."

Lena got out of the car, looking back at Henry. She put her hands together in a gesture of appreciation.

Henry smiled at her. "See you in a few minutes," he said.

Max squealed the tires as he pulled away.

Fifteen minutes later he roared up in front of the house again, his surfboard strapped to the roof of his car. He flung himself out of the Mustang and began unlatching his board from the rack.

Lena hurried out, glancing at the neighbors' houses.

"Not cool," he was muttering. "Extortion is not cool."

Once the surfboard was stowed safely in the garden shed, behind empty planters and bags of organic fertilizer, covered by a blue tarp, Lena breathed easier. When her mom came home with Cole, she was so deeply involved in her homework that she had almost put the surfboard out of her mind. Almost.

CHAPTER 18

The next Friday at lunchtime, Lena sat with Pem and Kai. She was adding a fresh coat of white nail polish to her nails, while Pem and Kai played chess.

"Kai, you hamster, that's the third game you've opened that way. Can't you play something besides the Queen's Gambit?" Pem shook her head, setting in motion the *I Dream of Jeannie*–like ponytail sprouting from the top of her head.

"Just play, Pemberley."

Lena watched but did not comment. Her conversations with Pem had been strained ever since the incident in Max's car.

"Are you going surfing today?" asked Pem, glancing over at her.

"No. Ani's not coming home this weekend. She has midterms, and she wanted to stay on campus to study. Besides, we're finished with the lessons."

"You are?"

"Yes."

"When did you finish?"

"Last Friday."

"How come you didn't call?"

Lena shrugged. "I figured you were busy."

There was a fraught silence.

Lena blew on her nails, hoping she'd stung Pem just a little with her remark.

Maybe she had, because Pem asked, "So, um, today . . . do you want to hang out at my house?"

"What about . . . ?"

"Max is working."

"Oh." Lena tried to ignore the implication that she was Pem's second choice. "Sure. That would be fun."

"Um, hi. I'm right here," said Kai, waving his hand around. "Official boyfriend and everything?"

"What?" said Pem.

"What if *I* want to hang out with Lena? You know . . . *alone?*"

A silence as awkward as an armload of beach balls rolled around their table.

Lena glared at Kai. He lifted his palms, as if to say, *What?*

Pem glanced at each of them, then stared down at the chessboard. "Oh. I didn't think about that."

"Pem!" said Lena. "I do want to come over. I didn't have plans with Kai. He's just being—"

"Boyfriendly?" said Kai. "Come on, Lena. I'm glad my sister taught you to surf, but we haven't been alone in ages. What with rehearsals, I never—"

"It's cool," said Pem. "We'll do it another day."

"No, it is *not* cool," said Lena, a flush rising on her face. "Kai, this is totally embarrassing."

A shade of blotchy red crept up Kai's neck. "Oh, really? How is it embarrassing that I want to spend time with my girlfriend? You didn't even ask me before you said yes to Pem."

Lena's eyes widened. "*Ask* you! You think I should have to *ask* you before I make plans?"

"No," said Kai. "I just meant—"

"Stop it," said Pem. She stood up. "I knew this would happen. You guys said nothing would change, that the three of us would still be best friends, even though you were *together*. But I knew it would never work." She walked away.

Kai gathered up the chess pieces while Lena struggled to keep her temper. She felt like knocking the chessboard to the floor. Finally she said, "Why did you do that? We swore we wouldn't be one of those horrible couples who make other people feel like they're in the way."

He reached across the table and took her hand. "I'm sorry. I just want to be with you."

"You're with me all the time!"

He shook his head. "I want to be *alone* with you, Leen." His thumb traced feather-light circles inside the palm of her hand. "Don't you want to be alone with me?"

She melted a little. Her hands were sensitive, and easily won over. "Of course. But why did you have to make Pem feel bad?"

"Leen. Come on. I said I was sorry. Don't make me beg." He lowered his voice. "Although I will if you want me to."

She laughed. There was that voice. "Uh, no. That won't be necessary."

"Please." He moved his hand up her arm. "Baby, please."

"Shh! Don't call me baby," she said.

"Let's do something after school, just the two of us. In fact . . ." He pretended to remember something, although

Lena could tell he'd known it all along. "No one will be home at my house. Ani's staying on campus, and my parents will be at work until five." He cocked his head appealingly at her. "We could watch a movie. Or listen to some music, or something."

Right, thought Lena. *Or something.*

□ □ □

Pem opened her front door and looked at Lena in confusion. "What are you doing here?"

"Can a sistah come in, or are you going to make me apologize on your doorstep?" said Lena.

Pem stepped back. "I thought you and Kai were going to—"

Lena entered the house, shrugging off her jacket. "I never said that. He was being presumptuous."

After a moment, Pem grinned and said, "And impertinent?"

"And exclusionary."

"And—" Pem paused. "Wow, that's a tough word. Uh . . . separatist!"

"Nice," said Lena. "Anyway, I'm sorry we made you feel like a third wheel."

"It's okay."

"No, it's not. Things have been weird, Pem, and I . . . I want them to go back to the way they were."

Pem gave a wry smile. "Too late for that."

Lena's lower lip trembled. "It's too late?"

Pem grabbed her arm. "Oh! Don't look like that! Sorry. I just meant that we *can't* go back to the way things were.

Everything's changed. You know, you're in love with Kai, and I'm in love with Max, and—"

Lena didn't know which tidbit to pounce on first. She settled for the latter. "You're in love with Max?"

Pem shifted her weight. "Well, yeah. I think I am. Yes."

"Really?!"

"Maybe you didn't notice because you're so swoony over Kai," teased Pem.

"But I'm not," said Lena. "Am I? I don't feel swoony. In fact, I'm not even . . . don't tell him, okay? But I don't feel like I'm actually *in love* with Kai."

Pem's eyes widened. "You're not?" She pulled on Lena's arm. "Come on. Let's go talk in my room. Mama Mia is lurking around here, wanting me to help her fix dinner. We'll go say hi to her, and she won't bother me once she sees you're here."

Lena confided to Pem that the whole being-with-Kai thing felt almost like watching a movie. She could see how they had ended up together, and she cared about him a lot—of course she did!—and she liked the making-out part, but she didn't get all weak-kneed and palpitating when he was around.

"Maybe that's how it is for some people," she said. "They hang out together for years, and suddenly one day they're madly in love and can't get enough of each other. But, um, that's not how it is with Kai and me. Or at least, that's not how it is for me."

Pem listened. Then she said, "Leen, the guy called you his *pearl* in front of a roomful of people. In front of your parents! I hate to break it to you, but he's totally smitten. So don't . . . you know, *hurt* him."

"I'm not going to hurt him," protested Lena. "He's my boyfriend. And also? If I hurt him, I'm afraid Ani will beat the crap out of me."

Pem laughed. "She is a force of nature, isn't she?"

"But if Kai expects me to turn into Kissy McSwoonypants, he's going to be disappointed." She twiddled the braided yarn anklet on her leg. Hers was black and white. She remembered saying to Pem when they made the anklets, "Mine has to be black and white to counteract all the pink in yours." Now she looked up at Pem. "So talk to me about Max. Are you really in love? Like . . . *love* love?"

Pem's expression softened. "He's so great. I know I had a crush on him last year, but this is different. For one thing, it's reciprocal. He's into me, too. I know you think he's just some gear-head who wears Hawaiian shirts, but there's more to him, Lena. He's so sweet and funny and cool."

"I'm sure," murmured Lena.

"And you know what?"

"What?"

"We're going out tomorrow. A real date, not sneaking around."

"Really?"

Pem nodded. "I even told my moms."

"You did? How did they take it?"

"They were okay, actually." Pem sounded surprised. "Of course I have to be home at, like, a ridiculous hour, but still."

"Were they freaked out that he's in college?"

"A little. But I explained that he only turned eighteen a few months ago. So we're only two and a half years apart."

"Good. I'm happy for you, Pem."

"Thanks." Pem glowed.

"Hey, Pem?"

"Yes?"

"I wasn't going to tell you this, but . . ."

"Oooh, sounds juicy," said Pem, scooting closer.

"No, not like that. But first you have to promise not to tell Max."

"I promise."

"Or Kai."

"Wow. Okay." Pem waited.

"Um, well, Martha and Leslie invited me to the movies tomorrow. And I'm going to go, but . . . um, I'm not really going to the movies."

"Huh?"

"I'm going to go surfing."

"What do you mean? I thought you just said you were going to the movies."

"I am . . . I mean, I'm going to have my dad take us to the movies, but then I'm going to sneak out and come back home for Max's surfboard, and go surfing."

"What?"

Lena nodded.

"But why? If your dad finds out, he'll—"

"He won't find out."

"How are you going to get there?"

"Walk."

"Walk? You're going to walk all the way to Back Yard with a surfboard?"

Lena hesitated. "No."

Pem stared at her, puzzled, then went still as a stone. "No," she whispered. "You don't mean Magic's."

"I do," said Lena.

"You're, like . . . messing with me, right? *Tell* me you're just messing with me."

"I'm serious."

"You can't be."

"I am."

"Lena . . ." She struggled for words. "You *just learned* to surf. Magic's is for extreme surfers!"

"I can handle it."

Pem grabbed her hand. "Don't do this. I'm begging you."

"I have to."

"*Have* to? What are you talking about? Lena, listen to me. Have you ever seen a girl surfing at Magic's?"

"Well . . . I guess not."

"Why do you think that is?"

"I don't know."

"Because they know you could get killed out there! Why do you think they call that one spot out there the Cauldron?"

"I'm not going to get *killed,* Pem. Jeez. Dramatic much?"

Pem glared at her.

"Theatrical?" added Lena, smiling.

Nothing.

"Uh . . . hysterical?"

But Pem would not play. "And there's the Boneyard," she said. "You know about the Boneyard, right?"

Lena hesitated. Oh, yeah. The Boneyard.

Pem leaned in so that her face was inches from Lena's. "It's that shallow spot, nothing but reef and rocks. It will cut you up like hamburger if you get washed out there."

Lena swallowed.

"Yeah," said Pem. "How do you like Magic's now?"

Forcing a light note into her voice, Lena said, "I won't wash out in the Boneyard. I promise."

Pem stared at her a minute longer, then sighed and shook her head. "If I can't talk you out of this, at least wear a helmet," she begged.

Lena smiled.

"I'm serious! If you're going to do this insane thing, at least protect yourself."

"I'm going to be *fine*. Nothing's going to happen. I just wanted to let you know. In case . . ."

"In case what?" Pem's face was strained.

"Nothing. I just wanted to tell you because you're my best friend." She stood up. "Let's get something to eat. I'm hungry. What is Mama Mia making for dinner?"

Pem stood up, too. "Lena," she said, "if the conditions are bad tomorrow, swear to me you won't go through with this."

Lena did not answer.

CHAPTER 19

"See you later, Dad," said Lena, climbing out of his car.

"Thanks, Mr. Whittaker," said Martha, who smelled unusually floral and who seemed to take a long time exiting the car.

Leslie got out of the car and joined Lena, rolling her eyes.

"You're welcome, Martha," said Lena's dad. "Leslie's mom is picking you girls up after the movie, right?"

"Yes," said Leslie.

When Martha took too long to close the door, Lena called, "Have fun on your date." Her parents were going to a wine-tasting event and art show in Santa Cruz—they would be gone for hours, which played a big part in Lena's scheme.

"I will. Call if you need anything. Bye, honey."

"Bye." Lena waved to him as he drove away.

The three girls walked into the mall and headed for the movie theaters. Lena stood in line with them, paid for her ticket, and sat down. She tried to participate in the conversation, but her mind was on her alternate plan. As the lights went out and the coming attractions blared onto the screen, Lena gripped the handrests of her seat. Any minute now.

The coming attractions seemed to go on and on. At last, the opening credits appeared for the feature presentation. Lena waited until the first scene was under way, then took a deep breath, leaned over to Leslie, and whispered, "My stomach is kind of bothering me."

Leslie looked over at her. "Yeah?"

"Yeah."

"You okay?"

"I think so."

"Okay."

She counted to two hundred in her head, then leaned over and whispered, "I'll be right back. I'm going to the bathroom."

"Okay."

Lena walked out of the theater and headed for the bathroom. She stood in a locked stall in the bathroom for several minutes. To pass the time, she went through the names of famous surf spots around the world: Phantoms, Himalayas, Alligators, Outer Logs, Pipeline, Lance's Right, Blacks, Haleiwa, Thunders, Pit Stops, Telescopes, Avalanche, Bowls, Gas Chambers, Dungeons . . .

Magic's sounds almost safe, compared to some of those places, she thought.

Finally she stepped out of the stall, washed her hands, and returned to the theater, making her way past rows of people in the dark.

As she sat down, Leslie whispered, "I thought you were never coming back!"

"I know . . . it's my stomach."

"What's the matter?"

"It must be something I ate." Lena felt her face heat up with the lie. Good thing it was dark in the theater.

"Oh, no," said Leslie.

"Yeah. I think I'd better go home."

"Want me to call my mom?"

"No. I'll just call my dad."

Martha leaned over. "I thought your parents were going somewhere."

"Shhh!" hissed someone behind them.

Lena leaned across Leslie so Martha could hear her, too. "They'll still be home. It's no big deal. I'll talk to you later."

"You sure?"

"Yeah."

"Want us to go with you?"

"No!" she said. "No. You guys stay and watch the movie. I'll talk to you later."

◻ ◻ ◻

Lena zipped herself snugly into her wetsuit and slid on her shoes, then risked a glance out the door of the garden shed. She could see Cole and his babysitter, Janni, in the family room. They were playing on his Mindbender.

It was now or never. Lena took a deep breath, then grabbed her duffel bag and Max's surfboard. Crouching low, she hurried around the side of the house, in the opposite direction of the family room. When she reached the sidewalk, she hitched up the heavy surfboard under her arm, adjusted the strap of her duffel bag, and headed down the street.

She was sweating before she even reached the parking area. *I'm going to be exhausted before I ever get there,* she thought. *But beggars can't be choosers . . . I need to do this while I have Max's board.*

By the time Lena reached Magic Crescent Cove, the sun was no longer high in the sky. She checked her watch. 4:15. She sank down onto the sand, tired and frustrated. After all this planning and lying, she wouldn't even have much time in the water, now that she was finally here. But it couldn't be helped. Sneaking around was harder than it looked.

Lena's heartbeat slowed as she gazed out at the sea. Her breathing calmed. She didn't try to study the conditions; she just drank in the soothing ocean breeze and the hypnotic sound of the surf. When she felt at peace, she turned her attention to waxing Max's board and reading the waves.

They were coming in regular sets, but they were huge—fifteen-foot rolling pins of heavy water. Lena had seen the waves at Magic's bigger than this . . . but not often.

Just my luck, she thought with a sigh. *The one day I manage to snag a board and get away for some stealth surfing, the waves are almost un-surf-able.*

No one was in the lineup, but there were four guys in wetsuits hanging around onshore. The size of the waves must have discouraged them.

Not me, thought Lena. She stood up. "Okay, mermaid," she whispered. "Here I come."

CHAPTER 20

The other surfers eyed Lena curiously as she headed toward the water.

"Hey," called one of them.

Lena glanced back.

It was a youngish guy with blond dreads. "You're not going in, right?"

Lena nodded and turned away.

"Aw, go home to Back Yard, little girl," he jeered.

Lena quickened her pace a little.

Someone else called, "Miss? Hey. Wait up."

Fighting an impulse to snap, "What?!" Lena looked over her shoulder.

A middle-aged guy with a dark beard was walking in her direction. "You're not really going in, are you?"

"Yes, I am," she said, and kept going.

"Don't do it," he called. "They're breaking too big. You'll never make it outside."

Lena didn't slow.

"I'm serious," added the guy, raising his voice. "This is the kind of day people need a tow."

Lena lifted a hand to acknowledge that she'd heard him, but she didn't stop. She knew that surfers sometimes got "towed in" to the big waves by friends on Jet Skis . . . it saved having to swim out past these monster breakers.

"Fine," yelled the dreads-guy. "Don't come crying to us when your board snaps in half."

There was laughter, but Lena ignored it.

As if having a bunch of guys yell at her wasn't bad enough, she heard Ani's voice in her mind, "Magic's is only for advanced surfers, and even then, it's dangerous."

But she also told me it takes some people years to develop the kind of instinct I already have, Lena reminded herself. *I'm a natural.*

Today the surfing was secondary. Lena had come here to look for the mermaid.

Lena splashed into the surf, letting a few small waves surge past her before she set Max's board down in the water. Then she lay down on the board and started paddling.

After a couple of minutes, she realized she was farther down the shoreline from where she had started. She would be busy enough just paddling parallel to the rip tide. She kept up a steady butterfly motion with her arms, pulling herself and the board through the water. A wave broke a few yards in front of her, and a froth of tumbling white water rushed toward her. Lena clutched the rails of the board and turned turtle.

For the next several minutes, Lena battled the punishing breakers, which seemed intent on throwing her back onto the shore. She had to turn turtle over and over as the waves towered above her, far too big to jump. Twice she rolled too late, and the waves crashed on top of her, tossing her violently around under water. She was more aware of the ocean's power than ever before, and of her own insignificance. "This isn't a swimming pool," she heard Ani's voice in her head again.

When she paused to get her bearings, she saw that she had been dragged closer to the Boneyard. One more smashing wave, coupled with a bad rip, and she would be scraping across the reef. *Maybe Pem was right about the helmet,* she thought.

Gritting her teeth, Lena whipped her arms as fast as she could, the surfboard slicing through the water, carrying her closer and closer to the next swell. With a giant intake of breath, she rolled with the board once again. The wave passed overhead . . . and then she was on the other side of the breaking waves.

Lena lay on her belly, resting and catching her breath.

A sleek head popped up in the water nearby.

Her heart leaped. Then she saw it was a sea otter. She rested her cheek on the deck of the surfboard, waiting for her heart to quit hammering, and trying to stay still.

The otter floated on its back, apparently unconcerned about Lena's presence. It had a flat rock on its chest, and it used its agile little paws to smash a clam against the rock. Lena watched, giddy at being so close to the wild animal. After its meal, the sea otter blinked at her and slid smoothly beneath the surface of the water.

Magic, thought Lena. *It feels magic out here. She has to be here.*

But the ocean remained empty, a huge, shifting blue and gray tapestry. No other living creatures appeared.

The sun will be going down soon, she thought. *I should catch at least one wave. I can paddle back out after.*

She couldn't bear to think that the mermaid was not here. Not yet.

A nice big swell was forming, and Lena began to paddle quickly, using butterfly strokes as the wave rose up. She popped up at the last minute, and then she was flying, racing through the dark blue barrel, faster than she had ever gone. This wasn't so much like riding on the back of a dolphin as it was falling off a house.

The lip of the wave began to crash just behind her, then the walls of white water caught up to her, and she was flung under water with what felt like an avalanche of ocean on top of her. She felt her leash snap, then she was tumbling, waiting to see which way was up.

Ani should have been here to see this wipeout, she thought. After what seemed like a full minute but was probably only a few seconds, she was able to orient herself as to which way was up. She swam toward the surface, hands above her head as Ani had taught her, in case she came up under her board.

She broke the surface and took what felt like the biggest breath she had ever taken. She could see Max's surfboard near the shore. But she'd hardly had time to take a second breath when the next wave was rushing toward her. She ducked. This time the wave surged harmlessly over her instead of picking her up and smashing her beneath. She broke the surface again and began to swim for shore.

Exhausted, she picked up Max's board and trudged onto the sand.

"You got nads, girl," said dreads-guy. "Either that, or you're just plain baked."

The weak sun would be setting any minute. And she had broken her leash. *So that's it,* she thought. *I can't go back out without a leash.*

But this is why I came, another part of her protested.

Lena turned her face to the water again. She felt oddly un-afraid as she walked back into the sea.

"What the hell!" cried someone.

"Hey!"

Ignoring the calls, she lay down on the board and paddled out. Her arms were trembling with exhaustion, and it felt like she was pulling them through thick mud, trying to stay in one place. She struggled past waves as high as a two-story house, turtle-rolling several times to let the waves break over her.

Finally, she made it to the main point break. She barely had time to turn her board around before another big wave was rising up behind her.

Legs shaking, Lena hurried to pop up. She had just stead-ied her feet on the board when she found herself racing through the barrel again.

She maintained her balance on the board as long as possi-ble, feeling the lip of the wave curl ever closer to her head. Then it was breaking over her . . . and she was wiping out.

The houseful of water seemed to push her down endlessly. Lena did not panic; she knew that she would surface eventu-ally. *You can hold your breath a long time,* she told herself, Ani's words reassuring in her mind. Sure enough, the churning waves shot Lena waist-high out of the water, but she barely had time to take a breath before she was being sucked down under again. She felt her body being driven deeply into the underwater hole once more.

You can hold your breath a long time, she told herself again, more desperately this time. She felt that she should have been washed out closer to the shore by now and was scared to see that she was still in the same spot when she finally did surface.

This is it, she realized suddenly. *I'm in the Cauldron.*

Then she was sucked beneath the waves again. The waters churned, tossing her back and forth beneath the surface like a rag doll in a washing machine.

Pem was right, she thought, as a terrible weariness came over her limbs. *I should never have come.*

She was too tired to struggle to the surface again. She was not even sure which direction was up. She knew she should try to remain relaxed in order to surface. Now it felt strangely comforting to relax and allow the boiling waters to toss her. Black dots danced at the edge of her vision.

I wonder if I'm going to die, she thought, but there was no longer a sense of panic to the idea. *This is where Dad almost died.*

At that moment, Lena felt something touch her arm, then a hard object was pushed into her hand. She clamped her fingers around it automatically.

Before she even had time to wonder about the object, Lena felt two small hands grasp her beneath the arms and pull her out of the deadly grip of the Cauldron.

CHAPTER 21

Lena coughed and gasped, sucking in lungfuls of precious air.

As she dragged herself up onto the sand, she saw that the man with the beard was hurrying to her side. The other three surfers watched in the background.

"Are you okay?" he asked, leaning over her.

She nodded, unable to speak. All she could do was keep breathing—she would never take air for granted again.

"I thought we'd lost you!" said the man, his voice shaking. "I didn't think you were going to make it out of that hole."

Lena stared up at him, trying to catch her breath. She wanted to open her hand and look at what she was holding— what *someone* had shoved into her hand—but she didn't want this guy to see. She turned to look back at the ocean. The sun was setting, bleeding orange and pink and gray, and the waves were turning darker every minute.

"Who's out there?" she panted.

"No one. *You* were the only one out there."

She glanced up and saw a guy her age standing a little farther up the beach. Max's board had been pulled out of the water and was sitting on the sand. The other two surfers were leaving. The show was over.

Lena looked out at the ocean again and saw a dark head bob above the surface of the waves. She squinted into the setting sun.

It was the mermaid.

Lena splashed into the water.

"Hey!" the man yelled.

The dark head disappeared in the waves as suddenly as if it had never been there. Lena stared hard. "Don't go!" she cried.

"What are you doing?" the man called after Lena. "You can't go back out there, it's getting dark."

"Leave me alone!" yelled Lena, struggling through the surf, scanning the waves. *It was the mermaid who pulled me out of the Cauldron.*

"Listen," said the man. "Maybe you don't know—the sharks come into the shallows to feed at dusk."

They won't hurt me, she thought. Then the shock of that idea froze her in place. *Why did I think that?* She fell to her knees, exhausted and shivering, eyes straining to see the mermaid. *Oh, God, please don't go.* Tears mixed with the salt spray on her face.

"Erik!" called the man.

"Yeah, Dad?"

"Call 911. There's something wrong with this girl."

"No!" moaned Lena. "There's nothing wrong with me. Why can't you just leave me alone?" The water lapped around her.

"Sorry, but you're shaking and crying, so something is wrong."

Eyes fixed on the waves, Lena clutched the hard metal object. There was no sign of a head now. She struggled to her feet, suddenly so weak she thought she might fall. The idea of just lying down in the waves and letting them take her was very tempting.

"Whoa," said the man. "Let me help." He tried to take her arm, but she pulled away from him. "We've got to get you warmed up," he continued. "Where's your stuff?"

She gestured numbly at her duffel bag, and walked in that direction.

"Do you have a ride home? Someone you can call?"

"Um," said Lena, teeth chattering. "Yes. I'll be fine. Thanks."

"Why are you on your own? You should *never* surf alone . . . especially not Magic's. What if we hadn't been here?"

Shut up, shut up, thought Lena. *Just go away.* Turning her back to the bearded man, Lena opened her palm to see what she was holding.

It was a gold key.

Lena whirled to face the darkening sea. The sun was giving off its last fiery rays, and she had to shield her eyes against its brightness. Then she saw the silhouette of a head in the water and a glimpse of white face in the darkness.

Lena made a small sound in her throat. *She's real.*

Lena stared out at the face in the water. She was not imagining this. She was not crazy. A mermaid lived out there. She had saved Lena's life.

And she had given her a key.

Blinking against the setting sun, Lena lifted her hand.

A slim white arm rose out of the water in response, then there was a small splash as the mermaid disappeared, leaving behind the empty ocean.

CHAPTER 22

"My friends are going to pick me up at the highway," Lena lied.

"Fine. We'll wait with you until they get here." The bearded man was relentless. He seemed prepared to stay glued to her side until she proved she had a ride home.

"No!" said Lena. "Thanks for your help. I'm fine now, okay? If my friends don't show up, I can walk. I live nearby." The thought of trudging home in the dark on noodle-weak legs, carrying a heavy surfboard, seemed impossible. But there was no way she was going to accept a ride home from a stranger.

That would be dangerous, she thought wryly. *And I'm all about safety.* A choked laugh escaped her throat.

The man studied her intently. "Why don't you call them?" he persisted. "Or did you have a prearranged time?"

Tears leaked from Lena's eyes. She just wanted to go home, and this guy . . . this guy was so damn *concerned* about her, she was afraid he was going to follow her home to make sure she was okay. And once he knew where she lived, he might try to talk to her parents—he might tell them she'd been alone at Magic's.

"Look," she said, trying to project a sane, trustworthy vibe. "Thanks. But I *told* you I'm fine. I don't need any help."

"No, *you* look," answered the man, rather fiercely. "You almost drowned out there! You've been through a traumatic experience. You're shivering, you're laughing and crying, and your behavior is erratic. I'm a parent and a doctor, and I am *not* leaving you alone in this condition. Either you call your friends, so that I can see you're going to be okay, or you let us take you home. It's extremely important that you get warm as soon as possible."

Lena didn't answer, just reached for her duffel bag. She slid the key into an interior pocket, zipping it closed. Then she pulled out her cell and dialed Pem, walking a few feet away.

"Leen?" answered Pem.

"I need you to come get me."

"Are you okay?"

"I'm fine," said Lena. "I mean . . . it's a long story. Please, can you and Max come get me? Please."

"I thought you didn't want him to . . ." Pem trailed off. Lena knew she meant that Max wasn't supposed to find out she had surfed at Magic's.

"I know, but I . . . I need a ride, and I don't want to call Kai."

"You're at—?"

"Yes. You might as well tell him I'm at Magic's. I don't have the energy to walk anywhere else. I'll meet you at the highway."

"We'll be there in fifteen minutes."

"Thanks." Lena clicked off the phone and put it back in her duffel bag. She pulled out a big towel and wrapped it around her shoulders. "They're coming," she said to the bearded man.

"We'll wait with you," he answered with maddening courtesy.

Eyes widening, Lena looked over at the man's son, as if to say, *Is he always this annoying?*

The guy grinned, understanding her perfectly. "Yeah. He can't help it," he said. "He's a giver."

Lena gave him a small smile.

She picked up her duffel and the surfboard, and headed up the beach to the highway, the man and his son close behind. She no longer felt cold. She was warm with the glow of belief: there *was* magic at Magic Crescent Cove.

The three of them walked in silence to the man's car parked on the side of the highway. The boy glanced curiously over at her a couple of times.

"Here," said the man, handing her a jug of water. "So you can rinse off your suit."

"Thanks," mumbled Lena. She turned away, tugging off her wetsuit, conscious of the other two peeling off their own wetsuits. The three of them rinsed their suits, and the men tossed theirs in the trunk of the car, which was lined with towels. Lena dressed in the clothes she'd packed earlier, placing her wetsuit in the bag. She took the key out of the bag and slid it into her hoodie pocket, keeping her fingers loosely around it.

"I'd better call Mom," said the man to his son. "She'll be wondering what happened to us." He walked a few steps away.

The boy held out his hand to Lena. "I'm Erik."

"Right," she said, grasping his fingers briefly.

"Hey, haven't I seen you out there before?"

"Out where?"

"Surfing. With Ani. Not at Magic's, though. And not Back Yard. Farther down the coast."

"You know Ani?"

"Sure. She's a friend of my sister's."

Great, thought Lena. *Does everyone in this town know everyone else?* "Yeah, I guess you have seen me, then."

"What's your name?"

Lena hesitated.

"That's cool. You don't have to tell me. I was just curious. I don't know any girls who surf Magic's."

"I never have before."

"Really? What did you think?"

She shook her head. "It was too much. I probably won't do it again."

He laughed. "Yeah, I wouldn't go out there unless I had my dad with me."

She looked over at Erik's father, feeling embarrassed that she had been rude to him. "It's cool that you surf with your dad."

Erik's father finished his phone conversation and hung up. "She said they'd save us some dinner." He looked at Lena. "Listen," he said. "My name is Ray Lamott. And you've met Erik. If you . . . if you need someone to talk to, I work at the hospital on Coronado. Feel free to call anytime." He made a move as if to touch her arm, but stopped himself. "You're too young to remember this, but a woman killed herself at Magic's once. I was there."

Lena's eyes grew round.

"She jumped off the rocks." He pointed to Shipwreck Rocks, where the waves crashed and retreated. "She was crying and talking to herself. So I got a little upset when you started acting so strange. I couldn't help flashing back to that day."

Lena tightened her fingers around the key. "I didn't mean to act strange," she murmured.

"What's your name?"

Lena did not answer.

"All right. You won't tell me, I get it. But promise me you won't surf alone anymore. Or I will make it my business to find out who your parents are. You understand? Because now I'm going to be watching for you."

"I promise."

"Good."

Lena had never been so happy to see Max's Mustang in her life.

Max parked, and Pem leaped out of the car before it had even stopped moving. She ran to Lena and put her arms around her. "Are you all right?" Her eyes were wide and wary as she looked at the two strangers.

"Yeah. Thanks for coming to get me."

"Take her straight home," said Ray firmly. "She needs to get warm." He lifted his hand in farewell, and got into his car.

"See you later," said Erik. He got into the car, too, looking back at Lena as they drove away.

Max strode up to Lena and took his board from her to strap it to the roof of his car.

Lena buried her face in Pem's shoulder, tears of relief filling her eyes.

"Are you sure you're okay?" whispered Pem. "Who were those guys?"

"Just some people who were out there at Magic's."

"Get in the car," said Max shortly.

"Max—" began Lena.

"You are so done with my board," he said.

"I know. I'm really sorry. And I really, really appreciate you coming to get me."

He didn't answer, just put the car in gear and drove as quickly as possible to Lena's house.

"Please stop here," said Lena, at the corner of her street. She didn't want anyone at her house to see Max's car.

Max veered to the curb and put the car in park. He turned around to look at Lena. "Hey."

"Yeah?" She waited for his fury.

He did look angry, but also curious. "Did you really surf there?"

She nodded.

"You're crazy," he muttered. Then: "What was it like?"

She thought for a moment. "It was huge. But your board performed like a dream."

He smiled as she got out of the car.

"Thanks again. I'm sorry I ruined your date."

"You didn't," said Pem. "Call me tomorrow."

"I will."

Lena carried her duffel bag in one hand and kept the fingers of her other hand around the key in her pocket. She walked to the backyard and opened the garden shed. As she stepped inside to stow her duffel bag, she heard the sliding-glass door open.

"Where have you been?" asked her father in a tight voice.

CHAPTER 23

Whirling around, Lena faced her father.

"Where have you been?" he asked again, his voice rising.

She could see her mom behind him, and Janni and Cole in the family room.

"When Leslie's mom came to pick you up after the movie, and you weren't there, she called the house to make sure you got home okay," said her dad. "Janni told her that you weren't home, and that you were supposed to be with Martha and Leslie."

Lena swallowed.

"What have you got there in the shed?"

She didn't move. Her hand clutching the key trembled so much, she was afraid he would notice.

Her dad came out of the house and stepped past her to look into the shed. He picked up her duffel bag and pulled out her dripping wetsuit.

"What's this?"

Resisting the urge to answer smartly, *Looks like my wetsuit,* Lena just shrugged.

"Were you surfing?"

She stared down at her feet.

"Answer me!" shouted her dad.

Lena jumped. "Yes," she mumbled.

He threw her wetsuit down on the grass and stalked back to the house. At the door he turned around. "Get in this house," he said through gritted teeth.

Her mom and Cole were huddled on the sofa when she got inside. Cole's eyes were huge; he didn't know what was going on, but he knew voices were being raised . . . again.

Janni stood near the door. "I'm sorry, Lena. But I was worried about you."

"It's okay," said Lena.

"You are grounded, Lena. Go up to your room," said her dad, pacing back and forth.

Lena was only too happy to escape to her room. She would finally be able to examine the key in privacy.

When she reached her room, she closed the door and opened her fist.

It was a shiny, old-fashioned key, about two inches long, with an oval-shaped top and a single "tooth" at the bottom. After turning the key over and over in her hands for a few minutes, studying it from every angle, feeling each curve and corner, Lena looked around her room for a place to keep it. She knew her father would be coming up to talk to her eventually, and she didn't want him to see the key.

She sat down at her desk and slid open the drawer. She put the key inside, under some papers. She closed the drawer and sat there for a moment. Then, frowning, she took the key out again and went to her bed. She lifted the edge of her mattress and pushed the key underneath. Then she lay down on the bed and pulled Grandma Kath's sun-and-moon quilt over her.

She wasn't cold, but she felt strange, as if she might be feverish, or hallucinating.

Am I really awake? Or is this all a dream?

She pictured the key, gleaming under the mattress. What magic did it unlock?

Pushing back the quilt, she got out of bed. She reached under the mattress and drew the key back out. She couldn't bear not being able to touch it. Staring down at its shiny hardness, Lena realized, *This is what I've been looking for.*

Tears filled her eyes.

The mermaid was real. She was communicating with Lena. She wanted Lena to find the lock that fit this key, and . . . and . . . what?

Lena didn't know the answer. But her hands were no longer empty.

She lay back down on the bed, sliding the key under her pillow as she heard someone approach her room. There was a tap on the door.

"Come in," she said.

To her surprise, it was her mom who entered, not her dad.

"Hi," said Lena.

"Hi," said her mom. She sat down on the edge of Lena's bed. She didn't speak for a moment. Her gaze came to rest on the photo of Lucy that Lena had propped on her desk. Staring at the photo, her mom's hand drifted up to her ear, and her fingers began to twist one of her earrings.

"Lena," she said finally. "You were surfing?"

"Yes."

"When did you learn how?"

"Just the past few weeks. I know Dad was worried . . . but Mom! I'm really *good* at surfing. And I love it *so much*."

"Mmm." She looked again at the photo of Lucy, then seemed to drag her gaze away with effort. "I don't doubt it. You're good at everything, sweetie."

Lena met her mom's eyes. "Is Dad going to punish me? After all this, if he won't let me surf again, I don't know what I'll do."

Instead of answering, Lena's mom asked, "Where were you, Lena?"

Lena looked down. She was so tired of lying! But there was no way she could admit to her mom that she had been surfing at Magic's. "Back Yard," she said.

Her mom's shoulders relaxed. "Oh. Good. At least there are plenty of other surfers there. In case you got into trouble and needed help. Was Kai with you?"

Lena hesitated only for a second. "Yes," she said. Poor Kai. Getting dragged into her family drama. But maybe her parents would be less worried if they knew Kai had been with her. She longed to slide out of this tangle of lies, like sliding out of a tangle of seaweed. "Um, there was a doctor there, too," she offered. "So even if someone got hurt—which they didn't!—he would be right there to help."

"A doctor?" said her mom. "On the beach?"

"He was surfing. Ray somebody."

Her mom stiffened. "Bones Lamott?"

"What?"

"Ray Lamott?"

"Yeah! That was his name."

Her mom frowned. "Ray was surfing at Back Yard?"

"Um, yes?" *Why wouldn't he?* thought Lena. "You know him?"

"He went to my high school. He's a few years older than I am." Her mom studied Lena. "Ray was always a big wave hound. As I recall, he preferred Magic's."

Crap! thought Lena. *Lying is hard!* "He . . . was surfing with his son today."

Without answering, her mom continued to study Lena. Finally she stood up, and Lena felt as though a searchlight had been removed from her face. "You know, your dad was planning to tell you you could take surfing lessons in the spring."

"He was?"

"Yes. The waves are bigger in winter, so he thought spring would be a better time to learn."

"He was going to teach me?" Lena felt her lower lip tremble.

"No," said her mom. "He can't teach you himself. But he was going to sign you up for lessons in Santa Cruz."

"Oh, wow."

"It may not seem like it, Lena, but we do keep your happiness in mind." Her mom gave a rueful smile and left the room.

Lena waited until her mom was down the hall, then reached under her pillow for the key, anxious to feel its solid weight in her hand again. Already she knew it was *her* key, and she hated not having it with her.

It looked so old, but there was not a speck of rust on it. Didn't metal rust in salt water? Maybe gold didn't.

"Where do you belong?" she whispered.

The sheer profusion of possible locks in the world made Lena feel dizzy, and she lay back on her bed.

I may spend the rest of my life looking for the right lock, she thought.

She closed her eyes, picturing cupboards and trunks, suitcases and closets, attic doors and desk drawers . . . millions of locks, but only one a perfect fit for her key.

CHAPTER 24

You will find it.

When Lena woke up, those words were clear in her mind. The mermaid had given her the key for a reason. She wouldn't give it to someone who had no hope of finding its lock.

Lena felt around her bed in the dark, a small wave of fear surging over her when her hands encountered only bedding. Had someone come in while she was sleeping and taken it? She sat up and pushed back her covers, relief flooding her when she found the key. It had slipped farther down in the bed.

Vowing not to lose it again, even for a moment, Lena climbed out of bed and fumbled her way in the dark to her desk. She felt in the top drawer for her flashlight. They often lost power during windstorms, so every room in the house contained a flashlight.

Shielding her eyes until they grew accustomed to the light, she shone the beam into her jewelry box. She moved things around until she found the gold chain she was looking for, and held it up to the light.

No, too delicate. She was afraid the chain might break and the key would be lost. She clutched the key convulsively at the thought.

She opened her bureau drawers one at a time, slowly, so they wouldn't make noise. When she got to the bottom drawer, she withdrew a blue scarf knitted in velvet yarn. Her mom had gone through a short-lived knitting phase when she was pregnant with Cole, creating booties and a blanket for the baby, and scarves for Lena and her dad.

Perfect. It hardly ever got cold enough to wear a scarf, anyway. Lena took a pair of scissors from her desk and snipped the end of the scarf. Unraveling the thick strands of yarn, she pulled free a single strand measuring about three feet in length. She snipped the other end and fed it through the open top of her key. Then she triple-knotted the two ends of yarn together and slipped the homemade necklace around her neck, tucking it under her shirt. The softness of the yarn and the hardness of the metal felt exactly right against her skin.

She crawled back in bed, glancing at her clock radio. 3:39. She could sleep another three or four hours, thank goodness. Magic's had beaten her up, and she needed rest.

Lena's breathing grew regular and her limbs relaxed. Images of the mermaid drifted through her dreams. "Come to me," sang the creature. "Heed my call."

I'm coming.

Lena dreamed she was slipping out of bed and opening her door. Halfway down the stairs, a small sound broke through her dreams, and she paused. Cole was crying.

Lena woke up.

She felt the oak banister under her hand and grabbed it to keep from falling down the stairs. She might have stood there a long time, trembling and telling herself, "I'm okay, I'm okay. I'm safe in the house," but she heard another cry from Cole's room.

She hurried back upstairs and eased open the door to his room. He sat up in bed, mumbling, ". . . can't have it," then lay back down. Lena watched him for a minute, but he was asleep. She closed his door very gently. She crossed the hall to her own room and went inside, closing her own door very gently, too.

◻ ◻ ◻

The mermaid came as close to shore as she dared, and she rocked in the waves until dawn, waiting for the girl to appear. When the sky began to lighten, she uttered one lonely moan and slid beneath the surface.

CHAPTER 25

PemberLoca: How r u today? U didn't call.

Sea_girl: So so tired.

PemberLoca: No wonder! U got rinsed at magic's, huh?

Sea_girl: Plus the rents caught me so I'm grounded for life.

PemberLoca: !!!!

Sea_girl: Janni got worried n called them on their date. They were waiting for me when I got home.

PemberLoca: Gah! Were they rly rly mad?

Sea_girl: Yes n no.

Lena paused. It was so much more complicated than she could ever explain to Pem. How could she say, "Well, I told my mom I was surfing with my boyfriend, when in reality I'm obsessing about a mermaid who, it turns out, is real, and I can prove it, because she gave me a key, which must mean something, but what?! I'm not sure, and I'm trying to figure it out. Help!"

A feeling of loneliness washed over her.

Pem's world revolved around very human concerns like friends and school and Max. Lena's world had become a tangle of broken sleep and waking dreams . . . voices in her head and mermaids in the water . . . locks and keys and calls from the sea.

PemberLoca: U there?

Sea_girl: Yeah sorry. Just thinking. Thx for coming to the rescue.
Max is a hero.

PemberLoca: ☺

Sea_girl: I better get off since I'm grounded. Lets talk tomorrow.

PemberLoca: K bye.

Sea_girl: Bye.

◻ ◻ ◻

Lena greeted her dad warily at breakfast. He was eating a
bowl of oatmeal and staring down at his newspaper.

"Dad?"

"Mmm–hmm."

"I'm sorry."

"Thank you," he said. "I appreciate that."

It's time to tell him about the sleepwalking, thought Lena.

Her dad stood up and carried his bowl to the sink. "I have
to go in to work today. I'll talk to you later."

"On a Sunday?"

"Yep. Problems with the server." He left the room.

Wow, she thought. *He's really mad at me. He's never been that
cold before.*

◻ ◻ ◻

Kaiborg: U didn't answer ur phone.

Sea_girl: Mom took it. Im grounded.

Kaiborg: ??

Sea_girl: Long story. I lied about where I was.

Kaiborg: Oh? Where were u?

Sea_girl: No big deal. Just surfing at magics.

Even though Lena hadn't planned to tell Kai, now that she'd been caught and *had* to tell him, it gave her a little thrill to talk about Magic's.

Kaiborg: Haha. Very funny.
Sea_girl: . . .
Kaiborg: Leen??
Sea_girl: Its true.
Kaiborg: OMG.
Sea_girl: I know. Crazy. & amazing.
Kaiborg: But why?
Sea_girl: Just rly wanted to try it.
Kaiborg: I cant even . . . !
Sea_girl: Um theres one other thing too.
Kaiborg: ??
Sea_girl: I kinda told my parents u were there too.
Kaiborg: What? Why?!
Sea_girl: Its complicated.
Kaiborg: Explain then.
Sea_girl: Its too long to tell in chat. Will tell u Monday at school.
Kaiborg: Lena I kinda think u owe me an explanation. Call from ur land line when u get a chance.
Sea_girl: K. I will.

Kai logged off without saying goodbye. Now *he* was mad at her, too. With good reason. She touched the shape of the key through her shirt. Well, they could all be mad at her; she didn't care. This key was totally worth whatever price she had to pay.

▢ ▢ ▢

"Okay, remind me again," said Kai. "Your parents know you went surfing, and they think I was with you, but they don't know you were at Magic's. Have I got it straight?"

"Yes. For the hundredth time, I'm sorry."

"And for the hundredth time, help me understand. Why Magic's, Lena? I would go surfing with you anytime, anywhere. All you had to do was ask. I would even lie for you. But Magic's? *That* . . . I don't understand."

Lena glanced over at Pem, who was eating lunch with Leslie, Martha, and some other drama people. Pem flashed her a sympathetic look. She had told Lena earlier, "You're on your own with Kai. He's upset, not only about the fact that you dragged him into the lie to your parents, but about the fact that you're grounded and can't spend any time with him outside of school. He ranted about it to me for half an hour yesterday. So make nice with him."

Lena was *trying* to make nice, but Kai was persistent in wanting explanations. And she couldn't say, "A mermaid lives at Magic's . . . that's why I had to go there." All she could say, over and over, was, "I'm really sorry. I won't do it again."

Although . . . that was maybe not true.

She might surf Magic's again.

Lena decided to change tactics. She stood up and came around to Kai's side of the table. She waited until he turned around, then she sat down on his lap and put her arms around him, nestling close. She put her lips against his ear and whispered, "Don't be mad. Is there anything I can do?" She sighed against his ear and stroked the back of his neck.

As she had hoped, Kai melted. He shifted her on his lap and gave her a long, deep kiss. When they finally broke apart, he murmured, "More of this. Let's take a walk before lunch is over."

◻ ◻ ◻

Lena didn't mind being grounded too much, since it meant she would have the house to herself when both her parents were at work. She had decided to take a systematic approach to her search for the lock that fit her key. She would start by searching her own house and yard before she moved on to the wider world of keyholes.

However, her parents had apparently decided to keep her under near-constant surveillance. Monday her mom was waiting outside school when she came out, having left work early to pick her up. Mom gave Kai a level stare before lifting her hand in greeting. Abashed, Kai slunk away. Tuesday was an exact duplicate of Monday, except that her mom unbent enough to give Kai a small smile.

Wednesday, unbelievably, her *dad* was there after school, waiting for her.

"No way?" said Lena.

Kai hung back when he saw her dad's car. "I'm not going out there. I'm afraid of your dad," he said.

"You're afraid of my dad?" she said. "Have you met your sister? She could snap my dad like a twig."

He chuckled and squeezed her hand. "Um, my kiss is implied. I don't want to risk your dad seeing me." He went back in the school.

Lena opened the passenger door and got in the car. "Server fine now?" she asked coldly. She and her dad had hardly spoken since the surfing incident.

"What?" he said. "Yes."

"How much longer are you and Mom going to chauffeur me home?"

He looked at her with his gaslight blue eyes, unsmiling. "Until we feel we can trust you again."

Thursday must have been the day their trust returned, because zero parents were waiting for her after school. Either that, or neither one could get away from work.

Lena wanted nothing more than to take a long walk on the beach—she felt like she'd been away from it for weeks, instead of days. But she knew she shouldn't miss the opportunity to look for the lock that fit her key.

When she got home, she set to work searching the garage, opening as many boxes as she could reach, getting dusty and grimy. She carefully set up a ladder and reached for the boxes that were up high. Some were too heavy, and she had to leave them where they were and hope that they were just filled with books or something. After what seemed like hours, she pushed the last box back in place and sat down on the workbench.

Whatever it was, the lock that fit this key did not seem to be in the garage. And she'd never seen any kind of funky old trunks anywhere in the house. Maybe it was in her parents' room.

You will find it, she reminded herself.

She stood at the doorway of her parents' room, looking in. The thought of going through their drawers and closets made her feel slightly ill, but it had to be done.

Just not today.

CHAPTER 26

"Lena, want anything from the store?" called her dad.

"No, thanks," said Lena. "Wait! Yes, I do. Could you get me some sushi from Miso on Main for lunch?"

Miso on Main was always packed with day-trippers on the weekends. By the time her dad finished the grocery shopping, he would have to wait twenty minutes or more for a sushi order.

"Well, I wasn't really planning on going there."

"Oh, Dad, come on. I have a craving for shrimp rolls with seaweed."

"What a surprise," she heard him mutter from below. "Fine, I'll add that to my list."

She hung over the banister. "Thanks, Dad. Love you."

"Love you, too. See you in an hour or so."

Lena listened to the back door close, the car engine start, and the garage door open and close.

Then, with a reluctant step, she entered her parents' bedroom. Her mom was at a wedding and would not be back for hours. Cole was across the street at Austin's house. As squicky as she felt at the idea of invading her parents' privacy, Lena knew she might not get another chance to search their room. And her desire to unlock this mystery was stronger than her guilt.

For the past week, she had spent every spare moment looking through all the cupboards, drawers, and closets in the house, except in her parents' room. She had even wandered around outside in the front and back yards, fretting over a possible buried chest, and wondering if she would have to dig up every square foot of garden.

Somehow, after wearing the key close to her heart for seven days, she felt that it would not lead her astray. And she did not believe the lock she sought was underground.

Pulling the key from under her shirt, Lena held it loosely in her hand for a moment, as if seeking guidance. The sun had gone behind a cloud, making her parents' bedroom seem darker than usual. She smelled the scent of her mom's jasmine lotion and her dad's woodsy after-shave.

Where to start?

Lena looked at the bedside tables. On her mom's side was a stack of books, mostly mysteries, with a gardening magazine lying on top. On her father's side was just one book, a Stephen King paperback. Lena didn't know how he could read horror novels and then fall asleep, but he loved them. She glanced at her mom's dresser drawer and opened it. Mostly just lacy, silky things, wafting the scent of jasmine up to her more strongly. She closed the drawer hastily. She paused at her father's drawer.

Ew, what if there are . . . marital things . . . in there? she thought. Her mind skated over the idea like it was a patch of black ice.

Holding her breath, she pulled the drawer open and glanced inside quickly, making sure there was nothing like a locked box, then shut the drawer. Whew.

She turned to their big mahogany bureau next. Coins, scraps of paper, a book of crossword puzzles, and various other objects littered the top. A large cobalt-blue hand—used for holding rings and other pieces of jewelry—stood at one end of the bureau. It was, of course, a gift from Grandma Kath. Lena shuddered. That disembodied hand, frozen in a blue-fingered reach, had always creeped her out. Trying not to look at the hand, Lena opened and closed the drawers, scanning their contents cursorily.

She turned away from the bureau with relief and examined their closet. It was about five feet across, with two sliding mirrored doors pulled shut. Avoiding her guilty reflection, she opened the right side door and looked at the rows of shoeboxes on the shelf. Dragging a chair over to the closet, she stood up on it and opened the box closest to her. Cards and letters addressed to her mom from her dad. She closed the lid. The next box held old CDs. The third and fourth boxes were full of letters, postcards, and photos from other friends and family. None of these boxes seemed to contain anything that Lena should be looking through. Another pang of guilt nudged her.

Shoving aside the shoeboxes, Lena looked deeper on the shelf. At the very end on the left side was a larger metal box, like something for holding files. *Now, that looks promising,* she thought, noting its lock. She couldn't reach it from her position on the chair, so she got down, closed the right side door, and opened the left. Then she moved the chair to the other side of the closet. She paused to look at the clock. Her dad had been gone for about half an hour.

She climbed up onto the chair again and reached for the metal box. Disappointed, she saw that the lock was too small for her key, and anyway, the box wasn't locked. The tabs on the folders inside read *Archive Bank Statements, Past Tax Returns,*

Legal Documents, and *Old.* Strange that her parents kept this in the closet instead of in Dad's office.

Lena climbed down off the chair and sat on the floor. She pulled out the file marked *Legal Documents.* There were the birth certificates for Lena and Cole, and the marriage certificate for her parents: Brian Wayne Whittaker and Allison Lee Briggs.

She glanced at the last legal document. It was a death certificate.

Lena stared at it in dismay. There was her mother's name, Lucy Whittaker, no middle initial. Under cause of death was typed: *Suicide by drowning.*

CHAPTER 27

Lena let the paper fall from her fingers.

After a long, airless moment, she lay down on the floor, pulling her knees to her chest.

Here was the truth that her father had been unable to tell her. Here was a piece of paper that explained years of "I'm not ready."

Suicide by drowning.

Lena closed her eyes, willing herself not to cry even as her heart cracked deep inside. Her mother had been dead for a dozen years. Yet the stab of pain Lena felt at this new knowledge melted the years away, and that chamber in her heart where she stored her mother's loss opened wide, stacking new grief upon the old.

"Why?" she whispered. "Was being my mom so awful?"

She could feel the ache of tears behind her eyes, and she took deep breaths to help her focus on *not* crying. She bit down hard on her lower lip. Finally she opened her eyes and sat up. Forty-five minutes had passed since her father had left. She still hadn't found the lock for this key. If she didn't find it today, she felt certain that she could never bring herself to look through her parents' room again.

Lena put the files back in the metal box, in the exact order she'd found them. She placed the metal box on the shelf. She put all the shoeboxes back where they belonged, then closed the sliding doors and put the chair back in the corner. While she worked, she kept her mind carefully blank.

Almost an hour now. Her father would be finished with the shopping and on his way to the sushi restaurant.

Lena looked around the room again. She pushed open the door to their bathroom, but it seemed too small a room to hold any secrets. She knew that her mom hid the few pieces of expensive jewelry she owned in a tissue box, but Lena was not interested in those.

Standing in the middle of the room, Lena closed her eyes and clutched the key hard in her fist, as if she could squeeze an answer out of it. *Where do you belong?* she thought angrily. *I need to know.*

When she opened her eyes, the room seemed brighter than before. The sun had moved out from behind the clouds. But one corner of the room remained in shadow. Lena cocked her head, studying the antique chair in the corner. Why was it there? No one ever sat in it. There was no light nearby, so it wasn't a good place to read. It was hard and uncomfortable, and usually had piles of clothes on top of it.

Lena moved to the corner and picked up the chair. It was solid wood, but spindly, so she was able to move it out of the corner easily. She examined the wall behind the chair. It looked smooth and unblemished. She knelt on the carpet, feeling for bumps or irregularities, but there were none. She put her fingers to the edge of the carpet and tugged, but it was tacked down securely.

Baring her teeth, Lena tightened her grip on the edge of the carpet and wrenched upward with all the strength of her anger and frustration. The staples holding the carpet in place popped out of the floor. Lena pulled the carpet back.

The wooden floor beneath the edge of loose carpet had been cut into the shape of a rectangle.

In the tick of time between her heartbeats, Lena hesitated. What could be so important—or dangerous—that her father would hide it this thoroughly? She was still holding up the edge of loose carpet; now she pulled harder, revealing the full size of the cut in the wooden floor. It was about two feet long and one foot wide. She bent the carpet back and knelt on it to hold it in place. Then she fit her fingers to the cracks between the wood, and lifted until one edge was raised. She fit her hands around the piece of wood, and lifted it out, revealing a neat rectangular hole.

In the hole lay a dusty, brown leather sea chest.

Lena set aside the piece of wood and reached for the trunk. As her hands touched the cracked leather, she hesitated once more. Whatever was inside this trunk was something her father had clearly never wanted her to see. *Suicide by drowning* . . . the blunt, black words on crisp, official paper floated into her mind.

Then a vision of the mermaid replaced the image of the death certificate. There had to be a connection between the mermaid's key and this dusty old trunk. She couldn't stop now.

Trembling, Lena lifted the sea chest out of the hole in the floor and set it beside her. She took the key from around her neck. Taking a deep breath, she fit the key in the lock. She turned it, and felt a click as the lock released.

Lifting the lid of the trunk, the scent of salt air drifted into her nostrils. It was as if she had stepped outside. There were photos and letters lying on top. Lena thought she had seen all the photos of her mother that existed. Now she realized that her father had saved some and hidden them away in this trunk. Lucy looked impossibly young, hardly older than Lena was now. She was laughing in some photos, looking serious in others. More beautiful than anyone Lena had ever seen, with her long hair rippling over her shoulders and her emerald eyes shining with love. Then there were photos of her father with her mother, hugging and kissing and acting silly for the camera. Her father looked very young, too, in these photos. His hair was longer and shaggier, and he had a blond goatee. There were even a few photos of the two of them in the ocean, her father sitting astride his surfboard, and her mother treading water near him.

She doesn't have on a wetsuit, mused Lena. *She must not have minded the cold water.*

Here was one of Lucy, her dad . . . and Allie! They were all three smiling into the camera, sitting at a table in a restaurant. Her dad's arm was around Lucy, and Allie leaned close to them, as young and pretty as they were.

The last few photos were stuffed in a too-small envelope. Lena slid them out. The first one was a photo of a small shop—the sign read, BAY AREA BODY ART, in large black letters, with a smaller line below: TATTOOS, PIERCINGS, AND SPECIAL-OCCASION BODY PAINT. The photos documented her parents getting tattoos. First they took pictures of each other making pretend-scared faces for the camera, then her dad took a couple of shots of the artist working on her mother's tattoo. When it was finished, a small dolphin adorned the skin just above her left ankle. Then her mother must have taken the photos of her dad getting the tattoo on his left arm.

But it wasn't the Chinese dragon tattoo Lena had seen all her life.

It was a tattoo of a mermaid.

"What. Is. Going. On," she whispered.

Her dad had had the tattoo altered at some point. But why?

She glanced over at the clock. She knew it couldn't be long now before her dad came home.

She set the photos next to her on the carpet, intending to hide them in her room, where she could take her time looking at them.

Next was a manila envelope full of yellowed newspaper clippings. Lena slid one out and saw the headline: *Local Woman Missing*. The one below that read, *Missing Woman Presumed Dead from Suicide*. She shoved them back in the envelope.

The letters and envelopes that came next were addressed to her dad in unfamiliar writing—it must be Lucy's. Lena wanted more than anything to read them, but she set them aside for later as well. Her hands felt clumsy and numb as she gathered the pages together. Her name jumped out at her: Selena.

Lena pulled the envelope out of the pile and stared at it—a cream-colored envelope with no other adornment, just her name. It was sealed.

Her heart thudded painfully. Her mother must have written a goodbye letter before she killed herself.

Lena's hand began to crumple the envelope, almost without her volition. Then she flung the balled-up letter across the room. *I wish I'd never found it,* she thought.

She fought down an urge to slam shut the lid of the chest. *I can't go back,* she thought. *I can't go back to not knowing.*

A large piece of heavy folded paper was the next thing she pulled out of the chest.

Lena unfolded the heavy paper and saw that it was a print of a painting called *The Land Baby,* by an artist named John Collier. The painting showed a small naked girl, about four years old, standing on a yellow sand beach while a mermaid gazed at her from the edge of the water. The mermaid was shown from the back, hands placed in front of her on the sand, her slim hips melting into a long, curving tail. The expression on her face was not visible, but her posture and demeanor suggested longing. The child's expression was unafraid. Lena stared at the print for a moment, then refolded it and set it aside.

A comb and a mirror lay inside the trunk. Lena picked up the comb, which was heavy, carved of coral. The handle was studded with brilliant gems, blue and green and red . . . she had never seen anything like it. She held the comb for a long time, running the tips of her fingers over the delicate teeth and the brilliant facets of the jewels. It must have belonged to Lucy.

The mirror in the trunk glinted up at Lena. There was not a speck of dust on it.

Lena picked up the mirror and gazed into it. Her eyes were wide and amazed, as gray as a stormy sea—like her dad always said. For the first time, Lena could see that she was going to be beautiful someday, just like her mother. Her skin was not as pale as Lucy's had been, and she had her father's thick blond hair, but something in the structure of her cheekbones and pointed chin was evocative of Lucy.

As she continued to stare, mesmerized, she became aware of a shadow behind her in the mirror. She whirled around.

There was no one there.

Lena turned back to the mirror and looked deeper. There *was* a shadow behind her. But it was *in the mirror.*

Goose bumps rose on her arms, and her heart hammered. Lena watched as the shadow grew bigger and began to darken her reflection in the mirror. It shimmered and swirled, and Lena's own face in the mirror began to dissolve. As Lena watched in disbelief, her eyes were the last features to disappear, melting into the gray mist. She saw that what appeared to be a vaporous mist was swirling into a more liquid form. The depths of the mirror were filled with an underwater murkiness.

This is it, she thought, gripping the mirror harder. *This is why the mermaid gave me the key. She wanted me to see this.*

Even as Lena continued to stare, she began to make out objects in the water. Silvery shapes flashed by. Strands of kelp and seaweed drifted past.

The murkiness in the water lightened. Lena peered deeper into the mirror, able to make out figures. They seemed to be spinning slowly in a circle.

Lena's hands began to shake. As the mirror quivered in her grasp, she saw that by moving it in different directions, she could see different perspectives under water. Now she was able to look more clearly at the figures in the circle. There was no question: they were mer-people. Their chests rose and fell, breathing in the salt water. Their lower bodies consisted of glimmering tails instead of legs.

Lena twisted the mirror in her hands again, trying to see even closer. They revolved slowly in their graceful dance. There was one mermaid in the center of the circle.

Is it my mermaid? wondered Lena. *Did she want me to see her world?*

Lena's eyes were fixed intently on the images in the mirror. She no longer saw or heard anything around her. She was no longer even aware of being in her parents' bedroom. Her whole being was concentrated on the underwater scene unfolding before her eyes. It was like watching a live-action camera. The mer-people turned in their unbroken circle, swaying gently, hands joined to enclose the solitary mermaid in the center.

Now Lena could hear sounds, too. She could hear a mournful, sweet song reaching up to her ears from the depths of the sea. It was like no human song she had ever heard, sounding more like a thousand violins and flutes all playing at once. And now she could make out speech. It certainly was not English, yet somehow, Lena could understand it. The sounds whirled into her mind, and she knew their meanings: "child," "alone," "heart," "life."

The mermaid within the circle lifted her hands to her face, head tilted back, eyes open in silent supplication. Lena moved the mirror in her hand, trying to get a closer glimpse of "her" mermaid. The mirror, as if it could divine her wishes, as if sensing her destination, began to zoom in slowly on the solitary mermaid.

Long, floating hair . . . a sinuous, silver tail . . . slim white arms . . . delicate hands covering her face, as if grief-stricken.

What's wrong with her? thought Lena. *What could make her look that way? Maybe this is how they have funerals.*

The mermaid's hands came away from her face, and she stared mutely around at the circle of her people. Green eyes . . . heart-shaped face with a delicately pointed chin.

It was Lucy. It was Lena's mother.

Her lips opened again, and Lena could hear her. "Selena . . . Selena. I remember. I remember now."

CHAPTER 28

She's alive, was Lena's first thought.

Not "She's a mermaid." But "She's alive." Her mother had *not* killed herself, whatever that death certificate said.

I'm half-mermaid, was Lena's second thought.

As if the gold key had unlocked not only a dusty trunk, but dozens of mysteries in Lena's life, everything began to make sense, like an unseen hand sliding puzzle pieces into place.

Blood work . . . We're not leaving Diamond Bay . . . How do you think Lena's going to feel when she finds out the truth? . . . You're a natural . . .

It all made sense. Maybe it even explained why she fainted that day on the twenty-ninth floor. Maybe her body went into some kind of shock when she was too far above sea level.

"Lena, didn't you hear me? I've been calling you . . ." Her dad stood in the doorway. "What are you—?"

Lena realized that far back in her consciousness, she must have heard the garage door opening, then the back door opening, then her father's voice calling her. But she was so absorbed in the undersea world opening up in front of her eyes that she had not registered his arrival.

Her dad's face darkened as he saw the trunk sitting open next to Lena. Then the look of anger on his face was replaced by an expression of primal fear.

"You found the mirror!" he cried, rushing forward. He wrenched it from her grasp.

Lena stood up, her voice breaking as she cried, "She's alive! You told me she was *dead*. But she's alive! I can see her!" She tried to snatch the mirror back.

Her father held it above his head and stepped away from her.

They faced each other, breathing heavily.

"Daddy," she sobbed. "Why did you do this?"

With shaking hands, her father lifted the mirror to his face, as if afraid to see what it would show. He watched for a long moment.

"It's the memory circle," he whispered. "She remembers. Oh, my God, Lena. She remembers." Tears filled his eyes. "After all this time . . . I can't believe it." He grabbed Lena and hugged her to his chest, weeping with an anguish she had never seen before. "I waited for so many years. But she never came back, and I knew . . . I knew her memories were gone."

Lena wept, too, not knowing what her father meant, only knowing that her mother was alive, and finally, she was going to find out the truth. She stayed in her father's embrace for a long time, while he rocked her back and forth.

After they stopped crying and looked into the mirror again, they found that it reflected only their faces. The magic had run out.

"It will only show you those you love for a few minutes," said her father. "Otherwise, you would never be able to put it down. You wouldn't be able to tear yourself away." He looked sadly at his own reflection in the mirror's surface. "I learned that soon enough."

"Daddy, please," said Lena. "Please tell me everything."

But her father seemed to be aging in front of Lena's eyes, his broad shoulders bent with loss. He sat down on the bed, as if unable to support his weight another minute. He looked at the open chest, its contents scattered. "How did you open this? I keep my key hidden away from home. Did you pick the lock?"

Lena sat down next to him. "She gave me the key." Seeing his confusion, she added, "The mermaid . . ." She hesitated, then spoke the words aloud: "My *mother* . . . gave me the key."

Her dad turned to stare at her, his expression shifting from confused to stunned. "You broke the spell." He took her by the shoulders. "Sweetheart. She *saw* you. And she finally remembered." He closed his eyes, and another tear slid down his cheek.

"I . . . what?"

He let go of her and stared down at the mirror again, as if it might reignite purely from desire, showing him the image of his lost love once more. Then his lips twisted and he shoved the mirror at Lena. "Here. Take it. I nearly lost my mind to this thing once before. I can't even touch it without feeling like insanity is just around the corner. It's yours now, anyway. The comb, too."

Lena pressed them to her heart. She took the key out of the lock and hung it around her neck again. Now she had all of her mother's gifts.

All except one. She walked across the room and picked up the crumpled letter on the floor.

Her dad looked at the envelope, and closed his eyes again for an instant. "Your letter," he said.

"When did she write it?" asked Lena.

He took a few breaths before he was able to answer. "Not long after you were born. She wanted—" He paused again to control his emotion. "She wanted to explain in her own words . . . in case something happened to her. She wanted you to understand, when you were old enough."

"Understand what?"

Her dad closed the trunk. "Your mother left us because she found her cloak. That made her forget . . . everything. But now, after all these years, she remembers." He touched Lena's cheek. "She saw you. And she remembered."

Lena stared, wanting to understand.

"Let's go downstairs," he said. "I . . . I need a drink. I mean—" He tried to smile. "I could use a strong whiskey, but I'll settle for a glass of water."

Lena slid the letter in her back pocket. She didn't want to read it yet. She followed her dad down the stairs, still holding the mirror and comb.

Her dad went into the kitchen. Lena followed, watching him pour a glass of water and try to drink it with a hand that shook so hard he finally had to use both hands to lift the glass. She sat down at the kitchen table to wait. After a minute he sat down across from her. A decade of secrets trembled in the space between them.

"What cloak?" asked Lena. "You said she found her cloak."

Her dad looked at his hands. "I can't believe we're finally having this conversation. I wanted to tell you . . ." He looked pleadingly at her. "I did! But it was so . . . damn . . . hard."

Impatient, Lena said, "I don't care how hard it was. You should have told me! How did this happen? How could a . . . a *mermaid* be my mother?"

Her dad folded his arms and leaned heavily on the table. "I need to start at the beginning. I don't know how else to tell you. I first saw her . . . Melusina was . . . is . . . her real name . . . when I was surfing at Magic's." He smiled to himself. "I thought I was losing my mind. At first I thought she was an otter, or a sea lion. It's pretty common for them to swim up next to you in the water."

I know, thought Lena.

"But I looked closer, and I could see her face. Her beautiful face." He fell quiet again.

Lena waited.

"I was surfing with my buddies, so I didn't want to say anything to them. They would have thought I was insane, anyway. But also . . . I didn't *want* them to see her, if she was real."

Lena recognized the sentiment. It was the reason she had never even told her best friends about seeing a mermaid.

"I guess she saw me, too. She disappeared into the waves, then came up a little farther away. But she didn't swim away." He smiled again, and closed his eyes, the better to see into the past. "She looked right at me, and she didn't seem scared. We stared at each other for a long time, and we . . . I think we were falling in love even then." He opened his eyes. "Then one of my buddies called out to me, and she ducked under the waves. I waited to see if she would come back, but she didn't."

"So when did you see her again?"

"Well, I became kind of obsessed. I was just sure I was going to see her again. I started going back to Magic's by myself."

Sounds familiar, thought Lena.

"And she came back?"

"She did. I really think it was love at first sight. For both of us. I wanted to see her again, but she wanted to see me, too. She was the one taking the risks—coming close to shore too many times, allowing a human to see her."

"Then what happened?"

"We started talking." He laughed. "Just your average boy-meets-mermaid story."

Lena looked at the mirror in front of her, which reflected back a face composed of features from her father, the human surfer, and her mother, the rebel mermaid.

"We used to meet at Shipwreck Rocks and just talk. Well, first she had to learn English, but she learned so quickly! It was more like she could read my mind than I taught her the language. We asked each other questions, and we laughed. It was so wonderful. Every time I saw her, I fell deeper in love. And it was the same for her. After a few weeks, though, we realized that we didn't want to spend the rest of our lives apart." Her dad's words poured out, a dam of memories finally released. "I asked Lucy to marry me." He looked at the wedding ring on his left hand, a different one than he had worn all those years ago. "And she said yes."

"So she came on land?"

"Not at first. I wanted to ask her father for her hand in marriage." He shrugged. "Old school, I know. But it seemed like the right thing to do. So she took me beneath the surface with her."

"How did she do *that?*"

"She sheltered me under her cloak."

Lena stared in confusion. "But . . . how did you breathe?"

Her dad gave her a wry smile. "Heck if I know. It was magic, Lena—I can't explain it. She put some kind of, I don't know, enchantment on the cloak."

"What was it like? How do they live?"

"I don't know. I never made it to the village. All I know about their world is what Lucy told me."

"But what happened? Did you get to ask her father for her hand?"

"No, I—" He shoved his hand through his hair. "I didn't get the chance."

Lena started to ask him another question, then saw the way his face had hardened. She waited.

After a moment, he began to talk. "That was the day I got a concussion. I always told people I got hit on my head by my board. But it was more complicated than that. It wasn't a surfing accident; it—" He scrubbed both hands through his hair, as if to scatter the memories. "I don't really want to talk about what happened. But I did end up unconscious, and when I came to, I was alone on the beach."

"Where was Lucy?"

"She . . . she wasn't there."

Lena made herself pause and take a breath. She could see that her dad was getting agitated, and even though dozens of questions jumbled around in her mind, fighting to be first out of her mouth, she forced herself to wait.

After a long moment, her dad seemed to compose himself, and Lena ventured, "So you were alone when you woke up. And you said you don't want to talk about that part. But eventually Lucy joined you, right? Otherwise I wouldn't be sitting here now." She smiled. "I guess you were irresistible."

To her relief, her dad smiled, too.

"So what happened?" said Lena.

"I went back to Magic's," he said. "As soon as I could. But I didn't see her for a long time. Well . . . it was really only about a week. It *seemed* like a long time to me. I started being afraid that I would never see her again." His gaze drifted away. After a moment, he said so quietly that Lena almost missed it, "That felt like dying." He closed his eyes, turning away from the memory. "She finally made it back, though."

"Thank goodness," breathed Lena.

He nodded. "Thank goodness. That was when she told me about the other uses of her sealskin cloak."

"Sealskin?" Lena was horrified. "They kill seals to make their cloaks?"

"No, no! Seals are their companions. Otters and dolphins, too. Mer-folk would never harm them. The pelts are collected after a seal dies."

"Oh."

"In order for them to come on land, mer-folk need to wear a sealskin cloak for protection." Her dad reached for a paper napkin and a pen. Lena knew he felt better when he could explain things by writing them down. "It has a kind of hood, which the mermaid—or merman—can pull over her head." He sketched a crude drawing of a cloak. "If a human sees them swimming, they think they're just seeing a seal." He added a seal's face under the hood of the cloak. "Once a mermaid comes ashore, she can take off her cloak, but she has to be very careful not to lose it, or she can't return to the sea." He drew waves, and a fairly good rendition of Shipwreck Rocks.

Lena stared down at his drawing. "You said she *found* the cloak. So . . . that means you must have hidden it from her."

Her dad nodded. "She wanted me to. She wanted to live on land, as a human. With me." He smiled, shrugging a little, as if to say, *Me . . . can you believe it?* "If I hid her cloak, she would have to stay, and the light of the full moon would split her tail into legs. She would still be able to go in the water, but she would have legs."

You must not have hidden it very well, thought Lena, but she managed to hold the words back. "What happened then?"

"Lucy told me to hide her cloak so that she could never find it. If she found it, we both knew that she would forget everything immediately, and return to the sea."

"Why didn't you just get rid of it?"

"We were afraid to. Sealskin cloaks are talismanic. They protect the wearer from harm when they travel between sea and land. What if your mother got sick living on land, among humans? What if she needed to return to the sea? We couldn't risk getting rid of the cloak."

Lena sighed. "And she found it."

"Yes."

"How?" Lena fought to keep her voice level.

"I'm not sure. I came home, and you were asleep in your bed, and she was gone. I looked for the cloak, and it wasn't there." Her dad stopped talking, and the silence that replaced his voice was terrible.

CHAPTER 29

Lena's dad seemed to shut down after that.

The shock of finding Lena with the mirror, the image of his lost wife floating up from its depths, the revelation of so many old secrets . . . all seemed to drain his spirit. Lena felt like she was looking at a hollowed-out version of her father.

"Please don't stop, Dad," she begged. "I need to know everything."

"I know you do, honey," he said. But he stayed quiet.

The longer he stayed quiet, the edgier Lena became. Finally she burst out, "How could you lie to me all these years?"

He put his hand over his eyes. "I never lied to you, Lena."

"What?!"

"I always told you we *lost* your mother. There's a difference." As Lena opened her mouth to protest, he looked up and said, "The moment she found her cloak, we lost her. Even if I'd been home, I don't know if I could have stopped her from leaving."

"Dad," said Lena. "I get it. She was under a spell. But you let me think she was dead all these years! There is *no excuse* for that."

After a long time, voice cracking, he said, "You're right. I'm sorry. I am *so sorry*. But you don't know . . . you don't know how hard it was. You were four years old, and your mother was gone. You were traumatized. You even stopped talking. For months!"

"I'm not four anymore," said Lena bitterly. "I haven't been four in a long time."

When her dad put his hand over his eyes again, Lena snapped, "Stop doing that!"

He dropped his hand, which trembled. "I'm—" He stood up and paced. "Cole will be home soon. We'll have to talk later." A troubled look came over his face. "Allie. She'll be home soon, too."

Lena suddenly remembered the photo of her father, her mother, and Allie, sitting together in a restaurant. Smiling. As if they were the best of friends. "Mom knows, doesn't she?"

"Yes, she does. She was closer to Lucy than any other human besides me. She's wanted me to tell you about her for a long time. And . . . Grandma Kath knows, too. She was present at your birth. We . . . we weren't sure what would happen when you were born."

Lena blinked. *Oh,* she thought. *They didn't know if I would have legs or a tail.* Then a surge of fury flooded her mind. *That's really great,* she thought. *Everyone knew about my mother but me.* "Fine," she said, standing up. "If you don't have time to talk, I guess I'll read my letter." She pulled the wrinkled envelope out of her back pocket, darkly pleased to see the expression of pain that crossed her dad's face.

But he didn't try to stop her.

Carrying the comb and mirror and letter, Lena went upstairs to her room. She set the comb down on her desk, then just stood for a long moment staring at the envelope with her name on it.

It was too much. First finding her mother's death certificate saying she'd killed herself . . . then finding out she wasn't dead, she was *inhuman* . . . it was too much. Lena's heart felt ragged and damaged. She set the letter down on her desk.

Picking up the mirror, she lay down on her bed, wrapping the sun-moon quilt around her. Stroking the satiny white moon, she gazed into the mirror again, hoping to see the mermaid. *Her mother.*

But it showed only her face . . . her father's blond hair and her mother's pointed chin and her own stormy eyes.

□   □   □

Time, faraway and formless, spun out while Lena lay wrapped in her quilt. The light in her room changed from the soft gray of a cloudy afternoon to the deepening shadows of evening.

I must be in shock, she thought, *because I can't move.*

She heard Allie come home, and pictured her dad breaking the news to her about Lena's discovery. The absence of normal Mom sounds from below—keys landing on the counter, closet door opening and closing, chatty conversation—told Lena the news was being absorbed in silence.

Then Cole came home, filling the house with his high-pitched voice and happy babble. The noise was a welcome relief to Lena.

But no one came to talk to her.

After a long time, Lena mustered the energy to roll over. She pulled the quilt tighter around her and closed her eyes. But the sound of Cole's Mindbender game kept her from escaping into sleep. The murmur of her parents' voices intruded on her thoughts, and finally she sat up. She pulled out the mirror from under her pillow, but there was no magic in its reflection. She slid it back under her pillow and got out of bed, padding to the top of the stairs.

Lena paused. Part of her wanted to go back to her room ... but the larger part of her was lonely. She wanted to see Allie, and Cole. And even her dad. He'd been such a wreck earlier, she was worried about him.

Lena went down the stairs. When she walked into the family room, Cole jumped up to greet her, as he did every time they were separated for more than a couple of hours.

"Hi!" he said, throwing his arms around her.

Lena bent over his white-blond head, planting a kiss there. "Hi, bud." She mussed his hair and released him.

"Want to play with me?"

"Sure." Lena settled down on the floor next to him and picked up a controller. She glanced at her parents. They were both watching her, as if expecting some dramatic scene.

For some reason this irritated her, and she turned her attention to creating a female warrior.

"Purple hair?" Cole laughed.

"Yes. My player has purple hair, and her superpower is—" Lena scrolled through the options and clicked one. "Swimming."

Allie approached and laid a hand on Lena's hair. "Are you okay?" she asked softly.

Lena fought back the urge to answer, *I've just discovered that my mother, whom I thought was dead, is alive, and a mermaid. Sure I'm okay.* But she saw the worry in Allie's face, and said simply, "Yeah."

For dinner, Lena's dad made pancakes and eggs. Cole was overjoyed.

"Breakfast for dinner!" he crowed. "Can I have hot chocolate?"

"Sure," said Allie. Her fingers strayed to her earring, twisting it as she gazed into space.

Lena knew that Allie really must not be herself, after giving in to such a request without a second thought.

They ate their breakfast for dinner, and Cole regaled them with tales of past battles on his game. After dinner, Allie and Cole went upstairs, leaving Lena and her father alone in the kitchen. Lena began to load dishes into the dishwasher.

"Leen?"

She looked over at him.

"I'm ready to talk now."

Lena kept loading the dishwasher. *What if I don't feel like talking now?* she thought. *What if I want to pretend none of this is happening . . . just for a little while? What if I just want to chat with my friends or watch TV or something?*

But that life was over.

She still had friends and school and movies and chat, but she could not pretend she was a normal teen. A strange grief filled her over the loss of her old life.

"Okay," she said.

"Did you read the letter?" asked her dad.

She shook her head.

He studied her for a moment, then said, "I think it's time."

Lena didn't answer at first, then she said, "Can I . . . read it in front of you?" She found that she didn't want to be alone with her mother's words.

"Of course. I'll wait here."

Lena retrieved the letter from her room and came back downstairs. She and her dad sat down at the kitchen table again, and Lena opened the envelope.

CHAPTER 30

My darling Selena,

You are four weeks old today, and already I cannot imagine life without you.

I thought I knew what love meant before you came . . . now I know that mother-love is more powerful than any other kind. The idea of being separated from you is un-thinkable.

But I take up this pen today, knowing that if you are reading this, it means that we have been parted. The unthinkable has happened.

The only force that could take me away from you is as ancient as mother-love: magic. On this day in the future when you read these words, know that I would never leave you. I may have been taken from you by magic . . . but please know, my precious maid, I would never go willingly.

Your loving mother

"Would never *leave* me? She's swimming around in the ocean and I'm sitting here in the house with you and Allie and Cole. She left me." Lena was surprised to feel a lump in her throat again.

"No," insisted her dad. "I *told* you . . . the moment that cloak was on her body, she had no choice." He raised his voice, old loyalty flaring to life. "In fact, Lena, I'd bet my life that your mother made sure you were safe first, then walked down the street with a broken heart, not even knowing why she was crying. So let's show her some mercy, all right?"

Lena swallowed. "Okay. I'm sorry." She hesitated, then asked, "Dad? Where was the cloak?"

He stood up. Lena thought he was going to refuse to answer, but instead he headed for the sliding-glass door. "Come with me," he said, taking a flashlight from the desk drawer.

She followed him outside to the garden. It was dark. As in a fairy tale, the moon swelled above them, full and faintly yellow. Lena thought of her mother, hiding in secrecy, waiting for the full moon to transform her beautiful tail into legs.

They could hear the sound of the surf in the distance. Lena's dad turned on the flashlight, and they picked their way carefully through the obstacle course of Cole's toys in the backyard. He stopped and shone the light along the length of the fence. It was adorned with stone garden sculptures: a long-bearded god of wind, his cheeks puffed out, a smiling sun, a sleeping moon, a spouting whale, a dolphin, and a mermaid.

"Don't tell me you buried it under the sculpture of the mermaid!" exclaimed Lena.

He grinned. "No. I may not be a smart man, but even *I* am not that obvious."

She watched as he lifted the dolphin off the fence and turned it over. On the back of the dolphin sculpture, there was a hollowed-out space. It was empty.

"This is where I kept the key," he said. "I don't know how she found it." He shook his head, as if he still had trouble believing it. "I never saw her act like she was searching for the cloak, but I don't know. Maybe mermaids can't help searching for their cloaks, whether they want to or not."

Lena's knees felt weak, and she sat down on Cole's plastic picnic table. It seemed almost inevitable that events would lead her mother back to the sea. "Where was it?"

"The cloak was in the chest. I kept it hidden in the crawl space above the garage."

"What crawl space?"

He gave a half-smile. "See? No one even knows it's there. The chest was in a box that was taped shut, surrounded by other boxes, and covered with clothes. It just looked like a big pile of junk. I don't know how she found it."

Lena pictured her mother searching for the cloak—maybe not even *aware* she was doing it—then she thought of her own search to find the lock for the key. One quest had torn her mother from Lena, the other had given her back.

"Now it's my turn to ask some questions," said her dad. "You said Lucy gave you the key." He swallowed. "So you've seen her. You were . . . *with* her? At Magic's?"

"I was at Magic's," said Lena carefully. She didn't want to tell her dad she'd been close to drowning. "But I wasn't *with* her. I didn't know she was there at first. I was in the water, and she, um, put the key into my hand."

Her dad stared.

"I didn't know she was my mother. But I saw her once before. It was on my birthday!" she said. "And I kept looking for her after that."

"Lena," said her dad. "You *surfed* at Magic's?"

"I thought she might be there. And I was right."

Her dad shook his head, muttering, "I knew it." He pinned his gaze on her. "Now do you understand? Now do you see why I didn't want you to surf? Once you learned, how could I keep you from Magic's?"

"You couldn't," said Lena.

They sat silently for a moment.

Finally her dad said with a sigh, "I've been such an idiot. Trying to keep a half-mermaid from surfing!" Then he smiled wistfully. "How do you like it?"

Lena's face glowed. "Oh, Dad, I love it so much. When I'm out there, it's like I'm—" She sighed. "I don't think I can even describe it. I feel like I'm in church . . . like I'm close to God, or something. Like the earth is so huge, but while I'm in the ocean, it feels like I'm in all the oceans on the planet, or something. How can you stand not to surf?"

He looked away, turning his eyes to the moon. "I can stand it."

"Dad," Lena said, struck by a new question. "You met at Magic's. Wouldn't she have come back to Magic's eventually? Did you look for her?" *I would have haunted Magic's every day for the rest of my life until I found her,* she thought.

Her father was silent.

"Dad," she persisted.

He made an impatient gesture with his hands. "Lena, stop."

"No," she said, raising her voice. "This is *my* story. If you won't tell me, who will?" An idea struck her. "Except Mom. She knows everything, doesn't she? I can ask her."

Her dad rounded on her. "Leave Allie alone. This is hard enough on her."

"She's my mother!" shouted Lena, and for a second, she wasn't sure which mother she meant. They were both, truly, her mothers. One gave her life, the other gave her everything else.

Her dad paced back and forth. "Please, Lena. Please trust me."

"Trust you?" She made a sound of disbelief. "Are you kidding?" She moved toward the door. "Fine. Mom will tell me."

Her dad grabbed her arm, then let go. "Wait." He stared inside the house, as if looking for answers. After a moment, without turning his gaze to Lena, he said quietly, "I was safe in the water as long as I was with her."

"What?"

"I was safe . . . in the water . . ." He faced Lena. ". . . as long as I was with Lucy."

Lena looked at him in confusion.

"Your mother's parents—your *grandparents*—had found out about her plan to live on land, and they were . . . not happy. That day we were headed to Lucy's village, before we ever got there, a group of mer-folk accosted us." He paused, remembering. "It was chaos. All of these voices in my head . . . yelling . . . threatening . . ."

"In your head?"

"That's how they communicate. In thoughts."

"Oh." Lena almost asked, *In English?* But she didn't want to interrupt again.

"Someone grabbed me and started to drag me away. Someone else—I think it was her mother—ordered Lucy to be restrained."

Lena swallowed. *Her own mother?*

"She pleaded to go with me, but they wouldn't let her. The only reason I'm alive today is that Lucy's brother—your uncle—followed the mermen who took me away. When they stripped the cloak off me and left me half-conscious in the water, he carried me to shore. He risked his own life to save mine."

"But—" said Lena. "Lucy got away later. How?"

"They tried to feed her lotus blossoms, to take away her memory, but she wouldn't eat them. She stopped eating entirely. Rather than watch her die, her parents allowed her to leave, finally."

Lena sat still and silent, trying to absorb this tale of love so tragic, it rivaled anything by Shakespeare. After a time, she said, "I still don't understand why you didn't go back to Magic's after she left us. I know the surf is rough, but you were a great surfer, right? Once she saw you again, she would've remembered."

He massaged his head, as if that old injury had flared to life. "That day . . . that day under the water . . . there were so many voices. But someone . . . someone with power—I could feel the words in my head like thunder—someone swore that if I ever set foot in the sea again, they would destroy me."

"Who was it?"

He sighed. "I think . . . it was your grandmother."

Lena shivered. "But how could she do that?"

"I don't know. I just know Lucy told me I was safe in the water as long as I was with her." Her dad stared sightlessly toward the sea, remembering. "Once I lost her, I was willing to risk my life to find her. But I couldn't."

He opened the sliding-glass door and paused, turning back to say, "I've never forgotten those words." He closed his eyes, chanting:

"Man, beware: I banish you from the sea.
The cold salt clasp is forbidden to you.
Death will be quick should you fail to heed me,
And those you love will die gasping in blue."

With a bitter sound, he added, "Their version of 'sleep with the fishes,' I guess." He stepped inside the house. "Do you understand now? You, and everyone else I love, are safe in the water . . . as long as I stay out of it."

Lena watched him close the sliding-glass door and walk away, but she stood alone in the garden for a long time, unable to make her trembling legs work.

CHAPTER 31

Cole asked Lena to sing to him that night at bedtime.

"Uh—" said Lena. She felt as empty as an abandoned shell; she didn't have the energy for singing. But Cole was the only person in the house she could bear to be around right now. "Sure." She snuggled up next to him on his bed. *I can see clearly now the rain is gone,* she sang softly.

Cole sighed and closed his eyes. When the song was over, he murmured sleepily, "Sing the blueberry one."

Smiling, Lena complied. When she had finished, Cole didn't move. She kissed his hair and whispered, "Sweet dreams, Cole Dog."

"I'm not a dog," he mumbled.

Lena's parents were hovering outside the bedroom when she emerged.

"Thanks, honey," said her mom.

"For what?"

"For singing to Cole."

"I don't do it to please you," snapped Lena. "I do it because I love him." She headed for her room, ignoring the shocked look on Allie's face.

"Lena," said her father.

"What," muttered Lena. She knew why she was angry with her dad—he had lied to her all her life. She wasn't sure why her anger was spilling over onto Allie. Maybe because Allie had known the truth all along, too. Anyway, she was sick of her parents right now. All she wanted to do was go back to her room and see if her mother was visible in the mirror.

"Where are you going?"

"My room. Where do you think? God! Just leave me alone!"

"Lena," he said again. "It will break your heart to keep looking into that mirror." He paused, trying to master the anguish that came into his face. "Believe me."

She went into her room and closed the door gently. Then she slid down the door and sank onto the carpet, weeping.

After a while, she made her way to her bedside table and grabbed some tissues, wiping her eyes and blowing her nose. Enough crying. Her mother was alive. Mermaid or not, she was *alive,* and Lena could see her.

She reached under her pillow for the mirror. She held it up and looked at her reflection for a long moment. As before, the image began to shimmer and dissolve. She waited impatiently to see her mother's face. First the scene was murky and dark, full of flitting shapes, then it lightened.

Lena studied the glass hungrily. She did not see her mother. The "memory circle," as her father had called it, had disbanded, although she thought she recognized some of the same mermaids and mermen from the circle, drifting in the currents. What was a memory circle? There were still so many questions!

Lena turned the mirror this way and that, eager to see her mother.

She watched the distant, blurry shapes of the mer-folk as they went about their activities. Some of them were playing what looked like musical instruments: carved ivory flutes and some kind of small harp, which Lena thought were called lyres. The base of the lyre was a large shallow shell, with fibrous strings stretched across it. Other mer-folk were gathered around a huge stone table. They seemed to be eating. Mer-folk children flitted here and there, some laughing and playing, others sitting with their heads together, as if telling stories. The tails of the mer-folk shimmered blue, green, gold, and silver. Their hair was every imaginable color, and their skin tone ranged from translucent parchment to polished ebony. They were arrayed in strands of pearls and shells and jewels. Lena felt as though she could gaze at them for hours.

But where was her mother?

She turned the mirror in her hands again. Was that her, drifting away from the group? Lena looked harder, and as before, the perspective of the mirror began to zoom in on the figure she watched. It *was* her mother.

Melusina swam into an underwater cave and lay on a bed of seaweed, uncoiling her tail to its full length. At first she lay silent, then Lena heard a low, sad song drifting out of the depths of the sea to the magic mirror, filling her ears again with that language she did not speak, yet could understand. Again, she heard words like "daughter," "heart," and "sleep."

As the scene in the mirror began to fade, Lena lay down with the mirror in her hands, and her mother's song lulled her to sleep.

□   □   □

Lena awoke in the middle of the night, the memory of her mother's song fading from her dreams.

Someone had come in to turn out her light and cover her with the sun-moon quilt. She sat up, looking for the mirror.

It wasn't on the bed.

Fear flooded Lena's senses. What if her dad had taken it away? What if he wouldn't give it back? Even though she didn't remember putting the mirror under her pillow before she fell asleep, she checked to make sure. Her fingers touched the coral comb, but no mirror.

She fumbled for the light on her bedside table, trying to calm down. *Maybe it just fell on the floor,* she thought.

The harsh glare lit up her room, and after her eyes adjusted, she saw the mirror on her desk. With a rush of relief so strong it made her dizzy, Lena hurried to pick it up. A note in her father's handwriting lay on her desk next to the mirror.

My sweet girl,

it read.

This is your family, here in this house, and we love you. But I know you must want very much to see your mother. If you will be patient, and trust me, I will help you. This mirror is not the answer. Love, Dad

Lena balled up the note. *Sure you'll help me,* she thought. *Sure I trust you.*

She lifted the mirror to her face and waited impatiently for her reflection to dissolve. After a moment, darkness filled the mirror. Lena squinted; in it she saw not the fluidly drifting images of the undersea world but more of a deep gray mist. This was not the mermaid's home. The scene in the mirror was air, not liquid.

Lena listened intently, trying to figure out what she was seeing. Gradually, she heard the crash of waves on rocks and the muted sound of the foghorn. With a gasp, she realized that the sound of the foghorn coming from the mirror was echoing the call of the foghorn outside her window.

The gray mist lifted, and Lena could see a darkened figure on Shipwreck Rocks. It was Melusina, her face like a flash of moonlight in the blackness, her long hair dripping over her shoulders, her elegant tail curved around the rock upon which she sat . . . the perfect embodiment of the mythical mermaid.

"Mama," whispered Lena.

Melusina sat very still, as if waiting. The cold did not seem to touch her.

As Lena watched, she saw Melusina open her lips and lift her head. Then Lena heard, within the mirror and within her own mind, the sound of singing. It was clear and sweet. First there were no words . . . just the sound of a pure, inhuman voice full of longing and love. Then Lena heard that same strange language in her mind:

"Come to me, child of land,
To the water and the sand;

Come away from wall and door
To the rocks upon the shore."

Lena's breath caught in her throat. *She's calling me.*

For a single, swooning moment, Lena felt the summons of a mermaid. There could be no refusal, no denial.

Then it was her mother again, calling for her child.

Lena stared into the mirror, transfixed. When her song was finished, Melusina tilted her head, as if trying to recall something. Then she sang,

"By the light
of the blueberry moon
we sang this song
in Lena's room . . ."

Lena didn't know there were tears sliding down her cheeks until the scene in the mirror whirled away, leaving only her own face, wet and white. She grabbed her clothes and pulled them on. Then she put on her hoodie and zipped it up.

But the comb and the mirror wouldn't fit in her pockets. She tore off the hoodie and grabbed her jacket, sliding the comb and mirror into the deep pockets.

She opened her bedroom door.

The house was silent. She hurried downstairs, trying to be quiet, but adrenaline made her careless of the squeaks and creaks.

In the kitchen, she hesitated, wondering if she should leave a note on the message board.

No, she would be back before anyone woke up. Besides, what would she say?

Lena moved toward the sliding-glass door.

"Where are you going?" Allie's voice came from the corner.

Lena jumped and put her hand to her chest. "Oh, my God! You scared me to death!"

Allie didn't answer. There was a rustle from the shadows, and she stood up, holding a blanket around her. "What are you doing, Lena?"

"Taking a walk."

"No, you're not. You are not taking a walk at two in the morning."

"Yes, I am."

"Lena, I am very well aware that you have suffered a huge shock, and that your life is not the same as it was this morning. But whatever you may think you're doing, you are not leaving this house in the middle of the night. You're still my daughter."

"*Your* daughter?" Lena could not keep her voice down. "You lied to me, too! My mother is *not* dead—she's alive! She's waiting for me at Shipwreck Rocks right now."

Allie stared at her. "Waiting for you?"

"Yes. I saw her in the mirror. I'm going to her, and you can't stop me!"

"Sweetie, wait. Don't . . . it's not safe!"

"Leave me alone!" Lena wrenched open the sliding door and dashed out.

"Lena! At least wait for your father!"

Lena didn't answer, just rushed through the garden and out to the sidewalk. She could hear Allie screaming her dad's name. Lena broke into a run.

She flew down the street, past darkened homes, their occupants tucked up warmly in their beds. Tomorrow they would wake up, eat breakfast, do the dishes, watch TV . . . go on with their cozy, normal lives. Lena felt a fleeting moment of hot jealousy—her life would never be normal again—then she was racing across the gravel parking lot and down the path through the long grasses.

When she reached the sand, she felt a surge of relief. This was her beach. She knew its landscape even with her eyes closed. Her father might chase her all the way to Magic's, but he was slower than she was.

Without stopping to take off her shoes, Lena ran to the edge of the ocean, where it would be easier to run on the packed sand.

But the tide was coming in, and the sand was wet and springy. It sucked at her shoes, slowing her down. She glanced back once but didn't see her father.

She kept running, and before long, Shipwreck Rocks loomed in the distance.

There was no one there.

CHAPTER 32

A small sob came from Lena's throat. *She's there,* answered her mind calmly. *She's on the other side of the rocks, on the Magic side.*

Lena stopped to catch her breath, bending over to put her hands on her knees. When she had rested for a minute, she turned to look back down the beach. Far behind her, running across the packed sand, was a figure that could only be her father.

Too slow, she thought in triumph.

She straightened up and raced toward the rocks, where she knew her mother was waiting.

The moonlight lay on the water like a shining path to the edge of the world.

My mother's family is down there, thought Lena. *Maybe they're down there right now, looking up at the moonlight on the water, just like I am. Am I sleepwalking? I must be awake . . . I feel wind on my face and I hear waves crashing and I taste the salt spray.*

She was closer to the rocks now, and she began to sob. Unable to wait any longer, she screamed, "Melusina! Melusina! Mama!"

A voice carried across the sound of the waves. "Selena . . . my Selena . . ."

Heart racing, Lena screamed, "Where are you?"

"I am here. You must come to me."

Panting and weeping, Lena reached the rocks and began to climb. "Mama."

"Dearest maiden," called her mother's voice.

Exhausted now, Lena climbed over the highest rock and looked below.

Melusina waited, slim white arms outstretched, face up-turned, tears shining in her green eyes. "My daughter," cried the mermaid.

Lena stumbled down the rocks, scratching her hands and twisting her ankles, but feeling no physical pain. "It's you," she wept. She fell to her knees by her mother's side, where Melusina enfolded her in an embrace.

The mermaid's strong tail clung to the rock beneath her, keeping her balanced as she held her daughter.

Lena felt the cool smoothness of her mother's skin and the wet strands of her long hair. She hadn't remembered how small her mother was; the last time Lena had been wrapped in her arms, she was only four, and her mother had seemed as big as any other adult. But now, hugging the mermaid, Lena felt how little she was.

Lena drew back slightly, filling her gaze with her mother.

The lovely face was exactly as she remembered—her mother appeared not to have aged at all. Her eyes glowed with excitement, and her lips were curved in a tremulous smile. Her upper body was bare, except for long necklaces of white and black pearls trailing nearly to her bellybutton. Lena looked in awe at the lower half of her mother's body, which turned to brilliant silver scales below her belly and curved down the length of her lower half, ending in a long divided fin. At the base of her tail was the faint outline of a dolphin tattoo.

"Are you much frightened, my child?" asked Melusina, her brilliant eyes searching Lena's face.

"No." But Lena shivered as reality set in. She was sitting on a rock in the middle of the night with a creature who was not human. What if this creature didn't have, well, human-mother feelings? What if she wanted to drag Lena beneath the waves and drown her? What if all her dad's attempts to protect her had been for good reason?

The mermaid reached out and cupped Lena's face with her cool-warm hand, stroking the skin from Lena's cheek to her chin, a touch so light it was almost like a dream. A child-hood memory of her mother gently stroking her face, just like this, swept over Lena. She closed her eyes as time slipped back and forth.

"You had sweetly plump cheeks as a small maid," said Melusina. "Now your face is slender and fair. What lovely gold tresses you have, as well."

"Like Dad's," said Lena.

Melusina tilted her head, a mildly puzzled look on her face. She took Lena's hands in her own, then held them up to look at them. "Ah!" she said in delight. "The tips of your fingers are like pearls!"

"Oh . . . it's nail polish," said Lena.

"Polish?"

"Yes. I used white nail polish on my fingernails."

"Ah, yes, I remember now. A kind of paint." She continued to hold Lena's hands as she raised her eyes to inspect every inch of her daughter's face. "Your eyes have many depths in them," she said. "The color of a stormy sea. I remember now. Indeed, I am fair amazed that I should ever have forgotten these eyes. I used to dream of you . . . and always I would wake with grief fresh upon my face." Her lips quivered. "Yet again I would forget." She brushed Lena's hair back and caught sight of the pearl earrings. "You wear the pearls of our ancestors?"

"Um," said Lena. "Well, these were a gift. From my boyfriend."

The mermaid smiled. "Well chosen. Our people have worn the sea's gifts since time began."

"You have an accent," said Lena. "I didn't remember that."

"Ah, forgive my stilted tongue. The language returns to me a bit more each day." The mermaid slid her hands up to Lena's shoulders, as if she could not stop touching her, making sure she was real. "I wish I could have come to you, once I had my memories back. But as you can see . . ." She gestured at her tail. "I could not. I had to wait for you to come to me." A smile of unearthly beauty lit up her face. "And you heard my soul's call. You have come."

There was a silence between them, shy and expectant.

"Will you bide with me awhile, that we may remember together, dear Selena?" asked Melusina.

Lena nodded, then thought of her father running through the dark to find her.

"I want to," she answered. "But Dad's coming."

Melusina looked at her. "This 'Dad.' He seeks you even now?"

Lena stared at her mother. "Don't you know who I'm talking about?"

"I fear not. But I must not be seen by a human. I must take my leave of you, with the greatest sorrow." Melusina looked anxiously back at the sea.

"Wait! You don't remember my dad?"

"Alas, no."

"He was your husband! You don't remember him?"

Melusina shook her head slowly. "I know . . . I must have known a man on land. Else how would I have you, my daughter? Yet the memory escapes me until I see his face."

Just then they heard a shout in the distance. "Lena!"

Because they were on the far side of the rocks, Lena and the mermaid could not see Lena's father, nor could he see them. *What should I do?* thought Lena. *If we stay here, he'll find us. I just got my mother back . . . I don't want to leave her!*

"Lena!"

"He draws closer," said Melusina, beginning to move to the edge of her rock. "What will you do, my own heart?"

"I don't know!" cried Lena, her voice rising to panic. "Don't leave me!"

"Come with me," said the mermaid. "I have brought my cloak this night. I dared to hope you might return with me to the world beneath the waves. This cloak will shelter and protect you."

Torn, Lena looked back at the dark beach behind her, then out at the shining sea.

"Lena!" shouted her father. "Answer me! Please!"

She held out her hand to her mother. "Take me with you."

Relief bloomed on the mermaid's face. She grabbed Lena's hand. "Come with me to the edge of the rock."

Lena obeyed. "What about my clothes and shoes? Won't they be too heavy? They'll drag me down."

With a slight smile, Melusina said, "We are diving deep. Your clothes will not matter in our journey. But you may leave your shoes. Now come as close as you are able, and put your arms around my waist."

"Lena!" came a distant shout. "Baby, where are you?" Her father's voice cracked with anguish.

Lena fought her urge to answer him, glancing back in the direction of his voice. She slipped off her shoes. Then she moved close to her mother and put her arms around her.

Melusina picked up the sealskin pelt and wrapped it around Lena's shoulders. "Are you ready, tender maiden?"

Lena nodded, unable to answer. The cloak felt warm and velvety around her shoulders.

"Hold tight to me. You will be safe. The difficult part for you will be jumping into the cold water. As soon as I pull the cloak over your head, you are protected. Now we depart the land." Melusina slid off the rock, and Lena held tightly, feeling the scrape of the rock's surface through her clothes.

They slid into the water more gracefully than Lena would have thought, but it was true: the shock of the night-cold water made her gasp.

Melusina held her in an iron grip, keeping her head above water. She pulled the hood of the cloak over Lena's head, and whispered in her daughter's ear, "Now we begin our journey."

Squeezing her eyes shut, Lena gripped her mother even tighter, and felt the muscles in the mermaid's tail move strongly.

They plunged below the surface. As they dove with startling speed, Lena held her breath as long as she was able. Then she opened her mouth in a reflexive desire to breathe, and felt salt water pour into her mouth. Panic-stricken, she loosened her grip on her mother's waist.

Melusina's voice came into her mind now, instead of her ear. "You are safe, my child. You will breathe the ocean now. This cloak protects you."

Lena shook her head frantically and felt Melusina tighten her hold.

What have I done? thought Lena. *She really is going to drown me! Daddy . . . I'm sorry . . .*

◻ ◻ ◻

Brian was in time to see his first love plunge off the side of the rock, arms tight around their child, and his heart fell into the water with them.

CHAPTER 33

Even though she knew there was no air for her here, Lena instinctively took a terrified breath, and felt the salt water enter her throat.

Incredibly, the water moved in and out of her gasping lungs. She did not begin to drown. She began to breathe the ocean, as her mother had said. She could not speak, but amazement filled her mind, causing Melusina to smile and send a thought to her: "No, you are not drowning. You are diving."

Lena felt a half-frightened laugh bubble out of her mouth.

"How can I breathe under water?" she asked, using thoughts instead of words.

"I cannot explain this enchantment to you. It is because of the cloak, and because of my desire. When *your* desire is powerful enough, you will be able to breathe under water without the cloak."

"No way!" said Lena. "You're kidding, right?"

Melusina's response was bewildered. "I am not in jest, dear one. The way is true."

Lena smiled at her mother's sincerity. "I believe you," she said. "It just seems impossible."

"It is impossible for humans," said Melusina. "But you are not human."

Lena's heart faltered. *Not human.*

"Or rather," continued Melusina placidly, "not wholly human. The blood and magic of my people runs through your veins. See? Already it is proved."

"What do you mean?"

"We dive ever deeper. But your body ails not. Your heart, your lungs, your every cell, do not collapse from pressure. You are my daughter." A flash of pride lit up her mother's features.

"Amazing," whispered Lena. She became aware that her legs were kicking in time with the movements of her mother's tail. But she was not swimming the way Allie had taught her to swim; she was kicking with her legs together, as if she were a mermaid, too. *I am,* she reminded herself. *I am half-mermaid.*

On land, that idea would have felt preposterous. Deep beneath the surface, with her body behaving in a most fishlike manner, it seemed natural.

"Where are we going?" she asked after a few minutes.

"My village. My home. It is still farther."

"What will happen when we get there?"

"You will be welcomed. My people know I have the memories back. As soon as I saw you—my beloved child—the Recollection struck. I—" She faltered. "I was wounded by the memories as they returned. But my people saved me as I foundered. They are a great solace, always." She added with a smile, "They know about you now, daughter."

"But what about . . . ?"

Melusina waited for her to finish the thought.

". . . your parents."

"Ah," said Melusina. "They are not merely my parents, they are your grandparents! They will welcome you with joy.

My people have held many memory circles to help in the healing of my sore heart. Amphitrite and Merrow deplore my pain."

"Amphi—?"

"Your grandmother and grandfather."

"But . . ." Lena could not help pursuing the thought.

"Yes?"

"Dad said your parents didn't want you to marry him. They had him dragged away."

Melusina's strong swimming slackened for a moment. "Ah. I regret that the memory eludes me. I recall the feeling of betrayal. But that was long ago, and I have learned to forgive."

"But your mother said she would destroy him if he ever set foot in the ocean again!"

"What? No, my darling, never believe this! My mother would not command such violence. Her role is to protect our village, not mete out punishment."

Lena thought that Melusina might be too trusting of her mother, but she didn't say that. After a moment, she asked, "Is she the queen or something?"

Melusina chuckled. "That is a word she would love to own, but no, we do not use human titles that rank one above the many. Amphitrite is—" The mermaid used a word in her language, and Lena understood it to mean something like *guardian*.

They swam on. As their distance from the shore grew greater, Lena thought less about her father. At first her heart literally ached, knowing how scared he would be when he found her shoes abandoned on the rocks. But as she and the mermaid dove deeper into the sea, her worry seemed to diminish, as if it were attached to the land, and she was moving too far away to feel it.

"How much farther?" she asked.

Melusina laughed. "You are still an impatient child, I see. Soon the village will be within view."

Lena's clothes felt heavy. Obviously, she couldn't remove the cloak, but . . . "Can I take off my jeans?" she asked.

"Jeans? Oh, yes, the fabric that covers your legs? Certainly."

Lena unbuttoned her jeans, desperate to free her legs from the water-logged denim. "People will stare, won't they?"

Her mother squeezed her hand. "Yes, dearest. But they will stare whether your lovely legs are clothed or bare."

Lena kicked off her jeans, breathing a watery sigh of relief. Now she could swim more easily. And her jacket was long enough that it reached to her thighs, so she didn't have to feel totally undressed. She let go of her jeans, watching them sink out of sight.

Deeper and deeper they swam. Lena had not expected to be able to see much under water, but the deeper they descended, the clearer she saw. *It must be my eyes,* she thought. *There must be something about my eyes that is not human, too.*

There was a deep blue, almost purple quality to the water, and the temperature did not feel as cold as it had before.

At last, Melusina began to slow her swimming. "The village is quiet," she said. "Some of the mer-folk are still asleep."

"You sleep?"

"Yes, but not in the same way that humans sleep. When humans sleep, they are still and dreaming for many hours. We

must rise to the surface regularly for air. Our friends, the dolphins, need air even more frequently than we do. Half of their
brains are always awake, to remind them to rise. We share that
trait, to a lesser degree. Mer-folk may sleep for two or three
hours before needing air, then we must rise."

I'm in between, thought Lena. *Maybe that's why I keep waking
up lately. My body thinks it needs to surface.* "Seems like with all
that going to the surface, people would see you more often."

"No, we rise to the surface far from shore. We are able to
feel the presence of sailing vessels, and thus avoid them. And
when we wear our cloaks, humans mistake us for seals. If we
choose to approach the shore, it is for the love of being upon
the land, even if it is but a short while. It is a great pleasure to
sit on land, feeling the sun on our shoulders and the air in our
lungs, combing our hair and singing. It is so much more sat-
isfying to sing out loud. We all have our favorite places to visit
on the shore."

"You always go to Magic's?"

"Magic's?"

"The place where you met my father. The place where I
found you."

"Ah. Yes, I love that cove. I call it the Place of Beautiful
Danger. I have spent the time since I left the land in warmer
seas. But something kept drawing me back to my Place of
Beautiful Danger. And now I know that it was you."

"Were you away a long time?"

"Yes. A great many full moons. Oh! The word comes back
to me. Months, yes? I believe that it was more than one hundred months." She considered. "Closer to one hundred fifty
months."

Lena counted in her head. Her mother must have spent most of the past twelve years far away from Magic's. That was why Lena had never seen her before. That must be why Lena had begun to feel more powerfully drawn to the ocean. Once Melusina returned to Magic's, they were both looking for each other, without even knowing it.

"Why did you go so far away?"

"Upon my return to the village, after living on land, I grieved deeply, although I could not say why. Though the villagers performed the reunion ritual several times, I failed to thrive. The—" Melusina used another word in her language, which Lena understood to mean *healer*. "The healer fed me Loss Potion many times, without success. At last, my parents felt it would be wise to take me away from the scene of my sadness, until my heart was regained."

Lena thought of her mother, all those years ago, separated from her beloved husband and child . . . her heart broken, but unable to remember why.

"We travel often," continued Melusina. "Sometimes to the warm waters . . . sometimes to the iciest seas. Would you like to travel to the tropical waters with me?" Her face lit up with excitement. "We could swim with the manta rays and the giant turtles. Oh, but the white whales of the cold northern waters are wonderful, too, with their funny smiles! There is so much to share with you, dear one."

"White whales? I've never even seen a picture of a white whale."

"There is much to see. You will love this world, Selena. We will eat and drink and rest, then we shall explore this world together."

"What do you eat down here?"

"Oh, all manner of things! The sea is bountiful."

"Do you have caviar? Dad buys it for me sometimes. It's really expensive."

"You shall feast on the eggs of the salmon every day if you like, dear."

"Really?"

"Certainly. It will be my great pleasure to share food with you. It is a mother's joy to feed her child."

"And then we can explore?"

"Ah, my dear, first you must rest. We will have plenty of time for exploring. You shall stay as long as you like."

"But what about—?" Lena stopped. What about . . . *what?* Her loved ones on land? Yes, she supposed they would be anxious. But their faces were already growing fainter in her mind.

CHAPTER 34

In the distance, a giant kelp forest swayed, the ever-shifting currents of the sea rocking it hypnotically.

"It's so beautiful," said Lena.

"It is the verge of our village," answered Melusina.

"You live in the *kelp?*"

"No, dearest. But the kelp provides a shield. Our lookouts patrol this area—if danger approaches, they can disappear into the forest before they are seen, and alert the village."

"I don't see them."

"No," said Melusina. "But they see you."

Nervousness seeped into Lena's thoughts. *What if they won't let me in?*

Melusina squeezed her daughter's arm. "My people will welcome you, Selena. There is no need for fear."

As they neared the forest, Lena's mind filled with a sound that was a combination of calling and singing, loud and melodious.

"Melusina draws near," called a merman. "Near."

"She brings her child of sea and land," sang a mermaid. "Sea and land."

"Melusina draws near . . . gather here. Here."

"The child of Melusina is unarmed . . . you will be not harmed. Not harmed."

"What are they doing?" asked Lena.

"They are calling out to the rest of the village to announce our arrival." Her mother's voice in her mind sounded amused as she added, "Visitors are rare."

"But how can I understand them?!"

"Ahh, my child! It is the charm upon the cloak. Brilliant, yes?"

Even as her mother spoke, Lena became aware of many voices beginning to fill her mind. They were growing louder and more excited. Billowing out of the forest, a crowd of mer-folk swam in her direction. She gasped. There must be forty or fifty! It had been a shock to see *one* mermaid the day she first saw Melusina . . . the sight of throngs of mer-folk was almost overwhelming.

Lena shrank back.

"They wish to welcome you," said her mother. "They are your people, too, daughter."

They were all ages and sizes, tiny and plump to long and lean. Strong, young mermen and elderly, gracious mermaids. Some with long, streaming hair, others with cropped curls. The color of their skin ranged from unearthly pale to rich brown. Lena could see one very old mermaid whose skin looked almost blue.

"Auntie Lu," called a voice.

A young mermaid with flowing dark hair and dusky skin rushed toward them, ahead of the others.

She looks a little like Pem, thought Lena. A small frown came over her face. At the moment, she couldn't remember Pem's face. An image of a pink braid drifted through her mind. Lena looked down at her foot and was reassured by the sight of the yarn encircling her ankle.

"So this is your land child?" asked the mermaid. Her lustrous black hair looked like floating strands of silk. "She looks to be my age! Will you not introduce us?"

"Yes, of course, dear Lorelei. You have in common with your cousin the trait of impatience." She squeezed Lena's shoulders.

My cousin! thought Lena. Her heart beat faster. She felt almost dizzy. It was all so unbelievable. Was she really floating in the bright blue and purple depths of the sea, breathing liquid instead of air? Was she meeting a *mermaid* cousin?

"Lorelei, please meet my darling Selena," said Lena's mother.

Lorelei wriggled with barely repressed excitement. "Hello! I am Lorelei! You are welcome!" Then her brow furrowed and her voice grew louder in Lena's mind. "Can you understand me?"

Lena smiled and nodded, unsure how to answer. If she thought in English, would her cousin understand?

Melusina sensed her hesitation. "There is no barrier to your language here. As the cloak gives you comprehension, it does the same for your listeners."

"I am pleased to meet you," said Lena haltingly.

Lorelei beamed. "I heard your words! But will you also teach me that land-language?"

Before Lena could answer, two mer-folk who seemed to be Lorelei's parents approached.

"This is my brother, Nereus, father of the impatient Lorelei," said Melusina, indicating a merman with long reddish-gold curls. He smiled and kissed Lena's hand.

"Nereus?" said Lena, trying to pronounce the name correctly.

"Yes. All of our names have been handed down from generation to generation, some of them from ancient times. They are names from all the waters of the world."

Lena had an urge to thank him . . . but she could not remember why. He had done her father a kindness, she thought. Before she could speak, Lorelei darted forward. "Oh, look at the brightness of her fingertips! How they shine! Like abalone shell. May I touch your legs?"

"Lorelei!" scolded the mermaid next to Nereus.

"That is Iona, Lorelei's mother," said Melusina. "She comes from the warm waters. I journeyed with her to her native village when I was sorrowing over your loss."

Iona moved forward. "Welcome, child," she murmured. "We are so pleased to meet you." She frowned at Lorelei. "I apologize for your cousin's rudeness."

"It's okay—I don't mind if she touches my legs," said Lena quickly.

Lorelei came closer, eyes wide. She put one hand on each of Lena's legs, shyly feeling the long muscles and marveling over the hard kneecaps. "Is this what your legs looked like, Auntie Lu, after you were Riven?" she asked.

"Lorelei!" This time it was Nereus who reprimanded Lorelei. "That is quite enough. You have greeted your cousin, now be so kind as to allow others to meet her."

Lowering her head, Lorelei retreated.

Melusina's face had paled, and she did not answer Lorelei's question.

From the crowd of mer-people, an older merman emerged, coming closer to Lena. He was powerfully built, with broad shoulders and chest. His shimmering blue-green tail was single-finned and marked with several scars. A smiling mouth curved above his long beard.

"This is Merrow, your grandfather," said Melusina.

Careful not to dislodge the sealskin cloak, the merman put his arms around Lena, saying softly, "Welcome, child of my child." He patted her gently, then drew back to study her. "Ah, look upon the fairness of her face," he crooned. "Look upon her cunning legs!"

Melusina laughed. "Beauty and strength, indeed."

"Precious maid," said Merrow, his eyes shining . . . eyes the same gray as Lena's. "When Melusina had the memories back, and we knew of your existence, I longed to see you."

"Grandfather," said Lena. "I did not know about any of—" She looked around. "This. You."

Merrow hugged Lena more tightly. "Alas, we did not know about you, either. Else we might have aided Melusina to return to you long ago."

Lena nodded, feeling safe in her grandfather's arms. So many years lost, when her mother could have been with them on land. But what about Mom? She felt a stretch of blank confusion opening up in her thoughts. *Mom?* Her mother was right next to her! But there was someone else on land, someone she cared for . . . a woman, with kind eyes. Something about diamond earrings . . . Oh, Allie! She would not have been there if Melusina had come back. Lena felt a pang, but the vague thought drifted away as she rested in Merrow's embrace.

"Commence the greeting," called someone, and other voices added their agreement. "Yes, the greeting." "Bring her to the circle."

"Come," said Melusina. She took Lena's hand and led her through the crowd of curious mer-folk. Then they entered the kelp forest, swimming between the heavy stalks. Lena felt sure she would have become lost without her mother.

Where is my grandmother?

A couple of minutes later, they emerged in the village.

"Is there a castle?" asked Lena.

Her mother looked at her, perplexed.

Lena laughed. "There's a fairy tale called *The Little Mermaid*. In the kingdom below the waves, there's a big castle with, you know, fancy windows and gardens and stuff. I remember the line about the fishes swimming in and out of the windows."

"Ah, I fear I must disappoint you. Our village is not so grand, nor so permanent. We must live simply, with few possessions. When the threat of discovery seems nigh, we must leave this place until our scouts tell us it is safe to return."

"Leave?!"

"Humans are incorrigibly curious." Melusina smiled. "We leave the village, sometimes for days, sometimes for weeks. We take what we can carry. When the danger has passed, we return. Look there." She pointed to an immense stone slab. "To prying eyes, that resembles nothing more than a very large rock formation. To us, it is the communal dining table."

Lena looked at the huge empty slab. There were a few boulders around its perimeter, like makeshift chairs. She could see heavy gold bowls and shallow stone basins, some of them still containing food, as if their diners had rushed off in the middle of their meal.

They came to see me, she thought.

Melusina led Lena into a large clearing, which was bounded by a loose circle of stones.

In the middle of the circle, Melusina stopped. "Have no fear," she said. "This is the ritual of welcome." Then she squeezed Lena's hand and let go, leaving her alone in the ring of stones.

CHAPTER 35

As Lena waited, the mer-folk first gathered outside the circle of rocks, joining hands. They began to sing, wordless melodies at first.

"It is your song of welcome," said Melusina.

The delicate sounds shaped into words that Lena could understand: *"She is welcome . . . she is welcome . . . she is part of this world . . . she is not of this world . . ."*

The mer-folk released their hands and swam swiftly up to her, drawing close, then gliding away from her, still maintaining the circle. They flowed near, then backed away as rhythmically as the tides. In and out they moved.

"You are part of this world . . . you are not of this world . . . speak your name . . . speak your family . . ."

"Names are very important. Tell them your name," prompted Melusina.

Thinking as clearly as she could, Lena formed the word: "Selena."

"Speak the names of your people," sang the mer-folk, smiling and circling. *"Share the names."*

Lena looked questioningly at her mother.

"Tell them the names of your parents," said her mother.

"Melusina, Brian," recited Lena.

She sensed confusion among the mer-folk, and even from her mother.

"Brian is my father," she reminded Melusina.

"Ahh . . . Brian," she said, although Lena could tell she did not remember him.

With a sudden swish, an older mermaid appeared next to Melusina.

Lena started; she had seen only a glint of gold before the mermaid was beside her mother. *She must be unbelievably fast,* she thought.

"Selena," said the mermaid.

Lena nodded. Something about the regal bearing of the mermaid made Lena feel like she should bow or curtsy, or kiss her hand, or something. Her eyes were so light that it was hard to tell if they were blue or green, and they bored into Lena with unsettling intensity. Her hair was light as well, glowing with many shades of gold and silver. She wore her hair twisted into several tight plaits that encircled her head like a crown and trailed down her back. Lena could see pearls and shark teeth glimmering in her hair. Her double-finned tail was pewter gray.

She has a double-finned tail, too, like Mama, thought Lena. Then she peered closer at the mermaid's pointed chin, and realized she was looking at her grandmother.

"I am Amphitrite," said the mermaid. "You must learn the names of your people in *this* world."

"Grandmother." The word whispered through Lena's mind.

The mermaid smiled then, her expression softening. She did not embrace Lena, but reached out to take her hand. "Child of my child. You are most welcome here."

"Thank you," said Lena. It wasn't quite the same affection-
ate greeting her grandfather had given her, but maybe Amphitrite wasn't the hugging type.

With a grimace, Amphitrite's gaze swept down Lena's body
and legs. "Is she able to swim with those legs?" she asked
Melusina.

"Mother!" answered Melusina, in a tone universally em-
ployed between mothers and daughters: exasperation. "Of
course she is able to swim." With a proud smile, Melusina
reached down and stroked Lena's feet. "Look at her lovely
feet. They have grown so, since she was a baby! They were
perfect little moonbeam feet."

Amphitrite gave a frosty smile. "Yes, lovely." She addressed
Lena. "You must be glad to escape the land."

Lena blinked. Glad to escape the land? Did that mean
she was never going back? A tendril of worry touched
her mind.

But after all, why should she go back? She had missed her
mother. She wanted to stay with her.

A fleeting image of a child with blue eyes . . . a memory of
someone calling her name through the night . . . then the
hypnotic rocking of the sea drew those thoughts away from
her, gently, insistently.

Lena raised a hand to her brow, as if to hold her thoughts
inside her head. *It's like my memories are getting washed away,* she
thought.

Amphitrite noticed Lena's bewilderment and turned to
her daughter. "The child is exhausted, Melusina. She needs
food and rest. Let us not linger over the welcome circle."

"Yes, Mother," said Melusina, appearing flustered. She turned to Lena. "Selena, after you answer the welcome, our people will approach you. Do not be nervous."

Lena looked at all the mer-folk surrounding her, still circling in and out. "What should I say?" she asked.

"You must say what is in your heart."

Lena watched the mer-folk as they flowed inward and ebbed outward, their song fading to a whispering welcome.

"I—" She faltered.

They waited.

"I . . . think you are all beautiful," blurted Lena.

The mer-folk circled in very close, and many hands reached out to caress her. Three or four of the mer-folk merely bowed to her before swimming away, while others stroked her arms or hair. The little mermaids and merboys were fascinated with her legs, and took cautious pokes at them.

Instead of feeling afraid of so many strange creatures crowding near her, Lena felt the gentleness of their hands, so fleeting and light. Each touch was like a blessing. They were careful not to dislodge her sealskin cloak.

"Oh, here are my sisters," said Melusina, holding out her hand to two mermaids, both with white-blond hair and dark blue eyes, their upper bodies wreathed in identical sparkling sapphire necklaces. "Metis and Thetis. Twins, as you can see!"

The mermaids swept forward and brushed light kisses on Lena's cheeks.

Melusina continued the introductions: the husbands of her sisters, and all of the young cousins. "And this is young Amphitrite . . . named, of course, after your grandmother. And this is Piskaret . . . this is Fossegrim . . . and Calypso . . ."

Lena nodded and smiled, although the mer-folk were beginning to blur together in her mind.

Then she saw a broad-shouldered young merman lagging behind the rest of the group. He waited until there was no one left to greet her, then he approached.

As he drew near, Lena admired his chin-length green and brown hair, which radiated out from his head like a cloud. When he got close enough, she could see his dark, almond-shaped eyes and his full lips. The sight of his exotic beauty made her nervous.

Gazing at Lena with a rapt expression, the merman touched her arm.

The brush of his fingers across her skin caused Lena's heart to flutter.

Instead of bowing and leaving, as all the others had done, he backed slowly away, still gazing at her.

Lena discovered that it was possible to blush under water. The merman's lips were slightly parted, as if he might speak to her, and Lena longed to hear her name in his voice.

"Nix is handsome, isn't he?" said her mother with a smile.

Instead of answering, Lena looked down at her cloak, fussing with the way it rested on her shoulders. *Nix*.

◻ ◻ ◻

"Melusina," called Lena's grandfather. "The child must be sinking, after that long journey. She needs food and rest."

"Yes," agreed Amphitrite. "The welcome circle is complete, and the vote has been cast. She should join us for nourishment. What does she eat?"

Melusina smiled. "My daughter loves the eggs of the salmon! She shall have as many as she likes."

Vote? thought Lena.

"The kelp juice is excellent for regaining one's strength," said Merrow.

Following Amphitrite and Merrow, she swam with her mother to the large stone table. Mer-folk were now bustling around it, heaping the bowls and plates with food. Goblets filled with some kind of liquid, heavier than the seawater, rested on the table.

Nereus swam up with a primitive-looking chair. "Please," he said. "You are family. But today you are also an honored guest." He put the chair down by the table and bowed, indicating that she should sit.

"Oh," said Lena. "Thank you." She settled into the chair, which was hard and bone-colored. As she looked more closely at it, she realized it was made of actual *bones*. Some of them were clearly whale bones, but some looked decidedly human. She suppressed a shudder.

"You may try any of these foods, and decide which you like," offered Amphitrite.

Merrow held out a goblet, and Lena nodded her thanks, taking a tiny sip. It felt strange to be drinking under water. Her grandfather was right; the kelp juice *was* good, and she felt stronger already.

Amphitrite presided over the head of the table, passing Lena the gleaming plates with different foods on them: mussels and clams, shrimps and crabs, strands of seaweed and slices of sea slug.

"Try the periwinkle soup," said Merrow. "It has bits of rockfish in it."

"Oh. Thank you." Lena politely tried as many of the delicacies as possible. She reached for some small wrinkled bits of food. "These look like raisins," she said.

"Ah, the fish eyes," said Merrow. "Delicious!"

Lena's hand halted.

"The eyes were only harvested after the fish had died," Melusina hastened to assure her.

"Oh," said Lena, her own eyes wide. "Thank you. Maybe later. Mama, please tell me about the vote Grandmother mentioned."

"After the welcome song," said Melusina, "the village voted on whether or not you would be allowed to remain."

CHAPTER 36

Lena stared. "And? Do I have to leave?"

"No, dear one. The vote was in your favor. Do not trouble yourself about it," said Melusina.

"But when did everyone vote? I didn't see that."

"After the song," said her mother. "Those who placed their hands on you were bestowing their blessing for you to remain. Forever, if you like. Those who merely bowed and departed were indicating that you should be a visitor only."

Lena's lower lip trembled. What did it mean that some of them did not want her to stay?

"Come," said her mother. "We shall find a place for you to rest. I will bide with you until I must surface again. Have you eaten your fill?"

Lena nodded. "Don't I have to surface?"

"Not yet. The cloak protects you. Once you take it off, the enchantment is broken, and you will join me in surfacing."

"Take *off* the cloak? I can't take it off—I'll drown!"

"No, indeed, my child. You must trust in the magic."

Sure, thought Lena. *I'll trust in the magic enough to take off the cloak when I'm about five feet from the surface.*

Melusina swam with Lena past several large caves. Peering into the mouth of one of the caves, Lena could see mer-folk curled up on beds of seaweed.

A short distance away, Melusina led Lena into a different cave, slightly smaller. There were beds of seaweed clustered here, too.

"Here is the sleeping cave where I take my repose," said Melusina. "We all sleep at . . . what is the word? *Various* times, depending upon our need for air. Let me make you comfortable before I surface."

"You have your own cave?" asked Lena.

Melusina turned away, adjusting a bed of soft seaweed for Lena. "I am the only one who uses this cave."

"Why?"

"This is the cave for the Riven," answered her mother quietly.

"The Riven?" said Lena.

"Let us speak of these things when you have rested," said Melusina, avoiding Lena's gaze.

"No, Mama. Please. I'm not sleepy."

"Selena, my child," said Melusina. "You are stubborn as a limpet! You must rest." She caressed her daughter's cheek. "But I see that you will not be at peace until you have answers." She settled down next to Lena. "You may ask three questions. Then I must surface."

Lena nodded. "Okay. What is Riven?"

Melusina closed her eyes, as if gathering strength before speaking. "One who is Riven has chosen to forsake the world beneath the waves. She rises out of the sea and endures the riving light of the full moon upon her body. When legs take the place of her tail, she dares to walk upon the land. This transformation is against the most ancient laws of mer-folk.

Thus, when a mermaid returns to the sea, she regains her form, but is known ever after as Riven. Mer-folk do not abandon their own, but one who is Riven must always remain outside the circle, in some ways."

Lena's heart was beating hard. "Outside the circle? You mean they treat you like an outcast?"

"No, my dearest. Not an outcast. You see for yourself the closeness of our kind. When I returned to the sea, full of grief and woe, I was reunited with my people and tended most lovingly. But one who is Riven once chose land over sea, and that betrayal can never be forgotten." She touched Lena's hand. "Forgiven, but not forgotten."

"I don't understand why that means you have to sleep somewhere else, though."

"Mer-folk communicate with our minds, as you have learned. The dreams of mer-folk have the power to drift from one sleeper to another, much like our thoughts. My dreams are a danger to others, for at times I dream of my life on land."

Lena shivered. "So you remembered us, sometimes, in dreams?"

Melusina nodded. "Only in dreams. Each time I awake, the sea claims my memories again."

"But once you saw me—that day at Magic's—you remembered being my mom. Right?"

"Yes."

"If you could remember me, why couldn't you remember Dad?"

"Ah, yes. Dad," said Melusina vaguely. "I do not know the enchantment surrounding the memories of the Riven.

I remember the feeling of love. But I see only a blank face whenever I try to picture your father."

It seemed terribly cruel that Melusina should have lost all memories of her husband. After all, he was the reason she left her people to live on land.

"Do you remember *anything* about him?" persisted Lena.

"I remember the moonlight cleaving my tail into legs. I remember the love of a human had tempted me onto land."

"He loved you so much!" cried Lena.

"Did he?" Melusina looked interested.

"Yes! He didn't even get married again for a long time. But finally he thought you were never coming back, so he—" Lena did not finish her sentence. What was the name of his new wife? Lee?

Melusina frowned, as if focusing on some cloudy image in her mind's eye. "He was fair of face, was he not?"

"You mean handsome? Yes! Everyone says so."

"But kind, as well. My heart tells me this was true."

"He's very kind."

"You say he married again?"

"About seven years ago."

"Ah. Time is different for us. I cannot remember how long a year is."

"Well, there are twelve months in a year," said Lena. "So twelve full moons."

"Oh! Yes, yes. Now I understand. We do measure time by the full moon. But the passage of time is different in our world."

"It is?"

Melusina nodded.

"How do you mean?" asked Lena.

"Let me see," said her mother. "If there are twelve moons in a year . . . let me see. I would be sixty-two years old, in your world."

Lena looked at her lovely young mother in amazement. "Sixty-two?"

"Yes. I believe that is the number."

"That can't be right. How old is Amphitrite?"

"Well, let's see. She would be . . . hmm. One hundred and thirty-six years."

A long silence followed these announcements. Lena did not know what to say. Was time passing differently for her, too, in this undersea world? Had it been only a few minutes since she'd left, back on land?

"What about—"

"Selena, you have asked many questions! And now you must sleep. The cloak protects you until my return," said Melusina. "When you awake, we shall explore the world beneath the waves. But now I must surface."

"Yes, Mama." Lena settled down on the bed of seaweed, closing her eyes and plunging into slumber like an anchor falling to the seafloor.

◻ ◻ ◻

Brian's eyes remained dry while Allie wept—shocking, wracking sobs that rent the night sky. He sat on the sand, in the exact spot where he'd landed when the strength went out of his legs. He wanted to console her, but those words did not exist.

CHAPTER 37

Lena woke up under water.

For a moment, she was disoriented, remembering all the times she had woken up on the beach in the middle of the night. This watery cave was the reverse of those awakenings.

Every time I went sleepwalking, she thought, *I was trying to reach my mother. Something inside me—the mermaid part of me—knew she was near.*

Lena felt the sealskin cloak tucked warmly around her. She relaxed and closed her eyes again, feeling safe. She could hear voices—some of the mer-folk must be nearby.

She kept her eyes closed, trying to distinguish who was speaking. She had noticed earlier that the voices of the adult mer-folk sounded much alike in her head, although she could tell her mother's voice from everyone else's. Lorelei's voice had contained a distinctive ringing quality, and the children all sounded unique from one another. Lena supposed that the longer she stayed, the easier it would become to match voices to faces.

". . . because of the male human on land," she heard someone mutter. "Now we must live in fear that she will remember, and leave us yet again. It is not to be borne!"

"Shh," said a second voice. "You will wake the child."

"Ah, yes. The child." The first voice softened. "She's a lovely little land child. But she belongs to us now. And in time, her legs will cease to trouble me."

Lena huddled under the cloak, ashamed. Who couldn't stand to look at her legs? And what did that mean, "she belongs to us now"?

"We always knew there was a chance the human would seek her again," sighed a third voice.

"Not as long as I am alive," said someone coldly. "I warned him not to enter the sea again. And I spoke the truth. Had he disobeyed my command, I would have charmed the sharks to seek him out, even as he sought Melusina."

Lena could not restrain a small cry.

There was a swish in the water near her, then someone asked gently, "Are you awake, child?"

"Yes," said Lena, opening her eyes. Her grandfather leaned over her. She sat up and peered through the fluid light of the cave, and saw her aunts, Metis and Thetis, her uncle, Nereus, and her grandmother. Melusina's entire family seemed to be on guard duty over her!

"Good. I hope you are rested. You slept a long time."

"I did? How long?"

"Ah, let me see. Time is not something we measure, except by the moon. The moon has begun to wane, while you slept."

Lena frowned. The moon had begun to wane? Had she been asleep for days?

"Melusina has been to the surface a number of times. She asked us to keep watch over you while she was away."

Lena nodded her understanding. *I would have charmed the sharks to seek him out* echoed through her mind. She felt acutely self-conscious of her legs now, too. She was relieved to see Melusina approach.

"Did you sleep well, dearest maid?" asked her mother, swimming into the cave and settling near Lena. The others departed.

"Yes," answered Lena. "How long did I sleep?"

"Ah, a long time! You were profoundly weary."

"Hours? Days?"

"Oh, you want a measurement? Let me think . . . on land, the sun has risen and set again."

"How long before I need to surface for air?"

"Whenever you wish. Do you feel ready to take off the cloak?"

Lena stared at her in alarm. "Take it off *now?* I'm miles from the surface."

"Not miles, dear. And remember . . . I told you that when your desire was powerful enough, you would be able to breathe on your own in this world."

"But how will I know?"

"The only way to know is to search your heart."

"What happens if I *think* I'm ready, but I'm not really?"

Melusina looked puzzled. "But your heart will tell you truly."

Lena looked back at her mother. "But what if I'm wrong? I'll drown!"

"If you have doubt, then you must remain in the shelter of the cloak."

"Okay." Lena was relieved. No matter what her mother said, this would not be the place to discover she couldn't breathe under water.

"Now we shall eat. You must be very hungry. Afterward, would you like to explore the world beneath the waves with me?"

"Yes!"

Melusina took Lena's hand, and they swam together out of the cave. Mer-folk watched them shyly as they approached the stone table. A few swam closer to look at Lena, especially her legs, then flitted away again.

Melusina introduced Lena to as many of them as came near.

"Why does she wear that human garment under the cloak?" asked a mermaid who looked about Lena's age. She wore pearls in her hair.

"On land, it is protective," said Melusina. "It is called a—" She frowned.

"A jacket," said Lena.

"Ah, yes. Jacket."

The mermaid felt the slippery fabric of Lena's jacket, then smiled and swam away.

"They have many questions," said Melusina. "You will meet them as their shyness abates. Mer-folk are taught to be wary of humans, so it may take them some time to befriend you. Now let us eat. The sea cucumber is especially delicious."

They ate until they were full, then Melusina put her arm around Lena. "Ready, dearest?"

"Where are we going?"

"You shall see."

CHAPTER 38

Melusina led Lena through the village. Mer-folk bowed and waved to them. In the shifting, drifting crowd of mer-folk, Lena's gaze went unerringly to the green-and-gold-haired merman near the edge of the group.

Nix was watching her, and Lena felt her belly flutter. Everyone else seemed to blur and fade as Lena stared back at him.

"May I approach?" he asked, across the water. His voice was unlike any other—low, warm, with a gravelly undertone.

"Yes," she answered.

Melusina noticed their conversation, and smiled. "We shall greet Nix, but I wish to spend time with you a little longer, just the two of us, before others claim your attention."

As Nix swam in their direction, Lorelei rushed to greet Lena. "At last she wakes! Each time I returned from the surface, my cousin was still asleep. Auntie Lu, where are you going? I want to become better acquainted with Selena."

Nix paused. "I do not wish to intrude," he said. "I will return later." He directed a beautiful smile at Lena and, with a flip of his tail, swam away.

Lena felt a pang, watching him go.

"There will be ample time for visits, niece," said Melusina. "I am going to show my daughter this world."

"May I come, too?"

"Next time, Lori."

They left the village, followed by swarms of mer-folk children who raced circles around them, playing tag and begging Lena to explain how her legs worked.

"They work by magic," said Lena with a wink.

The children laughed and clapped and darted near to touch her, then swam away after Melusina shooed them off.

Mother and daughter swam for hours. Lena saw schools of fish and played with her mother's two favorite dolphins. Then they swam deeper . . . into the coldest part of the ocean, where bioluminescent fish cast their pale, otherworldly light, luring prey . . . sometimes becoming prey.

"The anglerfish," said Melusina, pointing to a fish that appeared to have a fishing rod with a glowing tip at its end.

"So cool," whispered Lena.

"It *is* cold," agreed her mother, and swam out of the depths with Lena.

Lena smiled, not bothering to explain what she meant.

As they ascended higher and higher, Lena became aware of a shadow passing above them, blocking out the rays of the sun. She turned her head as the massive shape shifted direction and began to skim downward past them.

"What is it?" she asked.

"A whale," said her mother.

The gigantic body of the gray whale seemed to go on and on, sliding past them until its enormous tail swept within inches of them.

"Its tail almost caught us," said Lena. "We would have been killed!"

"Not at all, dear one. The whale knew of our presence," answered Melusina. "The word in your language is echo—"

She paused to think. "Placement? No, *location*. Echolocation. It allows whales to know where things are at all times. If he had wanted to, he *could* have caught us with his tail."

"Big word, Mama," said Lena teasingly. "The language is definitely returning to you."

"There is another word." Melusina tapped her forehead with one pale finger. "The humans try to mimic the echolocation of the whales with their machines. But it affects our friends the whales. Man should cease his interference." She thought for a moment, then said, "Sonar! That is the word."

"Oh, sonar," repeated Lena. "I've heard about that. Poor whales."

They swam on. After a time, Lena burst out, "I can hardly believe I'm breathing under water! I'm afraid I'm going to wake up and this will all be a dream."

"But you *did* sleep, dearest. Then you awoke, and behold! You are still here."

Lena hugged her mother. "I love this world."

"I am happy to hear those words from you. This is your home now, as well . . . just as much as your home on land."

"Mama?"

"Yes, dear."

"That word, 'behold.' Was that you I heard that night when it was raining? It *was* you, wasn't it? You said, 'I beheld you, child.'"

"Yes, Selena, it was my touch on your heart from across the waves."

Lena took her mother's hand.

Once in a while, a mermaid or merman swam past them, bowing courteously. Some of them wore cloaks.

"Why do they have on cloaks?" asked Lena.

"Those who surface near land wear their cloaks. It renders us safe from view—we appear as seals."

"Don't you need your cloak, then?" Lena touched the pelt she wore.

"No," said Melusina, with an edge to her voice. "I never wear my cloak."

"Why not?"

"I will never wear it again!" she burst out.

Lena startled.

The mermaid took a calming breath. "Forgive me, my child. I should not have spoken so wildly. The cloak is a painful reminder of all I have lost. I have not worn it since my return." She smiled. "But it brings me joy now, as it protects my dearest treasure."

They swam in silence for a few minutes, then Melusina said, "I shall rise and take in air. We are far from the land, where no humans may see us. You must remain beneath the surface."

"Why?"

Melusina paused, then said slowly, "The cloak protects humans beneath the surface, just as it protects mer-folk above the waves. But once you rise above the surface, the enchantment of the cloak will cease for you and your body will require air."

"Oh," said Lena, wide-eyed. "I thought you said I could go without the cloak and still breathe under water."

"I did. But not *above* the water."

"Um, okay, I'll wait here."

Still holding her daughter's hand, Melusina rose for air. Lena watched from below, fingering the cloak.

"Let us return to the village now," said Melusina, when she slid back under water. "We will eat and drink, and you may spend time with your cousins. They have many questions to ask you."

"I can't wait!"

It was a long journey back to the village. As they drew near, Lena felt her heart lift. So many new family members to get to know! She found herself searching for Nix. *So soon?* she thought. *Do I have a crush on a merman just days after I find out I'm half-mermaid?*

Lorelei must have been watching for their arrival, because she hurried to join them. "Cousin Selena," she said. "Merrow is giving a lesson to the young ones about the world above the waves. Come listen! Perhaps he is mistaken, and you can tell us better."

Lena saw a group of small mermaids and merboys clustered around Merrow. "I doubt I can tell you better," she said.

"But you are *from* that world," insisted Lorelei. "Of course you know better! We should be taught the truth."

"Lorelei," chided Melusina. "Your grandfather teaches the ancient rhymes and songs. Those tales are meant to teach the young ones simple facts about the world above the waves . . . not detailed descriptions of modern human life."

Lorelei pouted. "Well, *I* want to know about modern human life!"

Melusina sighed. "Yes, Lori, you are always curious about the human world. I do not know, however, if it is wise for Selena to share her stories." She turned to Lena. "As you see, we do not teach using pen and paper. We pass along images and songs to our young ones, and that is how they learn. But

I am not certain whether we should hear your tales of human society. Perhaps they would be disturbing."

Lorelei scowled. "What a childish concern," she said. "I want to hear all about the humans."

Lena couldn't help smiling. It was a novelty to feel so foreign and interesting. "Maybe *you* should tell *me* some stories."

Lorelei shrugged. "Nothing ever happens here. Your arrival is the most exciting thing to occur in a hundred moons."

"What does everyone do all day down here?"

Melusina laughed, causing her pearl necklaces to dance. "Ah, Selena! We have much to do. We perform what you call 'work,' but not in order to gain—" She hesitated, again tapping her forehead. "I always forget the word. It means . . . hmm, it has something to do with getting things."

"Money?"

"Yes! We do not work to get money." She shook her head, as if disappointed that she couldn't remember the word. "We work to find food, and we spend time preparing the food. We have scouts who patrol the waters around us, to ensure the safety of the village. We have lookouts, as you saw, to announce the arrival of visitors, or to warn of intruders. We spend time teaching the young ones about our history, and about the other creatures of the waters."

"Is that it? Don't you do anything for fun?"

Melusina smiled again and leaned close, teasing, "No, no. We have no fun. It is nothing but work and drudgery here in the world beneath the waves."

Lena chuckled. "Okay, that was a silly question."

"We spend far more time in play than work, as a matter of fact." When Lorelei made a disbelieving sound, Melusina insisted, "It is true! We sing, we tell tales, we make music. We travel a great deal. There is so much to see! How could one ever grow weary of the sea?"

Lena watched a mermaid cuddle a tiny baby with a wee, wriggling tail. Nearby, a circle of children played what looked like a version of ring-around-the-rosy. In the distance, merfolk were pounding kelp and stirring pots, chatting as they worked. All around her, the villagers bustled with work and play, like any community. And ah! There was the handsome Nix carrying fresh seaweed into the sleeping cave.

Melusina noticed her riveted attention, and said, "Lorelei, I must beg your patience once again. Lena has others to meet. Will you dine with us? We have not eaten for hours."

"Yes, indeed," said Lorelei. "I will set out supper for us." She swam away.

Lena and her mother swam toward the place where Nix had gone. As they approached the cave, Nix reappeared.

"Hello!" he said, a look of pleasure lighting his face.

"Hello," said Lena.

Nix moved closer to Lena and took her hand. "I have been thinking of you."

Her heart tripped and sped up.

"May I hear my name in your voice? I am called Nix." The dark pools of his eyes were endless, and his large hand enveloped hers, making her feel that no one had ever held her hand properly before.

Pausing to fix his name clearly in her mind, Lena said, "Nix."

They floated for a long moment, staring at each other.

This kind of staring would never happen on land, thought Lena. *People would look away, feel embarrassed.*

But here there was no self-consciousness, only a deepening connection. Nix took her other hand, and Lena felt a dizzy warmth flow through her. *I think I'm swooning.*

◻ ◻ ◻

Brian did not look away from the waves, even when Allie sat down on the sand next to him. They no longer spoke. Allie's entreaties for him to come home had made no impression. How could they, when his heart was gone? She opened the plastic bag she had brought him yesterday . . . The food was untouched, but at least he'd drunk the water. Allie lay her head on his shoulder for a moment, and Brian felt a flicker of compassion. He was sorry to leave them alone—his second wife and child—but he couldn't abandon his vigil.

CHAPTER 39

Lena watched her mother sleep.

The mermaid's expression was troubled, and once, her hand rose up, as if reaching out to someone.

How horrible, thought Lena. *To relive your past over and over in your dreams, and to forget it as soon as you wake up.*

A figure appeared at the entrance to their cave, and Lena's heart lifted at the sight of a nimbus of green and gold hair.

Nix swam close to her. "Hello," he said, his voice deep and quiet in her mind.

Lena's face warmed as she answered, "Hello."

Then a silence hung between them. Nix gazed tranquilly at her, his bare, bronzed chest just inches from her. Lena looked everywhere but at him. She had grown accustomed to the sight of bare torsos in this world, but something about the nearness of Nix's skin made it hard to think straight.

"Do you wish to stay until your mother wakes?" he asked finally.

Lena glanced up at him, then at her mother's sleeping form. "I . . . I don't know," she said. "My mother and I have not been apart since we reunited."

He smiled. "I understand your reluctance. Perhaps you would be willing to allow me to keep you company?"

Lena nodded, feeling that she would be willing to try whatever Nix suggested.

—— L. K. MADIGAN ——

"Your face is so familiar," he said unexpectedly. "How is that possible?"

Lena shook her head. "I don't think it *is* possible."

Another silence descended. Then a frown crossed Lena's brow. "You're in the cave for the Riven."

"Yes?"

"Aren't you afraid her dreams will be upsetting?" She pointed to her mother.

Nix made an impatient gesture. "The old ways," he said, "are full of fear and superstition. I do not fear your mother's dreams." He watched Melusina for a moment, his gaze compassionate. "Her memories harm no one but her."

A lump came into Lena's throat and she nodded, grateful for Nix's sympathy.

His dark eyes settled on Lena's face again. She forced herself not to look away in shyness. After a long moment, she felt the same dizzy rush as the last time she and Nix had stared into each other's eyes. The water between them seemed to grow warmer.

That swoon is happening again, she thought.

Nix took her hand, drawing her closer.

Lena's breathing quickened.

"We could leave a message for your mother," said Nix. "She would know you are safe."

"Really? How do you leave messages?"

Nix lowered his gaze and looked around the cave. He let go of Lena's hand while he gathered up three smooth stones the size of his palm. He positioned them on the seafloor next to Melusina, their edges touching.

Lena watched him. "Why three?"

He hesitated. "I do not know. We have always used three stones for reassurance. I suppose one or two would appear to be accidental. But three stones placed just so"—he nodded down at the trio—"appear very deliberate." He offered his arm to Lena in a courtly, old-fashioned gesture. "Will you join me?"

Slipping her hand into the crook of his arm, Lena swam with Nix through the village, curious stares following in their wake.

◻ ◻ ◻

"Dearest maiden," said her mother, when Lena returned. "I felt your absence keenly."

Lena lowered her eyes, embarrassed. It seemed that mothers were overly protective no matter where they lived. "I was just out for a w—" She faltered. *Not a walk,* she reminded herself. "A swim with Nix. He was showing me around."

"Indeed," said Melusina. "I hope that I may trust Nix to keep you safe." She gave him a stern look.

"Mother," whispered Lena, mortified.

Instead of backing away, Nix met Melusina's gaze directly. "I will never put your daughter in harm's way. She is a treasure."

Lena's heart fluttered. Someone—a different boy—had once called her . . . what? A jewel? A feeling of déjà vu swept over her.

"Nix," she said. "Your words are sweet. Thank you. I enjoyed our time together." Even though her mother was right next to her, Lena could not help falling into the depths of his eyes. She wanted to reach for his hand again—not touching Nix was becoming unbearable.

Nix must have read her thoughts, because he moved closer to her, and took both her hands in his. "Selena," he said. "I will return to you. The time apart will be long."

Oh, she thought. *So this is what it feels like . . . falling in love. I wish I could tell—*

The image of a girl with long black hair and pink yarn around her ankle did not even take shape fully in Lena's mind before dissolving.

CHAPTER 40

"Fossegrim, please put aside your flute," said Merrow. He floated in front of the group of young children, waiting for quiet.

Fossegrim lay his flute on the seafloor next to him and beamed up at Merrow. "Will you teach us more about the care of seahorses? Mine keep dying."

Lena suppressed a giggle. In this world, pet seahorses lasted about as long as goldfish or box turtles did on land.

"Another time," said Merrow. "Today we will practice our Clouding."

"Oh, that's hard," sighed Syrenka. She turned to Lena. "You're not very good at it."

Now Lena's giggle burst out. "I know, Syrenka. I'm trying, though. Where I come from, we talk out loud instead of with our minds, so we don't have to learn Clouding."

Lena loved to take lessons with the children—on land, she supposed they would be five or six years old. For some reason, she was filled with happiness when she was with them, although sometimes the sight of their rounded cheeks and bright eyes caused a nameless ache inside her.

Merrow lifted his hands, as if conducting an orchestra, and began, *"Clouds are kind . . ."*

The children sang the rhyme that reminded them to obscure their thoughts when necessary:

"Clouds are kind to everyone.
Some thoughts are just for me.
Clouding works and it is fun!
Some thoughts are not to see."

It was true that Lena was still struggling to cloud her private thoughts from regular speech. But she practiced diligently, because she worried that too many people could read her thoughts about Nix. And those thoughts were definitely private.

Merrow described various methods of Clouding while the children listened. "Perhaps you may visualize a blanket of seaweed covering up your unkind thoughts," he said. "Or a large clamshell closing around your angry thoughts. What do you picture, Thoosa, when you want to hide your thoughts?"

Thoosa piped up, "I picture a cloud of squid ink!"

"Very good. And you, Achelous?"

"I picture an upside-down basket on top of my mean thoughts."

Merrow smiled. "Lena? Do you have a particular image that works for you?"

"Yes," said Lena. "I picture a curtain falling over my private thoughts."

"What's a curtain?" asked Thoosa.

"Oh," said Lena. "You don't have windows. Well, see . . . okay, let me explain what a house is. On land, humans live in these things called houses. And windows are—"

"Selena," interrupted Merrow. "Let us talk of houses another day. These children are a bit young to comprehend human dwellings. We teach those concepts when they are older.

I believe I know what you mean by a curtain, and that image will work quite well for Clouding." He continued on with the lesson. "Lealiki, what do you picture when you want to hide your thoughts?"

Nix appeared at the edge of the school circle, and Lena did not hear another word her grandfather said.

"Shall I teach you to find food?" he asked. His voice was quiet, but Lena felt the pull of his presence like the tide feels the moon.

She dropped a mental curtain over her own thoughts: *I can't believe that gorgeous merman wants to be with* me.

"May I be excused, Grandfather?" she asked.

Merrow nodded, and Lena swam quickly to Nix's side. He took both of her hands in his large ones. Warmth spread from Lena's fingers all the way to her toes.

"I shall expect a great bounty for my evening meal," Merrow called after them, and they laughed.

Nix released one of her hands but kept hold of the other one, and they swam slowly away from the village. "I confess my offer is made out of self-interest."

"Oh?"

"If I teach you to find food . . ." He looked at her slyly. "We will have time alone together."

"That's brilliant," sighed Lena.

As they foraged for abalone, Lena did her best to explain how humans acquired food.

"The food is already packaged," she said. "And sold in—" But there was no word for *stores* in their language. ". . . in public centers."

"Circles?"

"Um, no. In public buildings. You've seen human buildings, yes?"

"Yes." Nix loved to travel and had seen many human coastal towns, wearing his scalskin cloak as a disguise. "So workers gather the food from the ground and carry it to the centers?"

"Yes!" said Lena. "Farmers grow the crops, harvest them, and sell them in stores. I mean, public centers. Other people raise—" Again, there was no word for *livestock* in their language. ". . . certain animals for food. And of course," she said, smiling, "fishermen catch fish for people to eat, too."

"Does no one forage? As we are doing?"

"Well, not really. *Some* people do. They go out picking—" She thought of berries and mushrooms. "Um, foods that grow in the ground," she amended. "And some people hunt and kill animals for their own families. But most people just buy their food at the . . . public center. Using money."

"Ah, yes, money," said Nix. Lena had already explained the concept of money to him. "I like foraging," he said. "Wondering what the sea will yield . . . discovering a nest of turtle eggs or a new kelp forest. It must be strange to see so many kinds of food arrayed in one place, and never to know the people who provided it."

Lena smiled. "It does sound strange, when you put it that way. But we have so many, many people on land. Not like the village, where you know everyone."

Nix slowed in his swimming. "It seems a miracle, does it not? That you, from the wide world, should come to our small village." He spoke as if he still couldn't quite believe it.

"No, it's not a miracle," said Lena. "This is my mother's home. It was inevitable that I would come here."

"But you were separated for so long! What if your father had removed you from the town of your birth? You and Melusina might never have found each other."

"True," said Lena, shivering. "I only wish we had found each other years ago." She paused. A wisp of doubt niggled at her. *But if we had found each other years ago,* she thought . . . and her mind encountered a white space that had once been filled with memories.

"I would like to see the place where your parents met," said Nix. "Will you show me?"

"I don't know how to find it," said Lena, and the wispy doubt blossomed into a vague worry. What if she wanted to go there?

"Can you describe it to me?"

Lena pictured Magic's. "There is a large cove. On the northernmost point, there is a lighthouse." Luckily, mer-folk had a word for lighthouse. Roughly translated, it meant "tower of pulsing light." She closed her eyes to better see the beach in her memory. "On the southern end of the cove, there is a long, jagged jetty. Shipwreck Rocks. The beach between the rocks and the lighthouse is called Magic Crescent Cove. The waves there are sometimes huge . . . very dangerous to humans, but they cannot resist trying to conquer them." She opened her eyes.

Nix had a wondering expression on his face. "It was you," he said.

"What was me?"

"I knew I have seen you before. You are *the girl who greets us.*"

Lena looked at him in confusion, then in dawning comprehension. The sea lions! All those times she had waved at seals and sea lions . . . some of them hadn't been animals at all. Some of them had been mer-folk, *wearing their cloaks.* "That was you?"

Nix reached for her hand. "I knew there was a reason."

"A reason for what?" she said faintly.

"For the way I feel about you." Nix pulled her closer.

Lena's gaze moved from his dark, soulful eyes to his beautiful lips. *He's going to kiss me,* she thought.

But after a long moment, Nix pulled back, straightening her cloak. He seemed worried that he might have caused it to slip.

Lena looked down at the cloak. It might be protecting her . . . but it was getting in the way, too.

◻ ◻ ◻

After the day's catch had been deposited in the village kitchen— shark eggs and spiny king crabs—Lena and Nix stacked their collection baskets in what Lena thought of as the "supply closet," which was really just an area used for storing tools.

Then they floated together, not speaking, loath to say goodbye.

"May I be with you later?" asked Nix.

"Yes, please," said Lena, her gaze moving again to his lips. She felt her fingers twitch with the urge to touch those lips. They looked so soft, so full . . . Too late, she realized she should have Clouded her thoughts.

Nix took her hand and lifted it to his lips. With his eyes never leaving hers, he slowly kissed each of Lena's fingers. Desire suffused Lena, like sand soaking up water.

Nix released her hand, then backed away, finally departing. In a lovestruck daze, Lena drifted toward the village circle.

"Cousin!" Lorelei grabbed Lena's arm and pulled her toward a trio of young mermaids. "Is it true?" she asked, her eyes wide. "Are you going to marry Nix?"

"What?!" Lena's own eyes went wide. She looked around at the other mermaids, who were staring with interest at her.

"Everyone speaks of it," said Lorelei. "How Nix, who has never taken a mate, cannot be pried away from your side." Lorelei shook Lena's arm playfully.

"I . . . we . . . we're not getting married!" said Lena. "I'm only sixteen. People my age don't marry. Not where I come from."

"Sixteen?" asked a mermaid with light brown hair. "You are quite a baby. In that case, it is right that you send him away."

"Send him away?" Lena's bewilderment grew. "I'm not going to send him away. I love—" She hesitated. "Being with him. But we're not, um, *mated*. We're just getting to know each other. I'm sorry . . . I don't remember your name."

"Russ."

"Russ?" repeated Lena.

"Short for Rusalka," said the girl. "This is Wata." She pointed to another mermaid.

"And I'm Halia," piped up a third mermaid. "No doubt Nix is fascinated by your legs!" She giggled, oblivious to the effect her remark had on Lena, who was stung by it.

"I don't—"

"Well," said Lorelei. "It is a fact that Nix has never shown a fraction of the interest he shows you to any other maid. For a time it was believed he might want to mate with Scylla. Did you meet Scylla?"

"I . . . wait. Scylla? As in Scylla, the sea monster? Six mouths? Liked to eat sailors? I thought that was a myth."

"No," said Rusalka, shaking her head so that her long hair danced. "Not a myth. But our Scylla is perfectly lovely." Her white, translucent face quirked in a smile. "Our Scylla possesses one mouth only, and does not dine on sailors. It is her ancestor who was turned into a monster. And to be fair, *that* Scylla was a great beauty, before her unfortunate transformation."

"Never mind all that ancient history," said Lorelei. "As I was saying, for a time we believed Nix might want to mate with Scylla. He invited her to the Gifting of the Cloaks last spring, and he sometimes dined with her family. But Scylla says—" She lowered her voice. "His eyes were never alight with love in her presence. She could see no future in them."

Lena caught her breath. *I see love and light in Nix's eyes,* she thought. *And the more I look, the more I see the future.*

"But everyone notices how he seeks you out, and looks at you with intense desire. Do you think it is the legs?"

Lena glared. "It's not my legs!"

Lorelei looked surprised. "No? They're very clever." She reached down and touched Lena's kneecaps. "Especially these hard, bony parts. So unexpected."

"Why do you not remove your cloak?" asked Halia. "You have been here ages, and yet you still wear it."

"I want to remove it," said Lena. "But I need it to survive down here."

"Oh," said Lorelei, looking sympathetic. "Did Auntie Lu not explain? When your heart tells you true, it will be safe to take off the cloak. Then you will breathe like the rest of us."

"She told me," said Lena. "But how will I know for sure?"

"I just told you. Your heart will tell you true."

Lena rolled her eyes. What did that *mean*?

Wata touched her arm. "You must not feel uncertainty. Do not remove the cloak if you do." Her expression was worried.

"I won't," said Lena. She shifted under its weight. "Although I *want* to take it off! It feels so heavy now."

"Ah." Lorelei looked relieved. "That is the beginning."

The other mermaids nodded.

"The beginning of what?" asked Lena.

All four mermaids chorused together:

"When the weight of fathoms presses down on you,
The moment for doffing the cloak is due."

Lena laughed. "Does *everything* have a song?"

"Of course," said Rusalka. "How else does one remember things?"

Lena noticed that Halia was staring at her legs. "Um, did you want to touch them?"

The mermaid startled, then tried to pretend indifference. "I do not envy you your clumsy legs." But her avid gaze said otherwise.

Lena shrugged. "They're only clumsy down here."

"Well, since you offer," said Halia, and she stretched out a hand quickly, feeling the muscles and sinews of Lena's leg. Then she grasped Lena's foot, examining it with the scrutiny of a scientist. After a long moment, she said to Lorelei, "They *are* clever, aren't they? So much stronger than they look. And so very many bones! It would be a shame to give them up."

"Give them up?" said Lena. "What are you talking about?"

"Won't you ask for a tail?" said Halia.

Lena just stared.

"Halia," said Lorelei. "I do not think—"

"Surely you intend to transform," persisted the mermaid.

"Halia! You speak nonsense." This time it was Wata who chided Halia. She said to Lena, "It is a myth. We do not know of any humans getting tails."

"But—" said Lena. "Up until a few weeks ago, I would have said that mermaids were a myth."

The mermaids shifted uneasily.

"I spoke hastily," said Halia. "Pay no mind." But her amber eyes held a sly light.

"How does someone ask for a tail?" said Lena. "*Who* does one ask?"

But the mermaids were drifting away from her.

"I believe I hear my mother calling," said Rusalka.

The others nodded, as if a chorus of mothers had begun clamoring for them. And they fled.

◻ ◻ ◻

Brian woke up on the beach.

He jerked upright, scanning the waves with eyes that

peered out of a sunburned face. What if she'd come back while he was sleeping? But the surface of the sea remained empty. For the first time since Lena's disappearance, tears rolled down his cheeks, now thin and covered by a beard.

She's not coming back.

He stood and looked down the beach, almost hoping to see Allie heading his way. But it was barely dawn, and Allie was asleep at home. He moved stiffly toward the rocks and clambered up. When he reached the place where Lena and Lucy had jumped, he stared down into the dark, inviting depths.

It would be so easy . . . Two more steps and he would be in the clasp of the sea.

Brian picked up Lena's shoes—still waiting on the rocks—and turned to head home.

CHAPTER 41

Time drifted in loose, lazy ripples. Lena forgot to keep track of how long she had been in the world beneath the waves. Her mornings were spent attending lessons with the youngest children, and her afternoons were spent with Nix. When it was time for sleep, she retired with her mother to the cave for the Riven. They talked until they grew drowsy, and then Lena slept, dreams of sunlight and half-remembered faces flickering through her subconscious. When she awoke, it was always a relief to find herself still among the mer-folk.

Sometimes she sat cross-legged, studying the way her legs and feet bent to accommodate her weight. She plucked idly at the yarn braid on her ankle, no longer remembering where it came from. *If I had a tail,* thought Lena, *I could swim as fast as everyone else. As fast as Nix.*

Lena found that her thoughts returned obsessively to the idea of a tail. Was it a similar process to being Riven . . . except, well, the opposite? Did it hurt? Certainly, it would make life easier here in the world beneath the waves. She was a proficient swimmer, but there was no question that even the youngest mermaid child swam faster than she did. Nix seemed not to mind, but she hated knowing that she slowed him down when they foraged together. She wanted to be his equal.

And she had to admit: it would be nice to blend in, instead of being stared at all the time. Her legs were still a source of constant fascination to most of the villagers. Lena stretched them out in front of her, running her hands down the muscles of her thighs. How would it work? Would her muscles melt . . . or would her legs just kind of seal themselves together?

But really, all questions boiled down to one: was it permanent?

❑   ❑   ❑

"Where did you find those pearls for your ears?" asked Nix.

He was seated across from Lena at the large stone dining table. They had unloaded baskets of mollusks from their most recent forage, and were enjoying some refreshing kelp juice. He reached across the table to brush Lena's hair back from her face, caressing her cheek.

"They were a gift," she said.

"Yes? Who gave you such precious gems?"

"A sea otter," she answered, her face warming under his touch.

Nix laughed. "A sea otter? I have never heard of such a thing."

Lena laughed, too. "You're right. How can that be?" She tried to remember. "It was . . . oh! On my birthday! The pearls were in a little pink box. Hmm. It seems impossible, but I keep picturing a sea otter holding out the box to me."

"Then it must be so. What a generous otter."

Lena smiled. "I first saw my mother on my birthday. It was the best day of my life."

"Was it?" he said softly. "This is the best day of my life." He left his side of the table and settled next to Lena. Cupping her face with both hands, he leaned close.

Lena had an instant to think, *I hope he doesn't stop this time,* before the universe narrowed down to the two of them, lips joined, arms sliding around each other. The table, the village, the sea, disappeared. There were only lips and tongues and teeth.

After several long, sweet minutes, they broke apart. Lena grabbed Nix's hand, and held it hard against her chest, so he could feel her heart race. Nix took her other hand and pressed it to his chest, so she could feel the answering rhythm. "I love you, Selena," he whispered.

"I love you, Nix," she said.

At last they became aware of their surroundings once more, realizing that half the village seemed to be transfixed, staring unabashedly at them. A voice called out, "Blessings on their love!" and when Lena turned to see who it was, she saw Lorelei, her face bright with happiness.

Most of the villagers were smiling and nodding . . . even Scylla, Lena noticed. Then she caught sight of her grandmother, who merely studied them for a long, appraising moment, then swam away.

◻ ◻ ◻

Although it would have been unthinkable in her old life, in *this* world, the idea of marrying Nix did not seem outrageous.

"Never leave me," he sometimes whispered in Lena's mind, and she tightened her arms around him, promising with her fierce embrace.

Even Lena's grandmother, disapproving at first, had finally relented. "I see you are not to be separated," she said. "I feared for your heart, Nix, but it appears that the land child intends to stay." With an expression of amusement, she added, "Perhaps one day she will even relinquish that wretched human garment."

Lena was used to being teased about her jacket. She intended to remove it . . . after all, she couldn't wear it forever, but first she needed to take off the cloak. And that thought made her a little bit apprehensive. She wanted to be quite certain her desire to live among mer-folk was strong enough to support her body in this element.

Someday, perhaps she would go back to the land. Her father—was it Brian or Byron?—must miss her, but he would understand her desire to stay with her mother and explore the half of her heritage that had lain dormant for sixteen years.

And the others in her life?

Lena mused on them for a moment. There were surely people on land who would mourn her loss . . . but she could no longer remember them.

◻ ◻ ◻

"Mama," said Lena. "Who do I ask for a tail?" She lay with her head in her mother's lap, half-asleep from the caress of Melusina's fingers through her hair.

Her mother's hand jerked, and Lena could feel her body stiffen.

Lena sat up. "Mama?"

"Who told you that?"

Lena studied her mother's tight expression. "Why? Is something wrong?"

"You . . . you are not to ask for a tail." Her mother rose and began to swim around the cave . . . the undersea version of pacing. "Promise me, Selena!"

Lena stared, then said slowly, "I don't understand. Why can't I have a tail if I want one?"

Her mother's swimming grew more agitated. "They are your *legs*. Your beautiful legs! How could you even *think* of relinquishing them?"

Lena felt a flare of anger. "*You* are asking me this? You, who chose to be Riven?"

Melusina sank down on the bed of seaweed again. She put her face in her hands.

Lena could hear some of her mother's thoughts—she was too upset to Cloud them.

Her long, strong legs . . . her lovely moonbeam feet . . . How can I make her understand? . . . But how do I dare to object? . . . Why would anyone surrender the ability to walk? . . . Oh, no, no, no . . .

"Mama," she said. "Please calm down. I'm only asking. Can't you answer some questions? Or do I have to find someone else to tell me?"

Melusina looked at Lena with haunted eyes, but she managed to compose herself. "I will answer."

"Good," said Lena. "Well, I mainly want to know if it's permanent . . . or can I change back to having legs when I want to go on land?"

"You want to return to land?" Melusina's voice trembled.

Lena sighed. "Not right *now*. I'm just asking."

"No one knows with certainty," said her mother. "No human has transformed for many generations. Our legends tell of those who made the change, but they are unclear on whether or not those humans ever regained their legs."

Lena made an exasperated sound. "How can they be unclear? You guys have a song for everything, even one to tell a human when it's time to take off the cloak! There must be some little rhyme about transforming." Suddenly, Lena sensed her mother Clouding her response. "There *is*. You just don't want to tell me."

"Selena, you are far too young to make such a grave decision when the consequences are in doubt." Melusina tried to force a smile. "What a childish notion!"

Lena rose and faced her mother, unsmiling. "I am not a child. What I choose to do with my body is no one's business." She paused, then said deliberately, "Not even my mother's." She swam toward the entrance of the cave.

"Tender maiden," called Melusina. "Please stay. We shall talk more."

Lena left the cave.

◻ ◻ ◻

"Oh, cousin," said Lorelei. "Look at these garnets! Havfine found a pouch of jewels on his last exploration. I'm going to add them to my necklace. He's very sweet, is he not? And he has asked me to accompany him to the surface later." She fingered her necklace, already heavy with various gems and pearls. "Do you like him?"

Havfine was an adventurous young merman, always jaunting off to exotic locales. Lena *did* like him, but she was too impatient for girl-talk. "Hav is very nice," she said. "Lori, I want to know how to get a tail."

Lorelei's smile faded.

"Please. My mother won't tell me."

"Then I should certainly not!"

Lena put her hand on Lorelei's arm. "Lorelei. I am in love with Nix. You know I am."

Lorelei's expression softened. "Anyone who looks at you knows that."

"I want to be his equal. My legs slow me down."

"But what if . . . what if you want to return to land?"

"That's what I need to find out: whether the change is permanent. My mother says no one knows for sure, because it's been so long since anyone asked for a tail."

"It's—" Lorelei looked down at the blood-red jewels in her hand. "I've heard it's painful."

Lena nodded. That made sense.

Lorelei sang:

*"The twain of human legs, with their bones and blood and
    flesh,*
*Must knit with tears and pain, as the mermaid's tail doth
    mesh."*

"I understand. But . . . is there no song about getting the legs back?"

Lorelei looked uncomfortable. "There is *one* song."

"Good! Sing it, please."

"It's an ancient song, cousin. Your mother is right . . . no human has made the change in recent history. The song must be considered more legend than fact."

"Sing it, please," repeated Lena more firmly.

Lorelei closed her eyes and sang:

"The riving light will take a mermaid's tail,
cleaving it hard in two.
When she walks into the welcoming sea,
her tail returns anew.

The burning sand will take a human's legs,
leaving a strong sleek tail.
When she abandons the clasp of the sea,
her legs return, though frail."

"Her legs return," said Lena. "There's the answer!"

"Frail," said Lorelei. "Did you not listen?"

"I heard. So they're weak . . . the song doesn't say they're lame."

"Oh, curse Halia!" cried Lorelei. "It was she who put this idea in your head."

"I'm *glad* she did. How does it work? Who do I ask?"

Lorelei shoved her handful of garnets back into their pouch and turned away. "I have said enough. And I'm sorry, Selena, but I must get ready for . . . for . . . I need to surface."

Lena regarded her cousin for a moment, then said, "Then I will find Halia. She seems to know about transforming."

"No!" Lorelei grabbed Lena's arm. "Don't go to Halia. She is my friend, but she is perhaps not the kindest of maids.

I will tell you what you wish to know." Lorelei's voice grew hushed. "There is a goddess of the sand. Her name is Psamanthe."

"Psamanthe," murmured Lena. "A goddess of the sand? Like an actual Greek *goddess?*"

Lorelei said reluctantly, "She is the one you would ask for a tail."

"Can you take me to her?"

"She doesn't live *here* in the village." Lorelei shook her head as if the idea were preposterous. "She lives in an underground cavern near the shore."

"How do we find her?"

Lorelei fingered the leather pouch holding her garnets. Then she poured them out into her hand again, sifting them between her fingers. Finally she answered, "Hav will know. He travels far and wide. I will ask him, if you like. Are you quite sure, dear cousin?" She looked wistfully at Lena's legs. "They're such pretty limbs. Why would you risk losing them forever?"

"It's not forever. The song said so. And even if—" Lena swallowed. "Even if it were, I probably wouldn't mind. A tail would anchor me to this world."

Lorelei's gaze was full of sorrow. "Or perhaps it would merely imprison you."

CHAPTER 42

Nix pulled Lena onto his lap. "I used to enjoy the solitary nature of patrolling the verge," he said. "Now it is time away from you, and I count the minutes until it is over."

She pressed her lips against his neck, feeling a tremor move through his body. He tightened his hold on her, and she savored the knowledge that he wanted her. With deliberate languor, she rubbed her lips against his skin. Nix moaned and turned her face up to his, kissing her until she forgot where she was. She had no need of Clouding at times like this, because all her thoughts disappeared, and she became pure sensation.

"My Selena," whispered Nix after a long time. "I never knew the emptiness of my life until you appeared to fill it." He twisted a strand of her hair around his finger. "Like an other-worldly vision . . . except you are real." He pulled gently on the strand, bringing her face close again. "And you are mine."

"Do you think . . ." she whispered, kissing him between words. ". . . if we'd never met . . . we would have known . . . something was missing?"

But Nix took possession of her mouth again, and did not answer.

"Oh," said Melusina. "I beg your pardon."

Lena and Nix broke apart.

Melusina floated at the entrance to the cave for the Riven, eyebrows raised. "It seems I have intruded. I do apologize."

"No, no," stammered Nix. "I must depart. My patrol shift . . . I must . . . well, goodbye, Selena."

She giggled. "Goodbye, Nix."

"I will see you tomorrow," he said, backing away.

"Yes."

Melusina nodded as he went past, then came into the cave. "It seems that you and Nix like the privacy of the cave."

Lena blushed. "Sorry. We were just . . ." She trailed off, her cheeks aflame.

"Never fear, daughter," laughed Melusina. "Amorous mer-folk have been caught in sleeping caves since the beginning of time."

Lena moved toward the cave's entrance. "Oh. Well, I—" She glanced outside to watch Nix depart. Unconsciously, her hands came up to worry the edges of the cloak. It felt like a hundred-pound weight on her shoulders. She had a fleeting impulse to tear it off, before caution stayed her hand. *Soon,* she thought.

"I'm going out, Mama. I'll be back in a few hours. Havfine has invited Lorelei and me to go exploring."

Her mother smiled. "I am glad you have made friends, Lena."

Lena blew her a kiss and swam away.

◻ ◻ ◻

Havfine seemed flattered to be asked to show Lena and Lorelei the way to the Cave of Psamanthe, although Lena suspected he was most interested in spending time with Lorelei. He chatted politely to them about his travels—mer-folk were great scavengers, delighting especially in precious gems and gold jewelry—but after a time, Lena lagged behind. She wanted to allow the two of them to speak without her as a constant companion.

"I'm a little tired," she lied. "But I can follow, as long as you don't swim out of view."

Lorelei smirked, as if comprehending her ploy.

They swam on, stopping after another hour to dine on lobster. Havfine had acquired this delicacy through trade with a merman who hailed from the Atlantic Ocean. Lobsters were not to be found in the local waters.

"Have you rested, Selena?" asked Havfine. "The cave lies only a little farther."

"Yes," she said. "Thank you for the delicious meal! I'm ready."

Within another thirty minutes, they came to a rocky cove. Havfine led them through an undersea tunnel that led to a protected pool inside a huge, vaulted cavern.

"We will wait for you," said Lorelei, putting a hand on Havfine's arm. "Lena should speak to the goddess alone." She gave Lena an encouraging look. "Go on. We will be right here . . . just call if you need us."

Lena nodded and swam into the shallow part of the pool. She raised her head, inch by inch, until her eyes were above the surface of the water. She kept her mouth below the surface, since she was breathing water now and didn't know what would happen if she tried to breathe air. Her mother had said something about the cloak protecting her *below* the waves, not above them.

The cavern was empty.

Well, not empty. It was strewn with thousands of coins, rings, seashells, and fragments of terra cotta pottery. Some of the pottery looked like female figures, while others were shallow cups with handles. Looking closer, she saw that a few seashells were bronzed. Everything in the cave looked like it had lain there for a thousand years.

But there was no goddess—or anyone else—in the cavern.

Disappointed, Lena was about to report back to Lorelei and Havfine—*There's no one there . . .* —when she heard footsteps.

Lena sank beneath the surface and swam toward the shadows. She would hide until she could be sure it was the goddess. Peering up through the wavering surface, Lena saw a woman enter the cavern.

The woman was tall, wearing dark blue jeans and a sleeveless white shirt. Her short brown hair was streaked with blond.

Oh, no, thought Lena. *A human!*

The woman came closer to the edge of the water and looked directly at Lena. She said something in a language Lena did not understand.

Lena's heart hammered. She pushed herself backwards through the water. She felt as frightened as any real mermaid being seen by a human.

"Ah," said the woman. "Of course you do not speak Greek." She smiled. "Hello. There is no need to be afraid. I am Psamanthe."

Astonished, Lena raised her eyes above the water.

"Oh, dear. You're wearing a cloak. I didn't know humans

still did that." The woman slipped off her sandals. "Very well. I must come to you, then, since you cannot come ashore." She pulled off her clothes and plunged into the water.

Lena looked for her under water, but the woman was gone.

She had turned into a seal.

CHAPTER 43

Lena stared at the seal rolling and flipping in the water near her.

"Ahh, it feels good to shed that human form for a while," said the seal in her mind.

Lena continued to stare. The animal was a normal-looking seal, except for a streak of blond in her brown fur. "Psamanthe," she stammered. "You . . . I didn't know—"

"No," said the goddess. "No one ever does. My story is little known. I assure you, however, that I am a goddess. What is your name?"

"Lena."

"Where is your offering, Lena?"

With a sinking heart, Lena regarded her empty hands. *Ohhhh* . . . That was what all the other items in the cavern were—gifts offered up to the goddess in return for hearing an appeal. "I'm sorry," she said. "I didn't realize—"

The seal's eyes seemed to flash in the murky light under water. "You came on a pilgrimage to a goddess, and you did not bring a gift?"

"I'm so sorry!" said Lena. "I've never done this before."

"But my dear," said the seal, "I can grant no wish without an offering." She swam closer, her plush fur grazing Lena's arm. "However, I can listen to your appeal for a tail."

Lena's mouth fell open.

Psamanthe said patiently, "Of course I know what you seek, young supplicant."

"How——?"

"I did explain that I am a goddess, yes? I knew you were coming. Your need drew me back to my cavern." The seal made a sound like a sigh. "Only to find you empty-handed."

"I'm sorry I don't have an offering," said Lena. "What should I bring next time?"

"Oh, Lena. I rather doubt there will be a next time." Psamanthe flipped and rolled some more, then added, "Honey is the classical tradition. And I'm very fond of it. Certainly, I can acquire my own honey, but the taste of votive honey is so much sweeter."

"Honey?" said Lena. "But . . . I live in the sea. How can I get honey for you?"

Psamanthe's flippers appeared to lift. "Maybe you can ask an Ancient to get it for you."

"An Ancient?"

"The ancient sirens were half-woman, half-bird," said Psamanthe. "They lived on land, not in the sea. Some of them are still around, you may be able to find one willing to help a sister siren."

Speechless, Lena watched the seal swim around for a long moment. She glanced back at Lorelei and Havfine, who had been observing this exchange in amazed silence.

"Your question remains unasked, my dear," said the seal. "Your ambivalence is palpable. Thus I will broach the topic for you. No, the change is not permanent. But yes, it *is* painful. Just like a mermaid getting legs . . . a human getting a tail is not for the faint of heart. You have heard the song? The reference to burning sand? It is quite true. In the heat of noon-day, I bury you from the waist down in sand." She smiled, causing Lena to shiver. "There you remain for twenty-four hours. *If* you can endure it."

Psamanthe's voice in Lena's head had been perfectly friendly the whole time they were together, but a chill touched Lena's soul. After all, gods and goddesses were not famous for their kindness.

The seal regarded Lena, cocking her head. "Surely you do not deny your own ambivalence, young supplicant. Observe the cumbersome cloak, still hanging from your shoulders. If your desire to live in the sea were stronger, you would have stripped it off by now. And what of this?" The seal swam close to Lena's ankle, her whiskers tickling the skin of her foot. "This braid is a human memento. You wear it still because you have not fully embraced this life."

Lena reached down and touched the yarn around her an-kle and, for an instant, saw a human girl's face in her mind.

"I have enjoyed meeting you, Lena. No human has sought my favor in more than a century. But as I am unable to grant any wish for you, I must take my leave."

"You don't live here?"

The seal chuckled and rolled. "No, I reside among the hu-mans now. It's far more comfortable. But I will be here when-ever you decide to make a formal request." Psamanthe slid fluidly out of the water, and when Lena raised her eyes above the surface, the goddess stood on the sand in her human form again.

"That was refreshing," she said, shaking water out of her short hair. "It has been far too long since I enjoyed my seal form." She pulled on her clothes and came close to the edge of the water. "Selena."

Lena nodded, eyes wide.

"The problem is not that you must choose between the two worlds." For the first time, a gentle note came into the goddess's voice. "The problem is that you feel like an outsider in both worlds."

They stared at each other, then Psamanthe said, "Choose wisely."

She slid on her sandals and walked out of sight.

Lena watched her go, then sank beneath the surface. Lorelei and Havfine rushed to her side.

No one spoke for a long moment.

Then Lorelei burst out, "That was unbelievable! I thought Psamanthe dwelt in her cavern at all times, but of course! She is a goddess. She would have riches and a human dwelling and—"

Lena turned to Havfine and said, "I need your dagger."

He was staring at Lorelei, so it took him a second to absorb Lena's words. "What?"

"Please, may I borrow your dagger?"

Havfine unsheathed his ivory blade and handed it to her, hilt first.

Lena reached down and sliced through the braid around her ankle, letting the bits of yarn float away. *It's not an offering,* she thought. *It's a promise.*

◻ ◻ ◻

Brian told the lie so many times he almost believed it: "Lena has gone on a trip with her grandmother." The neighbors, the school, even his co-workers. He knew her friends were upset because Lena didn't answer their calls or messages. But he did not have the energy to craft a more convincing lie for them.

Since he could not look into his son's face and lie to him, Brian asked Allie to do it. She told the tale very plainly, but still Cole asked every day, "When is Lena coming home?"

CHAPTER 44

You feel like an outsider in both worlds.

Lena swam ahead of Lorelei and Havfine, those words as painful as the sting of a jellyfish. She didn't even try to Cloud her mind, so the source of her agitation was clear to Lorelei and Havfine.

When she could no longer tell which direction was the right way home, Havfine took the lead, touching her shoulder as he passed by. Lorelei stayed by Lena's side but did not attempt to speak to her. Instead she hummed a wordless melody that somehow calmed Lena's thoughts.

As they reached the village, Lena saw Merrow and Amphitrite dining with several of their grandchildren. She saw Fossegrim playing his flute, leading a number of children in a wiggly dance around the circle of stones. She saw her mother sitting with Nereus and Iona and another mermaid—she thought her name might be Sedna—sipping kelp juice while they talked.

I want to belong here, she thought.

Nereus glanced up and saw them. "Ah, the wanderers return."

Melusina turned and smiled. "Hello, Selena. Did Lori and Hav show you many sights today?"

"Yes," said Lena. "I'm very grateful to them. They would

have traveled much faster without me." She looked at her cousin and Havfine, and said simply, "Thank you."

Then a pair of strong hands encircled her waist, pulling her back against his chest, and Nix said, "I have missed you, my Selena. Will you dine with me? I must return to my patrol before long."

Lena turned to face him. She did not feel like an outsider when she was in Nix's arms. She pressed close to him. "I love you, Nix," she said. "I want to stay here with you."

Surprised by her vehemence, Nix did not answer at first. Then he kissed her and murmured, "I am glad to hear it. You know that my heart is in thrall to you."

Tears sprang to her eyes, and Lena could not speak. She pressed Nix's warm hand against her own heart.

"Tomorrow," said Nix. "Let us stand in the circle before the whole of the village and declare that we belong to each other." He kissed her lips, and her cheeks, and her forehead.

"Yes," said Lena. "Is it . . . like a promise?"

"It *is* a promise, my love. But tonight," he continued, "let us dine together, then I will rest with you until you fall asleep. I will surface, then I will complete my turn as patrol. And tomorrow we will be together." His thumb traced the curve of her cheek.

They ate quickly, more focused on each other than their food. Lena sat close enough to Nix that her leg was touching his strong tail, and their hands kept seeking one another, fingers twining briefly before slipping away.

Lena did not return to the cave for the Riven that night.

"I want to be alone with you," she told Nix, and he led her to a little-used sleeping cave at the farthest edge of the village, near the kelp forest. Perhaps the others saw them enter together, because no one followed.

They lay wrapped around each other, sighing wordless songs of love, until Lena fell asleep.

CHAPTER 45

When Lena awoke, Nix had gone. As she rose from her bed of seaweed, she saw three stones on the ground beside her, their edges touching.

Next time you see me, Nix, she thought, *there will be no cloak or human garment between us.*

The village was quiet—it was one of those rare occasions when almost all the mer-folk were asleep or surfacing. Lena swam into the cave for the Riven, where her mother lay.

"Mama," she said, touching her mother's arm.

"Daughter." Melusina smiled, opening her eyes and stretching.

"I am ready to take off the cloak."

Her mother sat up, searching Lena's face. Then she smiled. "I knew your heart would banish your doubt."

"What should I do? Is there a ceremony?"

Melusina shook her head. "Do you feel any anxiety?"

"No."

"Even in the most secret pulse of your blood?"

"No," repeated Lena.

Melusina put her hands on her daughter's shoulders, studying her carefully, then agreed, "I feel no trepidation within you." She smiled and took her hands away. "I feel only impatience. Close your eyes."

Lena obeyed.

"Allow your immutable belief in this world to fill your soul. Allow the never-ending love of your mother to hold you steady. Allow the support of our people to bind you to this place. And lastly, allow the purity of true love to light your desire."

Fingers caressing the sealskin cloak, as if in gratitude for its protection, Lena filled her mind with images from her new life: the mystical people of this undersea village, revolving around her in their welcoming dance . . . Lorelei's loyalty and humor . . . Merrow's warm embrace . . . playful dolphins . . . children with their flutes . . . her mother's joy at having Lena back . . . and finally, the dark eyes of her true love, drinking in the sight of her as if he would never have his fill . . .

Fixing this last image in her mind, Lena slowly pushed the sealskin cloak off her head and down below her shoulders. She inhaled. The life-giving ocean water continued to flow in and out of her lungs. There was no sudden need for air. She smiled.

"You are my brave daughter," said her mother.

Lena laughed and lifted her arms, now so much lighter, spinning around in pleasure. She put her hands on her jacket. "And now," she said, "I can finally take this off!"

Melusina clapped.

"I guess I'll take off the shirt, too," said Lena, hesitating.

"Of course."

"Even though my, um, chest will show."

"Ah," said Melusina, smiling. "You shall have a necklace to wear, if you feel modest."

"Could I have one like yours?" asked Lena. "With the white and black pearls?"

"We shall dive for pearls together until we have gathered enough for you. But it would bring me immense pleasure to have you wear mine, until we make you a necklace of your own. Yours should contain diamonds, as well, in honor of your village on land."

"Wait till Nix sees me." Lena began to slide out of her jacket, feeling something in the pockets as she did so. She put her hand into the left pocket and pulled out the coral comb she had found in her father's sea chest.

She blinked. "Oh," she said. "I forgot this was in there."

Melusina stared at the heavy coral comb. "My . . . that is my comb," she said in confusion.

Lena held it out to her. Melusina took it, turning it over in her hands. She lifted it to her head and drew it slowly through her hair, her eyes fluttering shut. "This was given to me when I was a small maid," she whispered.

With something like dread, Lena felt in her other pocket, and withdrew the mermaid's mirror. She lifted it to her face and saw her own startled reflection. Then, in a swift whirl of colors, the surface of the mirror began to change. She barely had time to think, *Now that I'm down here, what will I see in the mirror?*

And there, suddenly, in the crystalline glass, was her father. And Allie.

Lena's memories crashed back into her mind.

The cloak, she thought. *That damnable cloak. It stole my memory.*

Her parents were in their bedroom, yellowish light from a bedside lamp illuminating their still figures. It had been so long since Lena had seen electrical light that she squinted against its brightness. Her dad was sitting up in bed, a book in his lap, but he wasn't reading. He stared blankly in front of him, his face wan. His blue eyes were dull. Allie lay in bed next to him. Her eyes were closed, but she looked so rigid and miserable that Lena knew she wasn't asleep.

Lena began to tremble, which caused the mirror in her hand to shift perspective. Now she could see the rest of their room. The sea chest was sitting on top of their mahogany bureau, and next to it were her sneakers, the shoes she had left on the rocks at Magic's.

"Oh, no," she said.

Melusina opened her eyes and saw the mirror in Lena's hand. "My mirror," she whispered. For a long moment, she remained frozen, as if carved from marble. A combination of longing and horror came over her face, yet she did not move.

Lena heard her un-Clouded thought: *I will remember.*

Melusina lifted her eyes and looked steadily at Lena, as if to prolong this last moment between them before she looked upon the visions in the mirror. Then she lowered her gaze to the glass. Her lips parted.

"Brian," she said.

CHAPTER 46

A look of such terrible pain swept over her mother's face that Lena thought she would surely cry out. Instead, the sound of her mother's voice in Lena's mind was almost a whisper. "My beloved Brian . . . I remember now . . ."

Melusina's eyes remained fastened on the mirror, then she said uncertainly, "Allison?"

Lena put a hand to her mouth. She had forgotten her mother once knew Allie.

Comprehension flooded Melusina's face, and she backed away from the mirror, putting her hands to her head as if to block out the storm of memories crashing into it.

Lena's trembling increased as she looked from her grief-stricken mother beside her to her grief-stricken father and stepmother in the depths of the mirror.

Where was Cole? She turned the mirror until it obeyed her wish, and the view moved outside of her parents' bedroom, down the darkened hall, and into Cole's room.

Cole's room was illuminated only by the weak glow from his Raiders night-light. Lena zoomed in on the small form in his bed. Cole was awake. She could see his lips moving and bent her head closer to the mirror, listening.

"By the light . . . of the blueberry moon," he was singing softly. *"We sang this song . . . in Lena's room . . ."*

Lena dropped the mirror, moaning.

Melusina was shaking her head, her long hair floating around her agitated figure. "No . . . oh, no . . . Brian . . ."

She suddenly swept forward to catch the falling mirror, looking into it hungrily. "Who is this child?"

"That's Cole. My little brother."

"The child of Brian and Allison?"

Lena nodded.

Melusina looked hard into the mirror, her chest rising and falling rapidly. "He's beautiful."

"Yes."

"What is he saying?" Melusina held the mirror closer. When she heard his words, she looked curiously at Lena. "How does he know that song?"

"I remembered it a while ago. I started singing it to him at bedtime." Lena could not bring herself to look at Cole's little face again as he lay alone in bed. She was tempted to put her hands over her ears to block out the sound of his voice. What had her parents told him? Did he think she was coming back? Or did he think she was . . . dead?

When the images faded from the mirror's surface, Melusina put her hand down, still holding the mirror. Mother and daughter faced each other. They floated in silence for a long moment, neither one speaking, all of their shared and separate memories floating around them.

Kai! thought Lena. *Oh, no. And Pem! And—*

"You told me that your father didn't marry again for a long time," said Melusina.

"Yes."

"When?"

"I was nine years old."

"I see." Melusina spun in a circle, as if unable to contain her emotions. "I had been lost for five years?"

"Yes."

"And he married Allison."

"Yes."

"I knew her."

"Yes. I saw a photo of the three of you taken in some restaurant. I forgot about it until just now."

Melusina continued to spin, agitated. "We were friends. I never thought . . . I never would have guessed—"

Lena waited for her mother to control herself. But Melusina seemed to be spiraling deeper and deeper into her memories of the past, with fresh pain at every turn. Finally she sank down on a bed of seaweed, still holding the comb and the mirror. As if seeking to soothe herself, she began to comb her hair.

Lena moved toward the mouth of the sleeping cave, looking out at the village. Where was everyone? Her mother needed help.

I'll call Nix, she thought. Then she pictured him working, patrolling the verge . . . and he seemed too far away to call back.

Lena retreated into the cave. She knew she should put her arms around her mother, or say something to try to comfort her, or call for help. But she could not move. As long as she didn't move, nothing had to change.

So she floated motionless, breathing the seawater, looking at her stunned mermaid mother, hearing her agonized thoughts.

The image of her father's face came into her mind. She closed her eyes to shut it out, but that only made it stronger.

Then the sound of Cole's voice drifted into her mind again, and she could not shut it out. If she stayed here, Cole would grow up living with the loss of his sister every day. Could she do that to him? He was six, old enough to remember her. And Dad . . . he would have lost not only a wife, but his daughter.

"Mama!" she cried out, like a child waking from a dream.

Melusina jerked out of her inward reverie. "Yes, dear one."

"I—" Lena covered her eyes with her hand, much like her father when faced with something too difficult.

"What is it, my heart?"

Lena wept, her tears mixing with the ocean. "I have to go back!"

Melusina did not answer. She shook her head, denying Lena's words. She tried to speak, and failed. She finally pulled Lena close, stroking her hair. "The mirror has saddened you."

Lena nodded.

"It has saddened me as well. I have the memories back. My heart aches. So much sadness I left behind on land. A loving husband and a child who needed me. I felt this pain when I saw you on the shore, and remembered." She held Lena tighter. "But hush. We will lose some of the pain in the memory circle. We will ask the villagers for help."

"But Mama . . ."

"Hush, my dearest," said Melusina. "You must not think of bidding us farewell. What of Nix? Surely you would not abandon him, as I—" She stopped, stricken.

Lena's heart shuddered, and for a moment, she wondered if it would start beating again, or if this pain would kill her.

Like mother, like daughter. Two generations of women forced to abandon love.

She pressed a hand over the wound in her chest and made her voice firm. "I have to go back."

Melusina gazed at her in silence for what seemed an eternity, as if storing up new memories of her daughter's face to last her for the coming absence. Finally she nodded. "I shall not hinder you. I will take you to the surface."

She swam to the mouth of the cave and paused. "I will inform Amphitrite, so that the village may speed you on your way with a farewell circle. While I am gone, you may speak privately to Nix."

Lena went to her mother. Was this really happening? Was she just going to *leave* the world beneath the waves? "No," she cried.

Melusina waited, her lovely face marred by anguish.

I didn't have enough time, thought Lena.

Her mother stroked her cheek. "It's never enough."

"I don't want a farewell circle," said Lena. "I just want to talk to Nix." She clutched her head. "But I can't. I can't! How can I explain to him that I'm leaving? This is unbelievable."

"Not so very," said her mermaid mother.

"Will you call him for me? I can't bear to see anyone else."

Melusina started to leave, and Lena grabbed her arm. "Wait!" She squeezed her mother's arm so tightly that Melusina gasped. "I can't," she said. "Don't call him. I can't do it."

"Cannot do what?"

Calling upon every ounce of mental strength she had, Lena dropped a curtain over the turmoil of her thoughts. "I won't be able to leave if I see him," she said. Hardening her voice, she repeated, "Don't call him."

For a long time, Melusina waited in silence, waited for her to change her mind.

But Lena just looked at her with grim determination.

"As you wish," said her mother, and she pulled her arm away. "Let us go now, before the others awaken. I will explain . . . as best I can . . . once you are gone." She swam ahead of Lena.

With a wrenching pain, Lena followed.

How long have I been missing from land? she thought. *Weeks? Months? Dad and Allie still seem to be in shock. Maybe time is different down here.*

Dad.

Oh, Dad, I'm so sorry, thought Lena. *I never . . .* A surge of relief pounded in her chest. *At least he didn't do something stupid, like dive in after me.*

The idea of her father, obeying that cruel command to stay out of the sea, even after his daughter dove into it, caused Lena to stop swimming.

"Wait!" she said.

Melusina halted, a tentative smile touching her lips.

"I have to go back," said Lena, not wishing to give her mother false hope. "But there's something I need to do here first." She turned to look at the village, which was still empty and silent.

Lena swam toward the sleeping caves, entering them one by one until she found her grandparents.

Merrow and Amphitrite lay together on a large bed of seaweed. There was another family sleeping a short distance away.

"Lena?" asked her mother, who had followed her into the cave. "Do you wish to say goodbye to your grandparents?"

"Something like that," said Lena.

Merrow's eyes opened at the sound of their voices. His face lit up. "Dearest maids," he greeted them. "Ah, Selena, you are free of the cloak!"

Amphitrite opened her eyes, and anger darkened her face. She sat up and hissed, "You dare enter this cave, Melusina?"

Lena's eyes widened.

Melusina cowered. "I beg your pardon, Mother. I accompany Selena, who wishes to speak with you."

"Let her speak, then. You need not stay."

Lena's heart pounded with indignation. *Allie has never talked to me that way,* she thought. How could a mother speak to her daughter like that? And why didn't Melusina stick up for herself? A surge of love for Allie came over Lena. *I miss her,* she thought. *I need to tell her I'm sorry.*

"I want my mother with me," said Lena, taking Melusina's hand. "I'm here to tell you I have to leave the village."

"But why, child?" asked Merrow, looking distressed.

"I . . . they're suffering. My family on land."

Amphitrite frowned. "Your time among the humans was long. Your time here has only just begun, and there are many things for you to learn. I wish you to stay."

Lena did not move. "Thank you for the invitation. But my parents don't even know if I'm alive or dead. I have to go back."

Amphitrite's eyes became stony. "*My* daughter is your parent in *this* world. Do you not care for her feelings? She will be heartbroken. Not to mention the young man you profess to love."

Lena squeezed her mother's hand. "My mother understands. And as for Nix—" Here she stumbled over her words. "I . . . I was not free to make promises to him. I . . . the cloak is cursed! It doesn't just shelter someone between the worlds, it makes you forget! I didn't—"

"Enough," said Amphitrite, her expression dismissive. "The cloak is charmed to protect the wearer. Do you not realize that protection from the torment of memories is part of the charm?"

Melusina and Lena stared, absorbing this idea.

"You are free to go, Selena. Perhaps it is for the best. You are a lovely little creature, but your prolonged presence here would no doubt have led to dissension among our people. Nevertheless, you will be welcome whenever you return."

"Is that true?" asked Lena.

"Of course," said Amphitrite, her eyes narrowing. "How dare you doubt my words?"

"But what about the sharks?" she asked.

"Sharks?" All three of them looked at Lena in surprise.

"When will the sharks come for me?"

Melusina gasped.

The sleeping family in the cave had awoken and were listening to the harsh words in dismay. "Come," said the merman. His wife picked up their small drowsy mermaid, and they swam out of the cave.

"Your words are confused, Selena," said Amphitrite. "You are in no danger. No shark shall harm you while you are in the company of mer-folk."

"But Amphitrite, if you would charm the sharks to seek out my father, then you should do the same to me."

Amphitrite rose from the bed of seaweed and uncoiled her tail to its full length, her light eyes glittering. "You speak of things of which you know nothing, child of Brian."

"I heard what you said before. When I first arrived. You thought I was sleeping."

Amphitrite and Merrow exchanged a glance.

"I heard what you said about my father. You said that you would charm the sharks to seek him out if he ever set foot in the ocean again."

The expression on Amphitrite's face did not change. She did not speak. But her tail flicked slightly.

"You also told my father, long ago, that if he disobeyed your command, whenever anyone he loved set foot in the ocean, you would destroy them, too."

Silence.

"He never set foot in the ocean again. Not because he's afraid of you," Lena couldn't help saying defiantly. "But because he didn't want anything to happen to me, or anyone else he loves."

Still Amphitrite did not answer.

Lena kept her eyes locked on the mermaid. "I want to hear you take back your command," she said.

Amphitrite's eyes lit with an unearthly power. "We do not bow to the will of humans," she said.

And she swam out of the cave.

CHAPTER 47

Lena watched Amphitrite's retreating form, and her heart sank. Then she felt the gentle pressure of her mother's hand.

"She is formidable," said Melusina. "But so is her grand-daughter."

Lena nodded and kissed her mother's cheek. She swam out of the cave.

By the time she caught up to her, the mermaid was near the circle of stones in the center of the village. "Grandmother," she called.

Amphitrite turned.

Keeping her fears Clouded, Lena swam up to the mermaid and said, "Please let me speak. My father has obeyed your command for *so many* years." Her voice quavered, and she paused to gather her courage. "It has been a terrible sacrifice for him. He loves the sea! Surely you can imagine how hard it has been to see it and smell it *every single day,* but never to be able to touch it. He would have moved away years ago, if not for me. He knew I needed to be near the ocean, be-cause . . . because"—tears came to Lena's eyes as she realized for the first time what had kept her family in Diamond Bay— "to leave would have killed me."

The hard glint in Amphitrite's eyes seemed to soften, al-though she remained staring at the circle of stones. Melusina and Merrow floated just behind Lena.

"My father stayed out of the water for me. And everyone else he loves. Now I ask you to take back your command. I *beg* you."

Amphitrite looked at her then. "Yes . . . it would have been a terrible sacrifice," she admitted, "to forsake the embrace of the sea." She shifted her gaze to a point behind Lena. "However, I did not issue the command against your father."

Lena stared at her for a moment, then turned slowly, looking at her grandfather. "You?" she whispered.

Merrow did not answer. His expression—usually so warm and kind—was impassive.

Melusina gasped.

The four of them floated in silence for a long moment.

"Husband," said Amphitrite at last, "the child implores. Will you show clemency?"

The powerful merman, his scarred tail reflecting a century of survival in this harsh world, turned to his daughter. "Melusina."

"Yes, Father."

"What would you give up . . . to protect the human you once called husband?"

Without hesitation, Melusina said, "My life."

Lena shuddered. What was her grandfather planning to do?

"You have a loyal heart, daughter. But that will not be necessary," said Merrow. "However, you must cease your visits to the place where your husband and child found you."

Melusina's lips trembled, but she did not demur. "I agree."

Merrow looked satisfied. "Selena," he said.

Lena squared her shoulders. "Yes."

"You must give me your solemn vow that your father will not attempt to journey to our village, or bring disruption to our lives."

"I promise," said Lena.

"Be certain that you understand: he is welcome to enter the sea, but he is not welcome *here*."

Lena nodded.

"And there is one more condition."

Lena waited in dread.

"*You* must not attempt to contact anyone here."

Lena's stomach dropped, and her heart began to thump painfully, as if it wanted to push its way out of her chest in protest. "What?"

"You leave damage in your wake. Do not imagine all will be well in the village after you depart. Once you have gone, there will be no healing for Nix or your mother unless they know themselves free of your power."

"I . . . I don't have any—"

"Your word, Selena. Your word that you will surrender contact with our people . . . and I will give you *my* word that your father will be safe again in the sea."

Lena hesitated, then she nodded.

Merrow held out his hand, and Lena took it.

With frightening strength, Merrow pulled Lena into the circle of stones. He dropped Lena's hand and said, "Fix your gaze upon me as you speak your truth."

Lena stared into the merman's stormy eyes. After a moment, she felt the strength drain out of her body, and she would have begun to sink, except that she seemed to be held in place by the merman's gaze. The deep, ancient power of magic flowed from Merrow's eyes into Lena's soul. She could not move, she could not turn away, she could not speak untrue words.

"My land-father will not attempt to journey to the village," she vowed. "He will leave your people in peace."

Quietly implacable, her grandfather said, "And you relinquish your claim on the ones you love in this world?"

Pain flooded Lena's heart. "I do."

And she remembered that today—in this very circle—she and Nix would have announced their love.

Still Merrow did not remove his gaze. Lena felt the history of generations of mer-folk demanding vows in exchange for wishes granted.

Her grandfather raised his arms and spoke in a voice that exploded in Lena's mind like a thousand shouts: "Then my command is withdrawn." When he lowered his arms, a mysterious ripple spread out in all directions from his fingertips, surging through the sea. Its force pressed against them . . . a flash of electric power.

Then it was gone.

Lena felt herself released from a spell. She turned blindly to her mother, who gathered her into her arms.

Amphitrite swam closer to Merrow and put her hand on his shoulder. "Thank you, my love," she said. Then she gazed at Lena with her uncanny pale eyes. "You are brave . . . for a land-child."

Lena straightened her spine and answered with bitter pride, "I am a child of sea and land."

CHAPTER 48

The journey to the surface was long. Lena was weakened from the shock of her departure and had to rely on her mother to support her. Every mile that took her away from Nix felt like a fresh wound opening in her heart.

Close to an hour after they had left the village, Lena felt a tumult in her mind. She seemed to hear Nix's tortured cry as he discovered her betrayal.

She stopped swimming as the irresistible call of a merman came to her:

Heed my call.
Come to me.
We are bound.
Do not flee.

The pain and rage in his voice were so awful that she nearly turned back, instinctively wanting to comfort him. Then the image of Cole came into her mind again, and she forced herself to ignore the summons of her beloved. No human could have resisted the siren song, but Lena was not human.

When they reached the surface at Magic Crescent Cove, Lena's and Melusina's heads emerged from the waves simultaneously, far from shore. It was night, and rain speckled the surface of the ocean.

Lena took a breath of air and began to choke.

"You must breathe out the seawater," murmured her mother's voice in her mind.

But Lena sank below the surface again in a panic. Her lungs were breathing the ocean now. Would she be able to go back, or was she trapped here? She was afraid to leave this element.

"Do not fear," said her mother. "You can pass between the worlds now. Rise above the surface and breathe out the seawater. Go!"

Lena broke the surface again. Before trying to inhale, she forced the water out of her lungs, feeling tears come to her eyes with the effort. She coughed out the last of the salty liquid, then sweet night air was flowing in and out of her lungs.

Mother and daughter swam to the rocks where they had found each other, after so many years apart. Melusina found a place to pull herself up and reached for Lena's hand, helping her onto the rocks. Once out of the water, Lena began to shiver, her clothes and hair dripping, her legs bare. Rain pelted her, and after being immersed in water for so long, Lena felt like she could feel each raindrop individually.

"You must not linger," said her mother. "The night is cold, and they await your return."

Lena nodded. "Mama," she whispered.

Melusina held out the mirror, her eyes glistening with tears. "Whenever you wish to see your loved ones in the world beneath the waves, you need only look for us here. Merrow's edict did not forbid you to look."

Lena took the mirror. Now that she was here on land, about to lose her mother *again*—and abandon the man she loved—her determination began to fail. "What if—?" she whispered.

But Melusina's expression was blank and shattered. "No, darling," she said.

How will we survive? she thought. *When Mama goes back to the village without me . . . how will she manage?*

Although her hand tightened with her need to keep the mermaid's mirror for herself, Lena handed it back to her mother.

"You keep this," she said. "It's yours."

She put her arms around her mother's small body and hugged her tightly. "I love you, Mama."

Melusina clung to her daughter with primal strength, then released her.

Spent and despairing, Lena climbed across Shipwreck Rocks. With every step, she felt weaker and more chilled. Her soul was riven—she longed to slip back into the embrace of the sea, but she was desperate to get home to her family.

The journey across the jagged rocks seemed endless. Once she sank down on a flat stone to rest. She wanted to look back at her mother, but she was afraid that if she did, she would never leave.

When she reached the edge of the rocks, she jumped down.

Her legs buckled under her, and she fell to her knees in the sand.

❑ ❑ ❑

The mermaid watched her daughter's progress from the farthest point of the wave-splashed rocks. When Lena collapsed on the sand, Melusina cried out. She could not go to her.

"Selena!" she called. "Selena!"

Lena struggled to sit up, then lay immobile, a small, drenched figure at the base of the rocks.

"Oh, nooo," moaned Melusina, "please don't let her be hurt."

She struggled to make her way across the rocks in the direction where Lena lay.

Then she saw a solitary figure moving across the sand, and she froze.

The man came closer to Lena and knelt down beside her. He moved her hair out of her face and spoke to her. Then he helped her sit up.

Melusina pressed her hands to her face, weeping.

The man put his arms under Lena's shoulders and knees, then lifted her off the sand. Holding her in his arms, the man looked directly at Melusina. "She's okay," he said.

He Sees me, thought Melusina. *He has Seen me before. There is recognition in his eyes.*

"I knew you were real," said the man softly. "She's your little girl, isn't she?"

Melusina nodded, tears and rain coursing down her face.

"I'll make sure she gets home," he said. "Goodbye."

He walked away from the rocks, cradling Lena in his arms, his long coat blown by the wind.

EPILOGUE

On a warm spring day, Lena stood at the boundary between her two worlds—where land melted into the sea.

Magic Crescent Cove sparkled like liquid jewels today—the waves small and unthreatening. But Lena knew its pretty postcard appearance hid dangerous tides. Maybe someday she would surf here again.

But not today.

"I'll just be a minute," she told her dad. She walked closer to the water's edge, looking for the sight of a head in the water—she couldn't help looking—but saw nothing but gray-green ocean. She bent down a few yards from the high-tide mark and placed the three palm-size stones she was carrying on the dry sand, their edges touching.

Then she turned away from the lure of the sea. She walked back to her father and said, "Let's go."

He nodded, and they made their way up the beach to the edge of the highway, where her dad's car was parked, two surfboards secured to the top.

"Hi, Denny," said Lena. She approached the man who sat watching the cove, ever vigilant.

He stood up, brushing sand from his long coat. "Hello, Selena."

She hugged him.

"I want to see her again," said Denny, as he always did.

"Me, too," whispered Lena.

Lena's dad walked up to them and shook Denny's hand. "Will you come for dinner tonight?" he asked.

Denny smiled and shook his head, as he always did.

"Bye, Denny. See you soon," said Lena, and she opened the passenger-side door.

Her dad stood next to Denny, both of them staring out to sea . . . the immortal, immeasurable sea.

"Dad, come on," called Lena from the car window. She was afraid one day he might not be able to turn away.

To her relief, he laughed and jumped into the car. "Okay, okay, keep your wetsuit on!"

"The waves won't wait," she added.

He laughed some more. "Oh, Lena . . . the waves are eternal." The smile on his face fell slightly, and they looked away from one another, each thinking of a village beneath the waves and a beautiful mermaid who lived there.

Mother.

Wife.

Lena's dad started the car, releasing them from their reveries. He drove south on Highway 1, away from Magic Crescent Cove.

Ten miles farther down the road, he pulled into a spot on the side of the highway.

"Look!" said Lena, pointing. "There's Ani's Jeep! Oh, and Max is here, too. That's his car. Everyone is here!"

"Do you see Mom's car anywhere?" asked her dad.

"Not yet," said Lena. "Oh! There it is." She pointed at a green Volvo. Mom and Cole had not wanted to miss Dad's triumphant return to surfing. Lena suspected that somewhere on the beach, Mom had already been roped into a game of catch with Cole.

Lena's dad parked the car, and she jumped out to help him untie the boards.

She lifted down her brand-new custom-made Robbie Dick surfboard. The deck was sky blue with a smiling yellow sun on the nose, and the bottom was midnight blue with a bright moon in the middle and a spangling of stars across it.

Lena hurried down the verge to the sand. Her dad followed, carrying his own board, also a brand-new Robbie Dick original. It was a short board, with a green and silver Chinese dragon on the deck, and a yin-yang on the bottom.

Lena shaded her eyes against the blaze of the sun and studied the lineup. There was Pem. Farther down the row was Kai. Ani was riding a wave to shore, and Max was paddling out.

"Pem!" she shouted, waving. "Kai!"

Both of them saw her and yelled back. Kai was smiling.

It had taken some time, but she and Kai were friends again—mostly.

Lena's convalescence from her time under water had been difficult; she had run a high fever and couldn't speak. She'd been communicating with her mind for so long that while she was ill, she forgot, most of the time, to speak aloud.

Her friends had been told she'd caught a virus while traveling with Grandma Kath. Pem came to see her as soon as she was allowed, but Lena refused to see Kai. How could she, when the first word out of her mouth during her fevered dreams had been "Nix"?

Finally she agreed to see Kai. She tried to give him back the pearl earrings when she broke up with him, but he insisted she keep them. Lena was relieved that he didn't seem devastated by her rejection—he must have suspected there had always been something lacking in their love. Maybe it had been the siren in her voice that attracted him in the first place.

As for Nix, Lena spent every conscious moment during the weeks of her recovery wishing for the memory-stealing cloak to take his image from her mind. If he could only know of the ache that lived inside her, he might forgive her.

But that terrible time was months ago, also, and Lena had tried to find peace in her return to life on land.

Her family and friends were safe and happy.

And there was still the sea.

It would never forsake her.

Cole came racing across the sand, his sturdy legs pumping. "Hi!" he yelled, and threw his arms around Lena. She staggered a little. "Ooof," she said. "You're getting good at tackles. You almost took me down!"

Allie arrived a moment after Cole, and Brian kissed her.

"Group hug!" yelled Cole, and the four of them wrapped their arms around one another. When they broke apart, Lena saw tears in her mom's eyes. She leaned over and kissed Allie's cheek.

"Safe surf, guys," said Allie, smiling and turning to follow Cole, who had taken off down the beach again.

Lena knelt down on the beach to wax her board before its maiden voyage.

Her dad joined her, expertly applying wax to his own board. He beamed at her. "It's been a long time coming, sweetie," he said.

"Too long! And don't call me 'sweetie' out there in the lineup."

"What should I call you?" he asked, laughing.

Lena considered for a moment, then said, "How about Seagirl?" With a bubble of glee rising in her chest, she stood up and hurried into the surf, calling back, "I'm just kidding, Dad! You can call me sweetie if you want." She tossed her board onto the blue blanket of ocean. "Woo-hoo!" she yelled, flinging herself onto the deck.

She glanced back at her dad, who stood at the water's edge. His smile had faded, and he looked almost . . . *nervous.*

"Get on your stick, Dad!" she called. *You can do it.*

But nearly two decades of avoiding the sea at all costs, not even wading into ankle-deep surf, made him hesitate. His caution had kept his family safe. Now he was about to trust in the honor of an old enemy.

Lena couldn't bear to watch him waver. "Dad, it's a promise!" she yelled, then faced forward and paddled out.

Max greeted her as she joined the lineup. "Hey, it's the Leenatic."

"What?" She laughed.

"Anyone who surfs Magic's *has* to be a lunatic. Or in your case, a Leenatic!"

Lena rolled her eyes at Pem and Kai. But Kai looked jealous, as if he coveted her nickname, and Pem laughed heartily, as if Max was the funniest guy in the world.

Lena's dad paddled to a spot farther down the lineup, and Lena beamed over at him.

As the next set of waves rose up, Lena's friends hung back, and Lena and her dad popped up on their boards with identical poise, taking their first ride together.

Dear Reader,

I spent an hour this morning at Maverick's Beach. The waves were small, and the sea was sadly surfer-less.

But it was a beautiful sunny day, and I had the beach to myself—a rare pleasure.

As I walked across the wet sand, a sea lion stuck its head out of the water. We gazed at each other for a while; then I waved. It watched me for another long moment before sliding beneath the surface.

Wading in the cold surf, I watched a skittering of sand-pipers race close to the foam, digging their bills into the sand as the waves retreated. I admired a clique of pelicans skimming close to the water, and a solitary grebe bobbing on the surface. Then I sat on a rock and listened to the ocean's music. As waves curled around the Cauldron and washed over the Boneyard, I pictured Lena's fateful ride on a November day just like this one.

When it was time to go, I climbed the path leading away from the shore . . . pausing to pay my respects at the stone memorial to Mark Foo, a surfer who died at Maverick's.

My fictional town of Diamond Bay is based on the coastal towns south of San Francisco. Likewise, my fictional big surf spot, Magic's, is inspired by the real-life Maverick's. In writing *The Mermaid's Mirror,* I took many liberties with the geography, oceanography, and marine biology of northern

California. I'm an enthusiast, not an expert. Any errors in local flora, fauna, climate, or tides are mine alone.

If you are interested in learning more about marine life, the Monterey Bay Aquarium has an amazing website: www.montereybayaquarium.org. I'm grateful to Jim Covel in particular for answering a question about the region's bioluminescent marine life.

I relied on my favorite wave-rider—my sister—and several other sources to describe the rush and danger of surfing. Again, any errors are mine alone.

The Surfrider Foundation is a nonprofit organization dedicated to protecting beaches, promoting open access to beaches for everyone, fighting ocean pollution, and educating the public about the environment. Learn more about them at the website www.surfrider.org. I have chosen to make a donation to this foundation in honor of the *The Mermaid's Mirror,* which is, after all, my love letter to the sea.

L. K. Madigan
November 13, 2009
Half Moon Bay, California

ACKNOWLEDGMENTS

Mom and Dad, thank you for reading and praising my child-hood book about mermaids (eighty pages, complete with il-lustrations). And thank you for providing a home where creativity was applauded. Your early encouragement may well be the reason *The Mermaid's Mirror* exists today.

If this book manages to capture the heart and soul of surf-ing, it is due to the influence of my sister, Michelle. She shared her surfing experiences with me, and I did my best to convey her joy and awe. She lives far from the ocean now, but will always have the heart of a surfer. Love you, Peeps. I promise one day I'll finish the sequel.

Awesome editor Margaret Raymo shines a light on my work, illuminating places I forgot to explore. Thank you for believing in my story about the surfer girl and the mermaid. I am extravagantly glad that this book, which is so close to my heart, has finally made it out into the world. Oh, and thanks for letting me keep the zombie joke.

Deep appreciation to the entire Houghton Mifflin Har-court team, especially Karen Walsh, Lisa DiSarro, Linda Ma-gram, and Carol Chu.

Super-sharp agent Jennifer Laughran continues to astound with her wit, wisdom, and editorial insight. I am eternally grateful to have her as champion of my books.

I worked on this book sporadically over eight years, and many writers critiqued it in a variety of versions. If I tried to list them all, I would end up forgetting someone, so forgive me if I limit my thanks to the intrepid members of my current critique group: C. Lee McKenzie, Heather Strum, Melissa Higgins, Yvonne Ventresca, and Sara Bennett Wealer. They dare to read unwieldy first drafts and never run away screaming.

Special thanks to Lisa Schroeder, who reminded me of the differences between writing for middle-graders and writing for young adults. Not only is she a model of kindness in the wide world of children's literature, but she is one of my best friends. This author thing would be much harder without her.

Great love and gratitude goes to Beverly, who not only reads my books and comments thoughtfully, but sculpts beautiful mermaid artwork, of which I have been the lucky recipient.

My dear friend Jo read this book when it was a middle-grade manuscript and loved it so much that she read it to her fifth grade class. Her faith in my writing over the years has been a gift.

Lindsey Leavitt, Saundra Mitchell, and Sonia Gensler are . . . well, they're all really necessary to my writerly happiness. As are the Debs (www.feastofawesome.com).

Many thanks to my friend Martha for graciously allowing me the use of her name, and Leslie's.

Surfing sage and board-maker extraordinaire Robbie Dick read through the manuscript to check for surfing goofs. Thank you, Robbie.

Benita's singing inspired some of the song choices in the book; I have her to thank for "Bowlegged Women."

To my talented teen readers: thanks for the great comments on the manuscript, Taylor (T-Dog), and thanks for being my very FIRST teen reader, Brittany (so long ago you're out of your teens!).

I borrowed the idea of braided yarn anklets from my young friend Iris. She is a strong, smart teen who makes the demanding discipline of tae kwon do look easy, and I'm glad to know her.

I saved the best for last: Unending love and heartfelt thanks to my husband, Neil, who first listened to me describe the idea for this story almost a decade ago, and never stopped believing it would one day be a real book.

And of course, big love and heartfelt thanks to my son, who has adapted to life with an author mom and is proud of me. But not prouder than I am of him! Love you, NBW (more).

L. K. MADIGAN lives in Portland, Oregon, with her husband, son, two big black dogs, hundreds of books . . . and quite a few items of mermaid memorabilia. This is her second novel for young adults. The first book she ever wrote (in fourth grade) was an eighty-page epic tale about mermaids, so her inner child cannot stop beaming over finally having published a mermaid book.